# THE
# GIRLS *of*
# MERSEY SQUARE

# BOOKS BY PAM HOWES

*A Child For Sale*

*Fast Movin' Train*
*Hungry Eyes*
*It's Only Words*

# THE
# GIRLS *of*
# MERSEY SQUARE

## PAM HOWES

bookouture

Published by Bookouture in 2023

An imprint of Storyfire Ltd.
Carmelite House
50 Victoria Embankment
London EC4Y 0DZ

www.bookouture.com

First published as *That'll Be the Day* by Cantello Publications in 2014.

ISBN: 978-1-83790-999-5
eBook ISBN: 978-1-83790-574-4

*Dedicated to the memory of Buddy Holly, Ritchie Valens and The Big Bopper. Three young stars who lost their lives on 3 February 1959. They left us with a rich legacy of music never to be forgotten. For everyone with a bit of rock 'n' roll in their soul.*

# PROLOGUE

## LIVERPOOL PHILHARMONIC HALL, 20 MARCH 1958

After introducing the final act, compère Des O'Connor, billed as 'The Comedian with the Modern Style', bowed his way off stage to uproarious applause, stamping feet and loud whistles. A hush fell over the audience as the lights dimmed. The curtain rose and three teenage boys in the front stalls moved to the edge of their seats in excited anticipation.

They'd sat patiently through performances by Gary Miller, The Tanner Sisters and Ronnie Keene and his Orchestra but the moment they'd been waiting weeks for was about to happen.

Billed as 'The Great American Recording Stars', a smartly suited trio of young men filed on stage and took their places. The singer, tall, dark and bespectacled, looking more librarian than rock 'n' roll star, stood to the front, the drummer, smiling broadly, seated just behind, and the short, double-bass player, whose instrument threatened to dwarf him, stood to the right of the singer, and nodded shyly at the audience.

The silence was deafening as the drummer counted in and Buddy Holly and The Crickets began an electrifying performance of 'That'll Be the Day', a song that was to change the lives of the three enthralled teenagers forever.

# 1

STOCKPORT, CHESHIRE, JANUARY 1959

Lillian Mellor dropped the telephone back onto its cradle, stared at her reflection in the hall mirror and muttered, 'I'll swing for the little perisher!'

'What's up, Lil?' her sister Minnie asked as she hurried back into the parlour. 'Come and sit down and finish your cuppa.'

'Fred will go mad.' Lillian picked up her cup and took a sip. 'It's stewed now. I'll brew a fresh pot in a minute.'

'I'll do it. Who was on the phone?'

'The headmaster. Eddie's been playing truant again. He's in today, but he missed Monday and Tuesday.' Lillian shook her head. 'He goes out of here in the morning, smiling like butter wouldn't melt. He must think I'm daft. He'll either be hanging around the record shop or at Roy Cantello's house while Bob and Irene are at work. Since he, Roy and Tim started that group, he's gone off the rails. He'll never pass his O levels at this rate.'

Minnie struggled to her feet and picked up the teapot. 'I'll put the kettle on while you calm down. I don't know what to suggest. Having no kids of my own, I'm not best placed to give advice.'

'You don't know how lucky you are.'

'Oh, come on, Lil. Eddie's brought you and Fred a lot of joy. It's just a pity you didn't have him when you were a bit younger.'

While her sister made the tea, Lillian rehearsed what she would tell Fred when he arrived home. Eddie was their only child, born long after she'd given up hope of being a mother. With his big blue eyes, long dark lashes, hair the colour of ripened corn, now turned a rich golden brown, he'd been a beautiful baby. He could charm monkeys from trees with his dazzling smile and he knew it. She was the first to admit she'd spoiled him rotten. In spite of rationing, he'd been given every-thing a child could need and more. Now they were paying the price; sharing their home with a sulky sixteen-year-old who lived by his own rules.

* * *

Eddie sighed with relief as the four o'clock bell signalled the end of the long school day. He pushed his floppy brown fringe from his eyes and chucked his books inside the desk. He leant back on his chair and turned to his friend, Roy. 'I've had enough of this place. Who gives a toss about the war? It finished ages ago.'

Roy nodded. 'Not long now, Ed. Only five more months and we're free.' He stretched his long limbs and picked up his battered satchel from the floor. 'So, what now? You going home, or do you fancy hanging around town for a while?'

'Town,' Eddie said. 'Mum gave me hell for coming in late last night and she'll be raring to have another go as soon as I walk in. It was only eleven, but the way she went on, you'd think I should have been tucked up in bed for nine, like a good boy.'

'And weren't you?' Roy smirked, brown eyes twinkling as he took a comb from his trouser pocket and ran it through his immaculate black quiff. 'Thought you had a date with Angie Turner? Any luck?'

'Nearly! She's promised me she will next time, but she said that last week.'

'Birds are all the same.' Roy shrugged. 'None of them mean it, mate, and believe me, I should know.'

'Mellor and Cantello, I want those revised history essays on post-war Britain back by Friday morning, no later.'

Eddie looked up as Mr Crabtree, grey hair standing on end where his hands had woven agitatedly during the lesson, bore down on them.

'If they're handed in late again there'll be detention next week, make no mistake about that.'

'Yes, sir,' Eddie replied, and under his breath, 'No, sir, three bags full, sir.'

'What was that, Mellor?'

'Nothing, sir. Just clearing my throat.'

'Yes... well, Friday morning, on the dot.'

As the history master swept away, Eddie waved two fingers in the air behind his back then turned his attention to his classmate, Tim Davis, who was still at his desk, scribbling on a sheet of paper.

'Stop working, swotty. Let's get out of this dump.'

Tim looked up, blue eyes shining under a thatch of blond hair. 'I'm not working. Well, not schoolwork anyway. I've been writing down the words to Chuck Berry's "Carol" for tonight.'

Leaving behind the smell of chalk and carbolic soap, the threesome grabbed their blazers from the cloakroom and hurried down the corridor. They spilled out of the old Victorian building and into the playground, Eddie studying the paper that Tim had been scribbling on.

Roy reached into his satchel, pulled out a crumpled packet of Park Drive and handed them round. 'Don't light up yet,' he warned as Eddie took a box of matches from his pocket. 'Wait until we're off the premises. Crabby'll be on our backs again and it'll mean the cane or detention if we're seen. I for one don't fancy either.'

'Well, hurry up then, for God's sake, I'm gasping.' Eddie quickened his pace out through the wrought-iron school gates and leant against the wall. He lit up and inhaled deeply, closed his eyes and sighed. 'Ah, bliss! Love that first drag after a day in the hell hole. You coming to town, Tim?'

'Yeah. But let's go to Flanagan and Grey's. It's too cold to be hanging around on street corners. Looks like it might snow.' Tim glanced at the grey sky, which hung heavy with threatening clouds.

Eddie took another lengthy drag on his cigarette. 'Now that's exactly what I had in mind.'

Roy raised a quizzical eyebrow as they hurried towards the bus stop. 'Why might that be?'

'No reason. Just thought John could play us any new releases, you know, so we can keep up to date.' He smirked and added, 'And those three lookers from the grammar school usually go in about four thirty.'

'I knew it.' Roy laughed. 'You fancy that little dark-haired bird with the big brown eyes and ponytail something rotten.'

Eddie sighed. 'She doesn't like me. I winked at her last Saturday but she turned away. Think I embarrassed her.'

'I fancy her friend, the snooty one with the long brown hair and legs,' Roy said. 'Now she's got class.'

Tim scratched his head. 'They've all got legs, Roy!'

Roy tutted. 'Idiot. I mean the one whose legs go right up to her armpits. Bet she'd be a challenge, padlocks on her knickers, the lot.

Wouldn't mind getting my hands on the key.' He took a last drag on his cigarette and tossed the butt end over a nearby garden wall.

'Well, if you fancy *her*, and I like the dark one, that leaves the one with the blonde ponytail and blue eyes for Tim. Bet you wouldn't mind getting to know her, eh, Tim?'

'If I could only pluck up the courage,' Tim said wistfully, as the bus lumbered slowly into view.

\* \* \*

Flanagan and Grey's Record Emporium in Stockport town centre was the regular haunt for music-mad teenagers and John Grey, the store's young manager, greeted the boys with his usual friendly smile as they ran downstairs into the cellar-like shop. 'Afternoon, lads. How's it going?'

Eddie pulled a face. 'Can't wait to leave in July.'

'You've only just gone back after the Christmas holidays. Surely it can't be that bad?'

'It is. We've got double maths and geography tomorrow and we've got to redo an essay on post-war Britain before Friday morning. I just might skip school again and come down here instead.'

'Ah, that reminds me, Ed. Your mother called earlier. Asked me if I'd seen you this week. I told her you hadn't been in for a few days. I hate lying to her,' John finished as Eddie shrugged indifferently.

'You didn't tell her we'd been here Monday and Tuesday?'

'Course not, but she said the headmaster had been in touch again about you playing truant.'

'Hell. That means my old man'll be waiting for me when I get home. He'll go on about that stupid apprenticeship I don't want. We're musicians, we don't wanna do normal jobs,' he finished as Roy and Tim nodded their agreement.

John laughed. 'Buddy Holly's got a lot to answer for!' He'd been restless himself at that age and had talked his dad out of sending him to learn accountancy. He much preferred working in the family music business.

'What new stuff have you got in?' Roy picked his way through a stack of records on the counter. 'Anything worth listening to?'

'Nothing you lot would like, unless of course you fancy the latest by Michael Holliday. Or what about Alma Cogan?' John picked up a copy of 'Last Night on the Back Porch' as Eddie pulled a horrified face.

'Do us a favour! My mother likes that. Play "Johnny B. Goode" then, please.'

John pulled the record from the shelf. 'Go down to the end booth then.'

* * *

The boys crowded into the booth to listen to Chuck Berry. They snapped their fingers, tapped their feet and sang along to the music. As the song ended, Eddie nudged Roy and pointed. The three girls from the grammar school were leaning against the counter. They spoke to John and then strolled across to the adjacent booth. The tall snooty one with the long legs passed coolly by without a backward glance at Roy in spite of his loud wolf whistle in her direction. Eddie caught the eye of the dark-haired girl, and winked at her. She blushed furiously and turned away, disappearing into the booth with her friends to listen to the latest Buddy Holly.

Roy's dark eyes followed the tall slim girl, and he groaned. 'God, I could shag that! I've got to get to know her. I wanna find out if her legs really do go up to her armpits!' His deep voice carried into the adjoining booth.

Eddie grinned broadly at Tim as he heard the girl say, 'Hmm, he thinks a lot of himself.'

The boys said goodbye to John and left the shop, Roy trying his best to catch the eye of the tall girl, who ignored him. As they hurried down the High Street he turned to Eddie. 'So, rehearsal at Tim's later, yeah? We need a couple more songs for Saturday night.'

'Sounds great. Promised Angie I'd see her about ten in Mario's. That's if I'm in one piece after my dad's finished with me.'

'By the way, Mum said we can leave our gear in the garage,' Tim said. 'Saves us having to keep setting up.'

'Brilliant,' Roy said. 'I'll get Dad to collect you and your drums in the van, Ed. Pick you up about seven. I'd like to have a go at "Johnny B. Goode" as well as "Carol" tonight. I think I can remember most of the words.'

Eddie nodded. 'We've cracked "That'll Be the Day". It sounded great the other night. So, we only need a couple more and we're sorted.'

'What about "Rock and Roll Music"?' Tim said. 'That's another Chuck Berry song we could do.'

'Scribble the words down if you get the time,' Roy said.

They said their goodbyes and Tim set off to walk the short distance home, while Eddie and Roy clambered aboard the waiting number 92 bus which would take them across town to Jackson's Heath, where they both lived.

Eddie, sprawled out across one of the back seats on the top deck of the old red bus, and tried to blow smoke rings. Roy, sitting on the opposite back seat, did likewise. Neither had quite mastered the art yet. Eddie peered through the grimy window. He could see the three girls from the record shop walking towards Mersey Square, their long, red and grey scarves flying out behind them. He knew they all boarded the same bus, the number 74, and assumed they lived close to one another. One day, in the not too distant future, he resolved to pluck up the courage to speak to the one he fancied. The one Roy lusted after threw back her head in laughter at something the dark-haired girl was pointing at, but from where he was sitting, Eddie couldn't see what it was.

His thoughts turned to the group he, Roy and Tim had formed and the direction it was taking. They'd named themselves Roy and The Raiders and Mario, owner of the local coffee bar, had promised them a gig on Saturday night to entertain his customers. He wasn't paying them, it was a trial, he'd said, but they could have free coffees and Cokes all night and if they were any good, he'd pay them to play regular gigs in the future. With the optimism of youth, Eddie was quite sure that one day the group would be as famous as Buddy Holly and The Crickets, and maybe even bigger than Elvis. The stumbling blocks were school, and parents, who tried to rule their lives. Get the next few months out of the way and there would be no stopping them. Nothing on earth would be allowed to get in the way of the group's rise to fame. Eddie lived and died for The Raiders. It was the only thing he was interested in, apart from girls.

The bus pulled away from the stop and he craned his neck to catch a last glimpse of the dark-haired girl, who, for some reason he couldn't yet fathom, currently filled most of his waking thoughts, more so than Angie Turner did these days. Although last night, after she'd led him on and then said no, again, she'd certainly been on his mind as he'd walked home. He could have done without the lecture from his mother, who'd been waiting up for him. He'd been brought back down to earth with her stinging words quicker than any cold shower.

\* \* \*

Jane Wilson, her best friend, Sammy Hardy, and Sammy's stepsister, Pat Mason, hurrying quickly up the High Street towards Mersey Square, were unaware that they were being observed from the top deck of a nearby bus.

Jane pointed to the slight figure of a teenage boy rushing along on the opposite side of the street. 'There's Georgie Green,' she said. 'Shout him, Sammy. Go on, I dare you. Make his day.'

'Get lost!' Sammy threw back her head in laughter, tossing her light-brown hair over her shoulder. 'He'll want to come over and talk. We'll never get rid of him. People will think he's with us.'

'Sammy, you are mean. Poor George,' Jane said. 'He doesn't look quite as gormless as he did at primary school. He's not wearing that pink plaster patch over his eye anymore.'

'He's still got bat ears and thick glasses though,' Sammy said, frowning. 'He's not changed that much, Jane. Get your eyes tested, for God's sake.'

Jane shivered in the biting January wind that whipped and whistled its way through the broken pains in the old bus shelter. She turned up the collar of her thin red blazer, wound her scarf tightly around her neck and pulled her grey wool socks up to her knees. She blew on her cold fingers, reminding herself to look for her gloves when she got home. 'Are we going to the youth club tonight then?' she asked, stamping her feet to stop her toes from freezing.

'Yeah, why not?' Sammy said. 'There's nothing else to do. It's better than staying at home bored stiff, and at least we get to see Stuart Green.'

'I'll call round for you about seven then,' Jane said. 'That boy winked at me again in the record shop. I really like him. He's got the most gorgeous blue eyes I've ever seen. I wonder where he lives. I've only ever seen him in Flanagan and Grey's.

He doesn't go to the youth club, so I don't think he's from our side of the town.'

'Well, the uniform he wears is for Hope End Secondary, so he must live somewhere local,' Pat said. 'And you're right, he's very fanciable,' she added as the bus pulled up, spilling its alighting passengers.

'And in spite of his cheek, so is his dark-haired friend,' Sammy said as she pushed her way through the throng of waiting passengers, her long legs leading the way up to the top deck of the bus.

The threesome flopped down on the back seats as the vehicle slowly lurched its way out of the bus station. They parted company on the corner by the local parade of shops and Sammy and Pat wandered off in the direction of Primrose Avenue, while Jane hurried home to Rosedean Gardens.

* * *

'Eddie, in here, please.'

Eddie kicked off his shoes in the hall and dumped his battered satchel on the carpet. He followed his father's voice into the front parlour. 'What now?' he began.

'Don't take that tone with me, lad,' his dad said, sitting forward in his chair and dropping his newspaper on the floor. 'Your mother tells me you've been skipping school again. What have you got to say about that?'

'I've been to school. Look, I've got inky hands. Anyway, who told her that I haven't? They're lying, whoever they are. You can ask Roy, he was with me.'

His mother hovered in the doorway, nervously wiping her hands on a tea towel. 'Eddie, don't be cheeky to your dad. The head phoned. School board will no doubt be knocking later this week. I wish you wouldn't show us up, son.'

'I don't show you up. I'm hardly ever here. Anyway, I want

my tea and then I'm rehearsing tonight at Tim's. Roy's dad's picking me up in a bit.'

'You're going nowhere,' his dad shouted. 'You stay in tonight and do your homework. If you don't pass your O levels, you won't get the apprenticeship and then bang goes your future.'

'I *am* going out, you can't stop me. I don't wanna be a bloody draughtsman. How many times do I have to tell you? I'm a drummer.'

'Don't you swear at me like that or I'll take my belt to you. You're not too big for a good hiding. You've respect for nobody these days. I've a good mind to sell that drum kit. We bought it on the condition you knuckled down at school this year, but your mother and I have seen no evidence of it so far.'

'Touch my drum kit and you won't see me for dust. I'll walk out and never come back,' Eddie threatened.

'There's no need for that, Eddie.' His mother twisted the tea towel. 'Go and get your tea. It's sausage and mash, in the oven. Take this towel and mind you don't burn your fingers when you lift the plate.'

Eddie took the tea towel and stomped out of the room, slamming the door behind him.

Fred leapt up but Lillian put out a restraining hand. 'Leave it. Let him go out, otherwise we'll have no peace. Why don't you just try a little harder to understand him? I know he's cheeky, but he loves his music and while he's at Tim's place, he's keeping out of mischief. At least it gets him away from Angie Turner.'

'And that'll be the next thing; he'll be getting that lass into trouble. Where was he last night till all hours?'

'Babysitting with her.' Lillian chewed her lips. Fred had voiced the thoughts she always pushed to the back of her mind.

After all, Eddie was still a schoolboy, far too young for such carryings on. But Angie Turner was a forward little madam and she didn't trust her one bit. 'I don't think we need have any worries on that score, Fred. He might be cheeky, but he's not stupid.'

'Well, let's hope you're right.' Fred picked up his newspaper and lit a cigarette.

Lillian went back into the kitchen, where Eddie was finishing his meal.

'Thanks, Mum, that was good. I'll go and get changed. Roy's dad'll be here soon.'

'Okay, Ed. Please try and keep your attendance up at school, love. It'll keep your dad off your back.'

Eddie sighed. 'I'll do my best, but I don't want that apprenticeship. I wish he'd try and understand. When the group gets a few more gigs lined up, we'll be laughing. I'll earn a living with my music. Other people do it, why shouldn't I? If it doesn't work out, well, I've only got me to blame and then I'll look for a proper job.'

Lillian nodded. 'Go and get ready, then. Otherwise you'll keep Roy and his dad waiting.'

## 2

'I'm home,' Jane called and hung her blazer on the coat rack in the back porch. In the warm kitchen her mother, blonde curls flopping down into her eyes where her hairpins had worked loose, was making a pot of tea. Jane sat down at the table and sighed.

'Hiya, love. You look frozen. You said you were coming straight home after school. I bet you've been hanging around that record shop again, haven't you?' Enid pulled a knitted cosy over the teapot. She pushed her hands into the pockets of her apron and carried on talking before Jane could open her mouth to reply.

'Why don't you wear your gabardine raincoat over your blazer in this weather? It's daft going around frozen for the sake of fashion.' She sugared and milked two mugs of tea and handed one to Jane. 'Here, drink this, it'll warm you up. And another thing, don't hitch your skirt up so short. God knows what the neighbours must think. You'll be getting yourself a bad name. I'm surprised you don't get told off at school.'

Jane rolled her eyes as her mother paused to draw breath. 'I don't hitch it up till I get out of school, and I'd rather die than wear that awful raincoat. I told you you'd be wasting your money when you bought it.'

Enid tutted as she salted a pan of potatoes and placed it on the back burner of the stove. The gas ring plopped gently as she leant over to light it with a taper. 'Well, don't you come home moaning to me about being cold then.'

'I didn't, it was you that said I looked frozen. I'm going upstairs to do my homework. Please can I go to the youth club tonight with Sammy and Pat?' She crossed her fingers behind her back. The answer was often no.

'I suppose so, just as long as all your homework's done first and you're not too late back.'

Jane sighed. God, she could go on sometimes, always finding something to moan about. She picked up her heavy satchel and made her way upstairs.

Her younger brother Peter was in his bedroom, playing with his friend, Harry, from next door. Jane stood in the open doorway watching them. Sprawled on the floor, the boys were blowing a football up and down a cardboard pitch with straws. Peter looked up and smiled.

'Hiya, our Jane.'

'Hiya, you two.'

Harry nodded and wiped his nose on his shirtsleeve. 'Hiya, Jane.'

'God, Harry, you snotty little horror!' Jane exclaimed. 'Use your hanky.'

'Not got one. My sleeve'll have to do.'

Jane tutted and went into her own bedroom. She threw her schoolbag on the floor and flopped down onto the bed. Over in the corner stood an old oak chest of drawers and on top, in pride of place, was a cream and blue Dansette record player. Neatly stacked beside it was her collection of records.

She jumped up and pulled a record from its sleeve. The room echoed to the sound of Paul Anka singing 'Diana' and

Jane, oblivious to everything but the music, settled back down on her bed and sang along. She gazed at her surroundings, where, for the first time ever, she'd been allowed to choose the colour scheme. The pink floral curtains complemented the pale pink of the candlewick bedspread and set off the home-made rag rug that partially covered the floor. Her dad said he'd fit a carpet when he got a bit of spare money. The white walls were plastered with current favourite pin-ups: Buddy Holly, Eddie Cochran and James Dean.

Jane's thoughts turned to the boy with the gorgeous blue eyes and how he'd winked at her twice now and smiled, and how each time she'd turned away with embarrassment. He was just the right height for her, not quite as tall as his friends, had a warm friendly smile, and full lips that she was sure would be nice to kiss. Jane's cheeks flamed at the thought and her tummy did a funny little loop. She'd never kissed a boy yet. She couldn't wait to try and hoped her first kiss might be with him. She'd love to pluck up the courage to say hello, but no doubt he thought she didn't like him, because she'd ignored him.

'But I do,' she muttered. 'I really do.' What if he never winked at her again? 'Please God, next time I'll smile, I promise. Let him wink one more time, and I'll never answer Mum back again, ever,' she bargained.

\* \* \*

Roberto Cantello, known as Bob to his friends and family, helped Eddie set up his drum kit in Tim's mum's garage, while Roy proudly carried his Fender Stratocaster guitar and small amplifier in from the van.

'Do you two want picking up later, Roy?' Bob asked.

'No, thanks, Dad. Tim's mum said we can leave our stuff here until we get a regular place to practise. And we're going to the coffee bar for the last hour.'

'Okay. Well in that case, I'm off for a pint. Don't be home too late now, Roy. You know what your mother's like. I'll be the one that gets it in the neck for encouraging you!' Bob grinned, looking exactly like his only son for a moment. His late father had been Italian by birth and Bob and Roy, who was known at school as the 'Italian Stallion', had inherited his dark good looks.

'Hey, and another thing, no drinking. Your mother swears she could smell booze on your breath the other night,' Bob added as he was leaving.

'I was chewing bubblegum. I won't drink, I promise,' Roy called, closing the garage door as Tim produced a bottle of cider and three tumblers from a shelf behind him.

'Here you go, lads.' He handed the tumblers round, slopping cider into each one.

'Where did you get this?' Eddie took a large swig from his tumbler.

'Our Carol. I did her garden last Sunday. She paid me in ciggies and cider.' Tim's cousin Carol was the proud owner of a large house with a garden that closely resembled a jungle.

'I need this drink,' Eddie said. 'Had a row with my dad. He even threatened to get rid of my drums. Has the head spoken to your folks about us playing truant, Roy?'

'They haven't said anything but they've been in the shop all day. School only has the home phone number.'

'They'll probably send the school board instead but at least you're forewarned now. Right then,' Eddie said, draining his glass. 'Two hours practice and then the coffee bar for an hour, eh?'

'Sounds okay to me.' Roy tuned his guitar and fiddled with the knobs on his amplifier. Tim produced several sheets of paper on which he'd scribbled the lyrics of the Chuck Berry songs.

'Switch the tape recorder on, Tim,' Eddie said. 'We'll start with Johnny B. Goode. I'll count us in and you take lead vocals on this one, Roy.'

The enthusiastic trio began and quickly followed up with Eddie Cochran's 'Summertime Blues', Roy taking lead vocals. Two Everly Brothers songs followed – Eddie and Roy's voices blending in perfect harmony as they gained confidence. As 'All I Have to Do Is Dream' came to a melodious ending they stopped for a break and another glass of Tim's cider.

'That wasn't bad,' Eddie said, wiping his sweaty brow with the back of his hand. Tim wound back the reel-to-reel so they could listen. '"Summertime Blues" sounds pretty good, if you ask me. We need to do a lot more work on "Johnny B. Goode", but it was okay for a first attempt.'

They seated themselves on upturned boxes, alongside numerous gardening implements and bits of an old motorbike that Tim was in the throes of dismantling, listening to the tape, feet tapping in rhythm.

Eddie nodded his approval. 'A few wrong notes from Roy here and there on the guitar solos, but those harmonies on "All I Have to Do Is Dream" are really good.'

'Good! They're bloody brilliant,' Roy marvelled. 'We even sound like the Evs. That'll get us the birds, you just watch. We'll be fighting 'em off at the weekend.'

'Let's redo "Dream" and "Summertime Blues". We've almost got those two perfect. You re-tape them, Tim, and then we can listen later in the week. We'll have to take Friday off and come and practise or we won't be ready for Saturday night. The Chuck Berry songs need a bit more polish if we're gonna play them.'

'Is your mum working Friday, Tim?' Roy asked.

'Yep.' Tim nodded. He disappeared into the kitchen and came back carrying a bottle of his mother's sherry. 'Here, have a drop of this, it'll loosen us up a bit more.'

'If Roy gets any looser he'll fall apart,' Eddie said with a laugh. 'And he promised his dad he wouldn't drink.'

'Promises are made to be broken.' Roy held out his glass. 'Ugh!' He took a slug of the sweet liquid and shuddered. 'How the hell do mums drink this?' He held his nose and knocked back the rest in one go, his eyes opening wide with surprise as the sherry hit his stomach. 'On the other hand, it's mixing nicely with the cider. I feel quite pissed, but mellow! Give us another drop, Tim.'

Tim tipped the sherry into Roy's tumbler and then held up the bottle. 'Shit, there's hardly any left. She'll bloody kill me.'

'Is there tea in the pot from teatime?' Eddie asked.

Tim shrugged. 'Probably. But why do you want cold tea?'

'I don't. Pour it in the bottle and put the cork back in. It's the same colour. Your mum'll think it's just gone off and tip it down the sink.'

'Ed, you're a bloody genius, if ever there was one.'

Roy grinned as Tim rushed off to do as Eddie suggested. 'You're not as daft as you look, are you, Ed?'

'Only sometimes!' Eddie said. 'But that's one trick I know definitely works, because I do it to my dad's whisky!' He picked up his drumsticks and twirled them round. 'Right, refreshment break is over. Ready for another bash?'

They re-taped 'Dream' and 'Summertime Blues' and packed away Roy's guitar and Tim's stand-up bass in their respective cases and Eddie threw an old blanket over his drum kit. The leather-jacketed trio locked the garage and made their tipsy way to Mario's Coffee Bar on Broadgate, near the town centre.

'It's a shame those girls don't come in here,' Eddie slurred as he popped a coin in the jukebox and selected a record, while Tim went to the counter to buy three bottles of Coca-Cola.

'Yeah, I often wonder where they go. I've only ever seen

them in the record shop and the bus station.' Roy flopped down at the only empty table by the window.

Mario's was a popular haunt for the town's teenage inhabitants and was always packed out. Tonight, all of the chrome tables and chairs were occupied. Eddie peered through the smoky gloom and spotted his girlfriend, Angie Turner, and her friend, Cathy, jiving together on the small dance floor. He waved to attract their attention.

As the music ended Angie ran over and plonked herself down on Eddie's knee, winding her arms around his neck. Her full, red and black polka-dot dance-skirt billowed out and engulfed them both.

'Hiya, Ed. How are you tonight? Been rehearsing for Saturday?' She pushed his hair from his eyes. 'Ed, you're pissed!'

'I'm not,' he protested. 'Come and dance with me.'

She yanked him to his feet, steadied him as he wobbled and led him over to the jukebox.

Eddie pulled her close and kissed her. 'What shall we choose?'

He ran his hands up and down her back while she selected 'To Know Him Is to Love Him' by the Teddy Bears.

'We can't jive to this, Angie, it's too slow.'

'We can smooch instead.' She grinned and held him close as he swayed with her.

'Are we babysitting on Friday night?' He smiled knowingly, looking into her eyes.

'We might be. Why?'

'You know why. You promised, remember?'

'Is that all you want to go out with me for?' Angie pulled away from him.

'Course not. I like you, you know I do. But you keep promising me, and then you always say no. I thought you loved me?' Eddie pulled her closer and nibbled her ear.

'If *you* loved *me* you wouldn't keep going on about it all the time.'

'And if *you* loved *me*, you'd do it to prove it. Let's go outside.' He pulled her by the hand towards the entrance doors, ignoring the look of disapproval on Cathy's face as they passed. He took her to the car park and pulled her into the darkened recess of the coffee bar's back door. The security light was broken, adding to the privacy.

'Ed, it's freezing,' Angie began as he put his arms around her, silencing her with a kiss.

'I'll soon warm you up,' he said, nibbling her neck.

'Don't leave marks where Mum can see them. She went crackers at the state of my neck last week. Even Pan Stik wouldn't cover them.'

'Shut up and kiss me.' He unbuttoned her black cardigan and slipped his hands inside, feeling the rush of heat to his groin.

'Oh, you're so cold.' She winced as his icy fingers touched her bare flesh. 'Someone might see us.' She peered anxiously over his shoulder at the deserted car park.

'There's no one around.' Eddie pushed her further back, his hands caressing her breasts. He kissed her passionately and ground against her, feeling more aroused by the second. 'We could do it here,' he whispered, pulling up her skirt and getting entangled in layers of net petticoats. 'Christ, how many of these bloody things are you wearing?'

'Four layers of net and one of skirt. Ed, do you love me?'

'Mmm,' he murmured. 'Course I do.' He heard her sigh with pleasure as his hand slipped between her legs and into her knickers. He couldn't believe his luck; she wasn't smacking him away.

'I love you too, Ed,' she whispered, 'but what about, you know, taking precautions?'

'We don't need to if we're standing up. Anyway, I'll be care-

ful,' he said, unzipping his jeans and guiding her hand to his
erection. He felt ready to explode as she stroked him and she
was ready for him too, warm and wet and writhing on his busy
fingers. He tugged her knickers down. She stepped out of them
and he pushed them into his pocket.

'Is that true, are you absolutely sure?'

'What? Course I'm sure. Everybody says so,' he said. He
didn't have a clue if the rumour in the school playground, that
you couldn't get a girl into trouble if you did it standing up, was
true or not but if she was willing to go all the way then he'd take
a chance and sod the consequences! He pushed her legs further
apart and kissed her again as he fumbled to guide himself
inside.

'Angie! Angie, where are you?'

'Shit, it's Cathy!' She pushed Eddie away as Cathy came
into view.

'Angie,' Cathy called again. 'You ready to go? I've got our
coats. Come on or we'll miss the last bus.'

'Fuck!' Eddie exclaimed. He struggled to zip up his jeans,
breathing deeply, as Angie pulled her knickers from his pocket
and slipped them back on.

'Friday. I promise you, Ed,' she whispered. 'If Sally's going
out we'll babysit, if not, we'll go to Norman's Woods.' She
buttoned up her cardigan and straightened her layers of petticoats as Cathy spotted them.

'What are you two up to?' Cathy frowned.

'Nothing, thanks to *you*,' Eddie muttered, glaring at her.

Cathy glared back at him. 'Well, it looks to me like I arrived
just in time.'

'If you say so,' he retorted. He grabbed Angie by the shoulders and kissed her on the lips. 'Friday, definitely!' He turned
and walked back into the coffee bar, silently seething. A couple
more seconds and he'd have been inside her. Damn Cathy,
damn, damn, damn her!

'Well, Mellor, did you get a shag?' Roy grinned, raising an eyebrow at Eddie's flushed face as he joined them at the table.

'Nearly, and then Cathy came looking for her. I was so close, you wouldn't believe how close this time.' Eddie groaned with frustration. 'That's two bloody nights on the run now.'

'Ah well, never mind, mate,' Roy sympathised. 'Get yourself into the lav with a dirty mag when you get home. We'll make an effort to get to know those grammar school girls. Rumour has it they're right little ravers at school. Drop 'em for anybody! John Grey's really friendly with them. He might know where they live and where they go at night.'

'Well, they can't just vanish into thin air when they get on their bus home, can they?' Eddie said.

'We'll find out, don't worry. You leave it to Uncle Roy.' Roy tapped the side of his nose and laughed.

* * *

Angie and Cathy walked briskly down Broadgate towards the bus station, shivering in the cold night air.

'You okay?' Cathy asked, looking at Angie's flushed cheeks and animated expression.

'Yep. Bloody freezing though.' She tucked her cold hands under her armpits for warmth. 'Wish I'd listened to my mother for once and put my scarf and gloves on.'

'I got the distinct impression that Eddie wasn't very happy to see me back then,' Cathy said. 'Did I really interrupt something?'

Angie nodded. 'We were just about to go all the way.'

'Oh, Angie, you weren't? Not at the back of the coffee bar, for goodness' sake. Think about your reputation. Why don't you wait until you meet the boy you want to marry, then it will be special for you?'

'Eddie is the boy I want to marry. I will do too, you just watch me.'

Cathy's frown held disapproval. 'You'll get yourself into trouble. Eddie and that Roy Cantello flirt with every girl they meet. Just 'cos they're in a group, they think they're God's gift!'

'They don't. Anyway, everybody does it and Eddie hasn't been out with anyone other than me,' Angie said. 'He never looks at another girl when we're together. He loves me, he just told me so.'

'Yeah, 'cos he wanted his wicked way. Anyway, it's when you're not together you need to worry about what he's getting up to.' Cathy cast an envious sideways glance at her pretty friend. With her curvy figure, light-brown curls caught up in a fashionable ponytail, sparkling green eyes, and a sprinkling of freckles on her nose, Angie could have the pick of the boys at school and the coffee bar. Although Cathy was tall and slim, with long, brown hair and big blue eyes, it was Angie's flirty ways and sunny personality that drew the boys to her wherever she went.

'You're only jealous because you don't have a boyfriend,' Angie said.

'I'm not getting into an argument with you over him, he's not worth it.' Cathy changed the subject. 'Are you working in the salon this Saturday?'

'Yeah. Can't wait to start my apprenticeship in August. It can be dead boring, just being a Saturday girl, but at least it's got me a permanent place for when I leave school.'

'Don't you get sick of brewing endless cups of tea for the old biddies?'

Angie grinned. 'Course I do, but we have younger clients too. I get to shampoo and take my turn at manning the reception desk. And sometimes, if I'm lucky, I'm invited to stand beside our gorgeous head stylist and observe how he does things. Richard's brilliant and he's been really nice to me. I think he secretly fancies me, but he's engaged.' Angie giggled as Cathy rolled her eyes in mock despair.

As they climbed aboard the bus and found seats upstairs, Angie rummaged in her handbag and took out her cigarettes and a small silver-plated lighter.

'Where's that lighter from? I haven't seen it before.'

'Ed gave it to me last week. Said he found it on the bus.' Angie lit a cigarette and blew a wobbly smoke ring into the air. She grinned at the result. 'My halo. Now that's something Eddie can't do yet!'

'Your mum would go mad if she knew he encouraged you to smoke.'

'Don't be such a square, Cath. Anyway, my mum would go mad if she knew half the things Eddie and I get up to!'

Cathy shrugged. There was little point in arguing. Everyone said that Eddie Mellor was a bad lot, but Angie wouldn't hear a word against him.

* * *

As the bus left Mersey Square, Angie stared dreamily out of the window. She was totally besotted with Eddie, although recently she'd complained to Cathy that he'd started to put his music before her, spending more and more time with Roy and Tim.

She stubbed out her cigarette and shivered with anticipation at the thought of the coming Friday night. If Sally went out, as she usually did, Angie was planning to leave Eddie with no doubts as to just how much he meant to her. And afterwards, when they'd done it and he realised just what she meant to him, he might agree to them getting engaged when they left school in the summer and would hopefully leave the group and think about a proper job. After all, he'd just told her that he loved her, and if you love someone, you should always put them and their needs first.

## 3

About the same time as Roy and The Raiders were rehearsing in Tim's mother's garage, across the other side of town, Jane, Sammy and Pat were making their way to the church youth club. The Wednesday haunt was popular with teenagers from the estate, but to the girls it wasn't quite as exciting a venue as they would have liked. However, as Sammy had pointed out earlier, it was less boring than staying at home.

As they walked arm in arm through the church car park, gravel crunching beneath their shoes and the cold wind whipping their ponytails around their faces, Jane pointed to a tall, dark-haired boy climbing out of a car in front of the hall.

'There's Stuart. Shout him, Sam; you've got a louder voice than us.'

Sammy hollered his name and Stuart turned and waved.

'Just in time,' he called, his face splitting into a big grin. 'Come and help me carry this lot inside, please.'

They hurried over and took a box of records each from the back seat. Stuart lifted out a record player, said goodnight to his father and followed them into the hall.

Eighteen-year-old Stuart Green led a very busy life. He

worked as a disc jockey at several youth clubs, attended art college during the day and on Saturdays and college holidays he worked alongside John in Flanagan and Grey's, where Jane and her friends had first met him.

Inside the warm hall Stuart pulled two trestle tables together, lifted the record player up onto one of them and the boxes of singles onto the other.

'Right, let's inject a bit of life into this bunch.' He looked around at the gum-chewing, listless teenagers huddled in small groups and slouching against the wood-panelled walls.

'Get up and dance, girls, show 'em how it's done.'

The girls took off their coats and claimed a table and chairs as the unmistakable sound of Buddy Holly and The Crickets, 'That'll Be the Day', filled the room.

'Oh God!' Pat exclaimed. 'Here comes Doug Two Left Feet Murray. I'm going to the toilet.'

She shot out of the door as the lad, who'd been playing table tennis with his friends, swaggered across the room, patting his elaborate Tony Curtis quiff into place. 'Wanna dance?' he directed at Sammy.

'Err, oh... all right then,' she said ungraciously and followed the ginger-haired boy onto the dance floor. She glared over her shoulder at Jane, who'd deliberately bent to fiddle with the heel of her shoe rather than meet Doug's roving eye.

Jane looked up, an amused expression on her face. Doug was not the most graceful dancer in the world, she observed, as Sammy yelled in pain when he stood on her foot for the third time in as many seconds. Jane wrinkled her nose as she gazed around the room. None of the lads were much to write home about, and that included looks!

'I'll dance with Jane and Pat, it's safer!' Sammy snapped at the hapless Doug as she limped back to her friends.

'Suit yourself!' He spun on his heel and sloped back to where his mates sat grinning at his embarrassment.

'Poor Doug,' Jane said. 'At least he tries, but those drain-pipes are cutting him in two. No wonder he can't dance properly.'

'I didn't mean to be horrible,' Sammy said. 'But he shouldn't be so flippin' clumsy. He's better off sticking to table tennis! Just look at the state of my new shoes.' She rubbed her hanky over the footprints on the black patent leather, left by Doug's crepe-soled brothel creepers. 'Bet those nice-looking lads in the record shop aren't as left-footed as him,' she muttered, almost to herself.

'Which nice-looking lads, Sammy?' Stuart asked, his green eyes twinkling with amusement. 'Do you mean me and John?'

Sammy blushed and looked at Jane for assistance.

Jane's eyes sparkled as she spoke with an enthusiasm that belied her usual shyness. 'There's three lads go in the shop most nights at four thirty, and on Saturday mornings. They wear grey blazers for school, and black leather jackets for casual. We think they go to Hope End Secondary. Do you know them, Stu?'

'Might do, but there's loads of schoolkids come in the shop. What do they look like?'

'Nothing like the usual schoolkids,' Sammy chipped in. 'They actually look quite grown-up.'

'One of them has floppy brown hair and the most gorgeous blue eyes. The second is tall, blond and has a look of Eddie Cochran, and the third is very tall, with really dark hair and sort of sultry brown eyes. He looks like Elvis, but a bit foreign!' Jane finished with a dreamy sigh.

Stuart laughed. 'Bloody hell, Jane! Top marks for observa-tion. You've just described Eddie Mellor, Tim Davis and Roy Cantello to a T. I do know them as it happens, we're good friends. Do you fancy them, or something?'

Sammy nodded. 'Jane fancies Blue Eyes. He keeps winking at her, but she's shy and turns away.'

'That's Eddie Mellor. I've got a feeling he's dating a girl

from school, but if you like him, I'll introduce you anyway. You should come to Mario's Coffee Bar on Broadgate. The boys are in a group and they're playing their first gig on Saturday. They're called Roy and The Raiders. I'll be going with John Grey and you're welcome to join us.'

'I don't know if I'll be allowed to do that,' Jane said, disappointed that the blue-eyed boy may already have a girlfriend. 'You know what my parents are like. Took them ages to let me start coming here. I'll ask, but don't expect a miracle.'

'It'll be all right, Jane,' Sammy said. 'So... what's the one with the sultry eyes called, Roy or Tim?'

'That's Roy Cantello himself,' Stuart said. 'You wanna be careful, girls. He and Eddie have a reputation for being bad boys.'

'Why, what's wrong with them?' Jane asked. 'They look really nice, and they're very handsome.'

'Oh, they're handsome all right. But they always seem to be in trouble of one sort or another. They're a good laugh though and they're fun to be with. You just need to have your wits about you, so I've heard. A word of warning, make sure you're not alone with them until you get to know them properly, safety in numbers and all that. Roy's nickname's "The Italian Stallion", and not without good reason, I believe!'

Sammy grinned. 'Hmm, thanks for the warning. I'd love to go on Saturday. We've never seen a group play live. Ask your mum, Jane, see what she says.'

Pat nodded. 'She'll let you go. Just be nice for the rest of the week and try not to pick any arguments.'

'I'll do my best,' Jane muttered. 'It's all right for you two; Tom and Molly are much more easy-going than mine. You get away with murder.'

Sammy rolled her eyes and laughed. 'It's 'cos they're newly-weds. They don't seem to notice us half the time, which is very handy!'

'Yeah, but then there's the lovey-dovey aspect as well,' Pat said. 'They're always kissing and cuddling when they think we're not looking. I mean, they're in their thirties, they should be past all that at their age!'

'Yuck!' Sammy laughed and stuck her fingers down her throat in a mock vomiting gesture.

'Well, if you think you can make it, we'll be there from about eight,' Stuart said, laughing at Sammy's antics. 'Let's have some more music. A bit of Jerry Lee Lewis, I think.'

As a 'Whole Lotta Shakin' Going On' echoed around the room the floor quickly filled. Pat and Jane jived together and Stuart and Sammy took to the floor, her ponytail flying out behind her as he twirled her under his arm, his long jean-clad legs and tall, slim body complementing Sammy's slender form.

'Stuart can dance so well,' Jane said a few moments later as a breathless Sammy re-joined her and Pat.

'Can't he just,' Sammy gasped, taking deep breaths, her cheeks flushed and her cool blue eyes sparkling.

'You're not so bad yourself,' Jane said. 'You should enter one of those jiving competitions they do at the Town Hall.'

'Maybe I will. I need a regular partner first.'

'What about Stuart? You look really good together,' Jane said. 'And it's so obvious he fancies you.'

Sammy frowned. 'Stuart doesn't fancy me. We're just good friends. Anyway, there's someone else I had in mind actually!'

'Who?' Jane and Pat choroused.

'The dark-haired boy in that group, "The Italian Stallion!"'

'You never let on that you fancied him,' Jane said. 'Anyway, you heard what Stuart said, both he and Eddie have bad reputations already and they can't be much more than sixteen, if they're even that. You don't want to get mixed up with someone like Roy. He sounds like the sort who'd get a girl into trouble and then clear off.'

'Well, I like him. He's really sexy-looking. Like Elvis and

James Dean rolled into one. Anyway, he might not be as bad as Stuart seems to think he is, and he did say he was good fun, didn't he? And I want some fun!'

Pat sighed and looked at Jane, who shook her head in resignation. They put on their coats and called goodbye to Stuart as they left the building.

* * *

'Err, Mum, please can I go to the coffee bar in Stockport on Saturday night with Sammy and Pat?' Jane asked, standing on one leg in the kitchen with all her fingers crossed behind her back, waiting for the no she was sure would come. Though why standing on one leg should make a difference she didn't know, but it was something she'd done since childhood.

Enid pursed her lips. 'Oh, I don't know, Jane. I mean, it's one thing going to the youth club, but the coffee bar... I'm not sure I like the idea, love. I think you're a bit too young to be going out on Saturday nights. There are all sorts of scruffy youths hanging about places like that.'

Jane suppressed a giggle. As far as her mother was concerned, any lad wearing a leather jacket and tight jeans was a scruffy youth!

'Mum, I'll be okay. There'll be three of us and we're all sensible. You should trust me; I'm fifteen this year. Everyone from school goes out on Saturday night.'

'I do trust you, love. It's young lads I don't trust,' Enid said. 'I believe that coffee bar's full of lads in black leather.'

'John and Stuart from the record shop are going and they're ever so nice. Anyway, you've never been yourself, so how do you know what goes on in there?'

'It's not what I know, it's what I've heard!' Enid bent to pick up a basket of laundry from the floor. 'Ask your dad and if he says it's okay, then you can go.'

Jane sidled up to her dad, who was almost asleep in his favourite chair in front of the lounge fire, and pleaded her case.

'What did your mother say?' he asked, lighting a cigarette.

'To ask you.'

He rolled his eyes. 'Typical! I don't see why not. Just make sure you're home for ten thirty.' Jane dashed out of the lounge and up to her bedroom before he had a change of heart. Half ten was a bit early to come home, but it was the best offer she was likely to get and she could always add an extra few minutes by missing the earlier bus home.

'We've to be home by eleven anyway, so a bit earlier is okay with us,' Sammy said when Jane told her that she was allowed to go.

'Thanks, mate,' Eddie said as Stuart passed him a cigarette and light. It was late Friday afternoon and following another day of truant and rehearsals the boys were in Flanagan and Grey's, begging fags from Stuart and John.

'Did you know you had an admirer?' Stuart said.

'Who me?' Apart from Angie, Eddie knew he had plenty of admirers at school, but Stuart would be unlikely to know them.

'The three girls from the grammar school who sometimes come in at half four were asking me about you lot the other night at the youth club. The little dark-haired one, Jane, apparently has a crush on you, Ed.'

Eddie felt his cheeks heat as Tim and Roy laughed.

'Now it's his turn to blush,' Roy teased. 'He thinks she's lovely, don't you, Ed? Trouble is he reckons she's too shy to speak to him. He thinks she doesn't want to know.'

'Well, she does and she may be going to Mario's tomorrow night with her friends. I told them you lot are playing there so make yourself available if you want an introduction.'

'What about the tall bird with the long legs?' Roy asked, hopefully.

'What about her?' Stuart's expression was guarded.

'Well... did she say anything about me?'

'Not specifically. She's very nice though. She and I are quite friendly.'

Roy looked crestfallen. Eddie peered at him closely. Stuart obviously didn't realise that for once in his life Roy was serious.

'We're just friends, Roy,' Stuart said. 'I mean, if you fancy her, don't let me stop you. She's called Sammy, by the way.'

'Sammy? Oh, Samantha. That's sexy. I never had her down as a Samantha! You sure you don't mind, Stu?' Roy's tone was more hopeful.

'Not at all,' Stuart muttered. 'Anyway, she did ask me your name.'

Eddie looked at Stuart, and then again at Roy, sensing rivalry in the air. Roy was determined to get to know Sammy, and as a rule was usually so sure of himself that the prospect of her being friendly with another lad had probably not even crossed his mind.

'And I suppose you fancy the little blonde?' John chipped in, looking at Tim.

Tim's face lit up and he smiled.

'Now that's convenient. Well, they'll be in Mario's about eight, and we'll introduce you.'

* * *

'Have you thought what you'll do about Angie if this Jane is okay?' Roy asked as he and Eddie sat on the bus going home.

'I'm not doing anything unless I need to,' Eddie said. 'I mean, Jane might not like me once she meets me. She seems really shy. She might not even let me kiss her, never mind anything else!'

Roy nodded. 'You could always date them both. At least you know Angie's a cert. You're bound to get your leg over tonight.'

'Hopefully. She told me yesterday that Sally's not going out though so we won't be babysitting. We're going to the pictures and Norman's Woods later. She's off out with Cathy and her mates from the salon tomorrow night then meeting me after the gig, which is great. I don't really want her there for the first one. She'll only be pulling her face and it'll put me off. And also, it'll give me a chance to see what Jane's like without her hanging around, cramping my style.'

Roy nodded. 'What film are you seeing tonight?'

'Don't know and I don't really care. Angie said *Jailhouse Rock*'s re-showing at the Plaza, so probably that.'

'You're just going along for the grope on the back row, I suppose!'

'Something along those lines,' Eddie said with a lustful grin.

* * *

Eddie slid his arm along the seat and around Angie's shoulders. She snuggled into him. They were sitting on the back row of the upper circle in the double Pullman seats that were unusually quiet for a Friday night. No doubt the threat of snow had kept people at home. All the better for a bit of privacy. He hoped the snow would wait until after the planned trip to Norman's Woods. Angie had moaned about the cold earlier and was all bundled up in a big coat, jeans and boots. Not ideal clothes for what they had in mind, or at least he did.

'Take your coat off,' he whispered.

'It's too cold.'

'I can't get near you.'

She tutted and struggled out of it.

'Shove it on the seat next to you,' he said. 'Nobody's gonna be sitting there.'

He rolled his eyes as the usherette shone her torch in their direction and said, 'Shh.' She showed a man to the row just below them and Eddie stared in dismay as he took a seat directly in front. 'Why has she done that? Why couldn't he sit somewhere else? There are loads of empty seats. And why does he want a double?'

'Ed, stop it, he'll hear you.'

'I don't care. She's done that on purpose.'

Angie giggled and took a bag of boiled sweets from her bag. 'Probably doesn't trust us. Have a sweet and shut up. The film's about to start.'

'I don't want one. And I can't kiss you if you're sucking bloody sweets.' Eddie sighed and put his arm around her again.

She snuggled back into him. As Elvis rocked his way around the jailhouse, Eddie's fumbles and kisses grew more demanding. Angie had her hand on his thigh and he manoeuvred it so that she was cradling his balls. He moaned as she caressed him and slipped his hand under her sweater, cupping her breasts in turn. He moved his hand down between her thighs, stroking the best he could through the denim and wishing she'd worn a skirt. Their sighs and gasps drowned the noise coming from in front until Angie stiffened and pulled away. Her hand flew to her mouth and she pointed to the man, who was doing enough huffing and puffing of his own.

'What's he up to?' she whispered as the man's arm moved up and down and his grunting grew louder.

'Wanking himself off, the dirty bastard!' Eddie exclaimed. 'Where's that bloody usherette?' He jumped to his feet and waved his arms around to attract her attention but the woman was down at the front of the circle, her eyes firmly fixed on Elvis.

'Get your coat, we're going.' Eddie slapped the back of the

man's balding head and pulled Angie to her feet. 'Filthy perv,' he yelled as the man turned around. The usherette also turned and shone her torch in their direction.

'What's going on?' she demanded, pounding up the steps.

'Him, tossing himself off in front of me and my girl,' Eddie said.

'That's disgusting! I'll get the manager,' she said as the man got to his feet, apologising.

'Come on, let's get out of here,' Eddie said, giving the man a glare. 'It's no wonder you're on your own, mate.'

He led Angie down the steep stairs and out of the circle as the man went off in the opposite direction. 'Sorry about that,' he said to Angie. 'You okay?'

'Yeah.' She shuddered as he held her close. 'Ugh, makes me feel creepy. Dirty sod.'

Out on the pavement Eddie gazed in dismay at the snow-covered roads. 'Shit, we were only in there an hour. Christ, I hope the buses are still running.'

Angie sighed. 'Looks like tonight's a write-off, Ed. We can't go to the woods now.'

He took her hand as a bus came slowly around the corner. 'Nope, I don't suppose we should. I'd better get you home while I still can.'

'I'm sorry.'

'It's not your fault. I guess it's just not meant to be at the moment.' He was disappointed but even he could see it was a mad idea to have a shag in the snow. 'Maybe tomorrow night after the gig. There might be a dressing room we can use.'

She nodded. 'We'll see, eh?'

## 4

Jane took ages getting ready. Her wardrobe was far from extensive, so it wasn't so much the choice of clothes as how to wear her hair that was the problem. Long and straight with a fringe, she usually wore it in a neat ponytail. Loose and shiny, cascading onto her shoulders, she liked the fact that she looked so much more grown-up. With a fresh clean scent from her lemon shampoo, it framed her heart-shaped face. After a touch of pale-pink lipstick and a spray of In Love perfume, she carefully rolled on a pair of stockings and clipped them up with a suspender belt. She hated the way the suspenders dug in but she wasn't wearing grey school socks tonight. She pulled on a straight black-and-white check pinafore dress over a black polo-necked sweater and long black boots. It was far too cold to be wearing flimsy dancing shoes and the snow would come over the top of them. She stepped onto the landing to check her appearance in the full-length mirror. Twisting this way and that, she decided she looked okay and picked up her coat and handbag.

'Bye, Mum, Dad,' she said, popping her head around the lounge door.

'Bye, love,' her mum said. 'Now just be careful and what-ever you do, don't speak to any strange lads.'

'Yes, Mum, I'll be fine. See you,' she called, hurrying out of the front door before her mother could think of any other warn-ings to put a damper on the night. For heaven's sake, the whole idea of going out was to meet strange lads, especially one named Eddie Mellor.

She'd thought about nothing else and was praying that Stuart had been mistaken about Eddie having a girlfriend.

Pat and Sammy were waiting at the bus stop for her as the number 74 pulled into the lay-by. They jumped on board and settled back in their seats as the bus trundled up the road.

'You two look nice.' Jane admired their black pencil skirts and Sammy's red sweater and Pat's blue one. They too had on warm boots and had left their hair loose. Sammy's was almost down to her waist, while Pat's fell neatly onto her shoulders.

'Molly treated us to the sweaters and Sammy made the skirts,' Pat said. 'Clever devil, isn't she?'

'I had a little help from Mum with the cutting out, but they were dead easy. I'll make one for you, Jane, if you get some material. I feel we might need more going-out clothes after tonight,' she finished with a grin.

Jane stared out of the grimy window. 'It's starting to snow again,' she said, pulling a face. 'I hate this cold weather.'

'Me too,' Sammy said. 'Next stop, girls.' She got up and rang the bell as the bus approached Broadgate. It dropped them outside the corset shop and they collapsed in fits of giggles as Sammy pointed to a huge pair of pink bloomers gracing the front of the window. 'My God, look at the size of those. A family of five could use them for camping and still have one leg left over! Shoot me if I ever get to that size, please.'

Jane gasped with delight as she gazed in the window of Susan Smarts next door. She pointed to a pale-blue silk shift dress. 'Just look at that. It would look really good on you,

Sammy. The colour would suit your eyes and the style would show off your long legs.'

'You'd have to save up for years!' Pat exclaimed. 'Look at the price, eighty-nine shillings and eleven pence!'

'It's 'cos it's real silk,' Sammy said. 'I'll never be able to afford anything like that, not in a million years. Bet I could make one similar if I could get my hands on the fabric. It's a simple enough style.'

'You're really good at making clothes, Sammy,' Jane said.

'I plan to have my own dressmaking business one day.'

'You will do too.' Jane nodded. 'God, here we are,' she said as Mario's came into view. 'I feel really nervous now. Oh look, there's a poster advertising the gig.'

'Well, it's definitely the same three lads,' Sammy said, gazing at the black and white photo of the group. 'Look at those sexy, come-to-bed-eyes on Roy.'

'Sammy!' Pat exclaimed.

'Oh, Pat, don't be so bloody square! I only said he's got sexy eyes.' Pat blushed as Sammy tutted and grabbed her by the arm. 'Come on, let's go in.'

Jane peered through the crowd and the smoky gloom and spotted Stuart and John standing beside the small stage where a drum kit, proudly bearing the name Roy and The Raiders, stood behind a double bass and a Fender guitar, propped against an amp.

Stuart looked across and waved. He beckoned them over.

Jane pushed her way through the chrome tables and chairs, Sammy and Pat following and Stuart led them to a table where several people were seated.

'This is Jane, Pat, and Sammy, everyone. These are my friends Roy, Tim, Vincento and Rosa, whose dad owns this place, and this,' he finished, nudging Jane and pointing to a boy who was looking intently at her, 'is Eddie Mellor.'

Eddie nodded at Jane. She smiled shyly as his bright blue

eyes held her gaze. She took off her coat and sat down next to him before her legs gave way. Her stomach was already doing somersaults. It was him – it was definitely him, and he was alone.

Pat and Sammy sat down next to Roy and Tim, who'd moved over to make room. Roy wasted no time, sliding his arm casually around the back of Sammy's chair, lightly stroking her hair while Stuart went off to get coffee for the girls.

Jane was conscious of her cheeks heating as Eddie asked her how long she'd known Stuart, his eyes never leaving her face.

'We met him a few months ago in the record shop. Then we discovered he was the DJ at our youth club,' she said with a rush.

He frowned. 'Stu's DJ evenings are for young kids. So how old are you?'

'Oh, I'm sixteen,' Jane fibbed. She had a feeling Eddie would lose interest if she told him she wasn't even fifteen until November. 'How about you?'

'Same as you.'

'Are you at college?' She knew full well he was still at school, but didn't want him to know that she knew anything about him, just yet. Sammy had told her it was best to play hard to get at first.

'No. I leave school in July.'

'So, will you go to college then?'

'God no, I've had enough learning. I play drums. I want to be a professional musician.'

'What do you play?' Jane asked.

'Drums, I just told you!'

'No, I mean what sort of music, you idiot!' Jane laughed and he laughed with her, breaking the ice.

'Rock 'n' roll, of course. What else?' He still hadn't taken his eyes off her face.

Stuart came back with the coffees and Jane took a sip of

hers, grimacing. There was absolutely no taste of coffee about the hot frothy liquid whatsoever.

'Want one?' Eddie held out a packet of cigarettes.

'No, thanks, I don't smoke.'

'Really?' He pulled chewing gum from his pocket. 'Gum then?'

She shook her head.

Eddie shrugged. 'Jive then?'

'Please.'

On the dance floor he pulled her into his arms. Apart from his big blue eyes and long dark lashes, Jane noticed the dimple that hollowed out most of his chin. He also jived brilliantly, twirling her round until she was dizzy.

He smiled as they danced. 'Been dying to get to know you for ages. Thought I'd frightened you off when I winked at you. Fancy going out sometime?'

Jane's hands felt sticky in his and her stomach was flip-flop-ping all over the place. He mustn't be seeing anyone. He wouldn't ask her out otherwise. She nodded her head, hoping that when she spoke, her voice wouldn't go squeaky with excite-ment. 'I'd love to. I've, err, wanted to get to know you as well. But nice girls don't speak first to boys.'

'Is that right?' He grinned and pulled her close. 'You're funny, Jane. Roy fancies your friend, the tall one with the long legs.'

'She fancies him as well. Here they come now,' she said as an eager Roy led Sammy onto the dance floor. She grinned and winked at Jane and Eddie over Roy's shoulder.

'They look good together,' Eddie said as the young couple jived for all they were worth, their limbs flailing in all directions, Sammy's long brown hair flying out behind.

'They do.'

He glanced at his watch. 'I need to get changed. I'll see you after the first set.' He pulled her close, kissed her firmly on the

lips and took her back to the table, where she sat down, hands
shaking and heart thudding. The kiss had taken her by surprise
and she'd not responded because she wasn't sure how to. Hopefully he'd kiss her again later and next time she'd be ready to kiss
him back.

* * *

Dressed in black T-shirts and tight jeans, The Raiders
assembled on the small stage as Mario introduced them. People
moved forward as they started to play. Eddie counted in the
beat and Roy played the opening chords of 'That'll Be the Day'.
A cheer went up and couples began to dance again.

Jane looked at Sammy, eyebrows raised in surprise. 'They're
good,' she mouthed. Sammy nodded her agreement. Jane loved
the way Eddie shook his fringe in rhythm and she smiled as he
looked across and winked. Roy blew a kiss in Sammy's direction
and she pretended to catch it and blow it back. During the first
break Eddie asked Jane to dance again and held her close as
they swayed in time to Conway Twitty's 'It's Only Make
Believe'. The second set flew by, each Raider taking turns to
sing solo. But the best was still to come as Roy and Eddie sang
their Everly Brothers duets.

'Oh my God, they're wonderful,' Jane said as note-perfect
harmonies filled the silent room. The cheers and claps and
whistles that followed were overwhelming.

Sammy nodded, seeming lost for words. 'Can't believe it.
They should be doing proper clubs, not coffee bars.'

'Maybe that's what they plan to do when they leave school.'

As Eddie rejoined her, Jane realised she'd have to leave if
she was to get home in time. She told Sammy and Pat they
needed to go. The boys offered to walk them to the Mersey
Square bus stop before the last spot.

'Are you going in the record shop next week?' Eddie asked, reaching for Jane's hand as they hurried along Broadgate.

'We go in most days.'

'I'll see you Monday then.'

She nodded; thrilled that he'd made a date. There'd been no sign or mention of a girlfriend all night, so Stuart must have been mistaken. Anyway, Jane reasoned, if Eddie was seeing someone, surely the girl would have been with him tonight to celebrate his first gig?

He put his arms around her, pulled her into the bus shelter and kissed her. This time she did what came naturally and kissed him back. It was easy after all and the feelings were overwhelming. Butterflies and funny little tugging sensations flared low in her tummy as Eddie pushed her back against the wall of the shelter, kissing her for all he was worth. He stopped and looked into her eyes. 'Wow!' he whispered and sighed into her hair. She snuggled into him and he held her tight. Sammy and Roy were in a passionate clinch in a dark corner. Roy's hands, appearing to have a mind of their own, were inside Sammy's unbuttoned coat.

Pat, holding hands with Tim, shook her head in their direction. 'So much for playing hard to get.'

Jane and Eddie grinned. She no longer felt shy. He was nice to be with and she felt really at ease with him. The bus arrived and he gave her a last lingering kiss and said he'd see her Monday. She and Pat jumped on and found seats. Jane banged on the window to attract Sammy's attention.

'Hurry up,' she mouthed as Sammy emerged from yet another passionate embrace, Roy seeming reluctant to let her go.

Dashing on board, flushed and happy, she flopped down behind them. 'I'm in love,' she said breathlessly, straightening her skirt and fastening her coat. 'Wow, what a kisser!' She lowered her voice so the other passengers couldn't hear her. 'And I know why they call him "The Italian Stallion!"'

'Sammy!' Pat exclaimed, blushing furiously.

'Well, when he was pressed up against me like that, I could hardly miss it! God, I tell you, he's unbelievably sexy, arms like an octopus, but nothing I couldn't handle.'

'You don't want to be alone with him, he was bad enough with people around,' Pat said, frowning.

'Oh, but I do,' Sammy smirked. 'I'm meeting him tomorrow. We're going for a walk in the snow.'

'Was Eddie as nice as you hoped he would be?' Pat asked Jane, who was staring dreamily out of the window.

'Hmm, he was lovely. He's a good kisser too! What about Tim?'

Pat nodded. 'He's very nice. I'm going to see him again.'

'By the way,' Jane remembered, 'I told Eddie I was sixteen. I thought it might put him off if he thought I was just a kid.'

Sammy shrugged. 'Err, actually, I told Roy I was too.'

Pat nodded. 'S'okay, I won't blab.'

'It's all right for you two,' Jane said. 'You're both fifteen in a few months anyway. November is ages off for me.'

'Roy seemed happy when I told him I was sixteen,' Sammy said. 'He said, "Great, the age of consent!" He's a wicked boy, a handful in more ways than one!' She stood up as the bus pulled up at their stop. 'C'mon, you two, let's go and have nice dreams!'

Jane smiled. She couldn't wait to get home to dream about Eddie and his kisses that still lingered on her lips.

* * *

As the boys hurried back down Broadgate, Eddie's mind was firmly on Jane. He loved the feel of her in his arms and her lovely lips on his. Cold though it was in the bus shelter, he could have stayed there and held her all night. He was lost in reverie as Roy's deep voice broke his thoughts.

'That Sammy's hot stuff! Thought she might be a right stuck-up cow with her nose always in the air, but she's not at all. I'm gonna take her to Norman's Woods tomorrow if she can get out.'

Eddie looked at Roy's animated face. He'd had loads of girl-friends, dated virtually every girl in class, but he'd never seen him look this elated. He usually off-loaded them after the first couple of dates, moving on to the next. This time though Eddie had the feeling it might be different.

Back in Mario's, Eddie heard his name being called as he came out of the dressing room. He turned and saw Angie waving at him. She came over, kissed him and wound her arms around his neck.

'Did you find out if there's a dressing room we can use? I won't let you down tonight, Ed, I promise. Have we time for a dance?'

He sighed and loosened her arms. He'd forgotten about his suggestion of doing it in the dressing room but, in any case, it was too small with the groups' clothes and instrument cases in there, not to mention Roy and Tim walking in and out. He didn't want to hurt Angie's feelings, but wanted to sit quietly for a few minutes and recapture the memory of Jane in his arms.

'I'm a bit tired, Angie. Would you mind if we give tonight a miss?'

'Okay then. I'll dance with Cathy instead.'

He felt a bit guilty but now that he'd actually held Jane he couldn't imagine ever wanting to hold or kiss Angie again, let alone shag her. She shrugged and walked back to Cathy.

'You okay, Ed?' Roy asked.

'Yeah, fine, thanks. But I've upset Angie. I don't wanna dance, I just want to think about Jane.'

'Ah, the boy's in love!' Roy teased.

## 5

Jane yawned and rubbed her eyes. She'd been awake ages thinking about Eddie. She couldn't get him out of her head and wished he'd arranged to see her today like Roy had Sammy. The Sunday morning smell of fried breakfast made her tummy rumble. She slid out of bed and ran down the stairs.

'Morning, love. Did you have a good time last night?' Her mum, standing by the cooker frying bacon, handed her a plate of toast. 'Get that down you to be going on with.'

'Err, yes.' Jane hoped her face wasn't going red.

'So, who was there, anyone from school?'

'A few. But mainly people from the record shop. I've been thinking,' Jane changed the subject before her mum probed further. 'I'm going to ask John Grey if he'll give me a Saturday job. I'd like to earn a bit of money to buy nice clothes for going out.'

'Well, you spend enough time in there, you might as well as get paid for it.'

'Is it okay to go to Sammy's later to do my homework?'

'I suppose so.' Her mum plonked a plate of egg and bacon in

front of her. 'It doesn't matter where you do it as long as it's done.'

* * *

Pat was alone when Jane joined her. As soon as their parents' backs were turned, Sammy had donned lipstick and perfume and dashed out to meet Roy.

'Molly'll do her nut if she finds out where Sammy's gone,' Pat said. She handed Jane a mug of coffee. They sat in the dining room, books spread across the table. 'Hope she'll be okay. Roy was a bit of a handful last night, don't you think?'

Jane smiled and opened her maths book. 'He was, but she'll be having more fun than us. Can't wait to see Eddie. Tomorrow seems ages away.'

'I'm looking forward to seeing Tim again.'

'I felt wobbly and had strange feelings in my tummy when Eddie kissed me.' Jane chewed the end of her pencil. 'Did you feel anything like that when Tim kissed you?'

Pat frowned. 'Not really. But he only kind of pecked me on the cheek.'

'Hmm, well, they were nice feelings. Hope I get them again.'

'Must be love,' Pat teased. 'Right, let's get cracking then we can go upstairs and listen to some records before Dad and Molly come home.'

* * *

Sammy pulled her scarf tightly around her neck as she hurried along to the rec, where Roy had told her to meet him. It was still very cold but had stopped snowing. Her heart did a funny little skip when she spotted him leaning against a tree, smoking. He'd

flicked the fur-lined collar of his black leather biking jacket up
around his ears but still looked frozen. His face lit up and he
waved. He threw his cigarette down as she ran towards him, and
caught her in his arms, dropping a kiss on her lips.

'Where are we going?' she asked as he took her hand and
pulled her back up the path she'd just run down.

'Norman's Woods. It's nice down there in the snow. Then
we can go get a hot drink somewhere to warm us up. I'd take
you back to mine but my parents have got visitors today.'

They picked their way carefully down the sloping path that
led to the depths of the woods. Roy had his arm around her
waist and Sammy was glad he was saving her from falling as
they slipped and slithered along.

'I had a great time last night,' she said. 'We thought you
were brilliant.'

'Really?' He looked pleased. 'Mario thought so, too. He's
offered us a regular Saturday night spot. Come along next week
if you can.'

'I'd love to. I'll tell Jane and Pat.'

In a clearing Roy brushed the snow off an old bench. They
sat down, huddled together and he slipped his hands inside her
coat.

'That's better,' he whispered. He kissed and held her tight.
Sammy lifted her denim-clad legs up over his knees and moved
closer. 'Wish we had somewhere warm to cuddle up,' he said,
stroking her hip. 'Not very romantic, is it?' He pulled her right
up onto his knee, slid his hands beneath her sweater and
nibbled her neck.

She gasped as he cupped her breasts and rubbed his thumbs
over her nipples through the silky fabric of her bra. She pushed
herself closer, kissing him for all she was worth. She swung
herself around and straddled him, knees either side of his
thighs. He groaned as she lowered herself and wriggled against

the bulge in his jeans. He kissed her and squeezed her so tight, she squealed. She knew instinctively what would please him, but had no idea how she knew. Apart from snogging the odd lad she'd never had a boyfriend. She'd been so tempted to touch him last night in the bus shelter but hadn't dared. Now she slipped her hand between them and rubbed the front of his jeans.

'You'd better stop that, or else,' he groaned after some deep kissing.

'Or else what?'

'It'll be too late and I'd really like us to be somewhere a bit nicer than this.'

She smiled and climbed off his knee. 'Sorry.'

'Don't be. It was just a bit too good though.' He jumped to his feet. 'Let's go find somewhere to have that hot drink.'

'Will it go?' She looked pointedly at his groin.

'Eventually, now you're off my knee.'

She grinned, picked up a handful of snow and threw it at him.

'You want a snowball fight? Right, lady, you asked for it.' He rolled a snowball and chucked it at her. She threw one back and he bombarded her as she ran off up the sloping path with him close behind. Giggling and out of breath, she grabbed his arm to stop herself slipping, but too late, Roy lost his footing and they slid on their backsides to the bottom. They lay side by side, gasping, and then he turned to her and looked into her eyes and Sammy knew she was lost. They locked lips as he rolled on top. The kiss seemed to go on forever. His hands were everywhere but the damp seeping through the back of her coat and into her hair made her realise they were going too far.

'Roy, stop,' she whispered, shivering with cold and ecstasy.

'Okay.' He sighed and rolled away, then jumped up and pulled her to her feet. He brushed her clothes, picked twigs and clumps of snow from her hair and kissed the scratches on her hand where it had scraped against something on the way down.

'Better get you home and cleaned up before you catch your death,' he said. 'Your parents will wonder what the hell I've been doing to you.' He kissed her again and said that he needed her.

'Do you?' Did he mean he wanted to go all the way? She didn't like to ask because he'd know then that she was totally inexperienced and she was supposed to be sixteen.

He smiled. 'I do.'

She squeezed his hand as they set off for home, nervous butterflies dancing all around in her tummy.

* * *

'Psst,' Sammy hissed. 'They still out?'

Pat, at the dining table with Jane, turned and stared open-mouthed. 'Look at the state of you. Where've you been?'

'Norman's Woods.' Sammy stepped into the room, Roy on her heels. 'We fell down a slope. Bit muddy where the snow was melting. We need to get cleaned up a bit, Roy, can't go home looking like this.'

'Hurry up then, Dad and Molly'll be back soon. You look like you've been rolling all over the floor; they'll never believe you fell.'

Roy slung his arm around Sammy's shoulders and pulled her close. 'We did do a fair bit of rolling round though, didn't we, Sam?'

She felt her cheeks heating and dug him in the ribs. 'Behave!'

Pat tutted her disapproval. 'Stop messing about. Get him out of here, quick. Sorry, Roy, nothing personal, but the parents will stop us going out if they think she's been up to something.'

'I understand. I'll just use the bathroom and go.'

'Take your boots off first,' Sammy warned. They'd already trod mud on the green floral carpet.

'You should have taken them off by the back door,' Pat grumbled. 'Leave it, Sammy, I'll get the dustpan and brush. Just hurry up.'

Sammy followed Roy up the stairs.

'We're in Pat's bad books,' he said over his shoulder.

'Oh, ignore her.' Sammy picked up a cloth from the bath and sponged the mud off the back of his leather jacket. 'There, but you'll have to put your jeans in the wash.' She threw the cloth in the sink and moved into his arms.

'Mum's used to me being a mucky sod,' he said and kissed her long and hard.

'Sorry I fell,' Sammy said when they came up for air. 'I'm a clumsy so-and-so.'

He held her close. 'Oh, you are, but you're lovely with it. You'd better keep your neck covered.' He turned her to face the mirror and pointed to a couple of large love bites below her right ear.

'Oh shit! Mum'll go mad.'

'Sammy.' He looked at her, his face suddenly serious. 'Can I see you again? I mean, really see you, like go on a proper date, the pictures or something?'

'What do you think?' she said. 'Now go, before the parents come back. Meet me tomorrow after school in the shop and we'll arrange something.'

He squeezed her. 'Sorry about your neck,' he said as he waved goodbye.

\* \* \*

Sammy changed into dry jeans and sweater, but kept her scarf on. She sat down on her bed and took her books out of her satchel. She still felt all churned up inside and had hated Roy having to go home. She smiled as Jane and Pat came into the room.

'Put the record player on, Pat,' she said. 'Something nice and romantic. I'm just in the mood.' As Tab Hunter's 'Young Love' filled the room, Sammy lay down, her hands behind her head and sang along. She smiled. The lyrics of this song were so appropriate. 'I really enjoyed this afternoon,' she said. 'Roy's great fun to be with.'

'Are you gonna tell us the truth?' Pat sat down on her own bed next to Jane. 'We saw the state of your neck. Molly'll go mad.'

Sammy frowned. 'I told you the truth – we fell. I'll use Pan Stik. Mum won't see them.'

'Roy looked a bit smug,' Pat said.

'We had a heavy necking session, that's all. Anyway, it was too bloody cold and wet to get up to anything else. I like him. He makes me laugh and I can handle him so stop worrying. I have got some sense, you know?'

'Yes, but has he?' Pat said.

'Oh, for God's sake, Pat, shut up. Wait until you're alone with Tim. He's probably just as bad – in fact, I bet he's worse!' Sammy rolled over onto her stomach to tackle her homework. There was no way she was saying anymore. She might tell Jane at school tomorrow that she'd let Roy touch her breasts. She'd enjoyed it, and he certainly had, and she knew it was only the cold and the fear of being seen by someone that had stopped them going any further.

* * *

Roy felt happy as he hopped on the bus across town and then walked the short distance to Tim's home. He reached into his jeans pocket for a cigarette only to find the packet damp and squashed and the cigarettes crushed. Oh well, never mind. It had been worth it to get Sammy in a clinch, and boy, what a clinch. He'd got further with her than he'd done with any other girls he'd dated, and if they'd been somewhere more private, who knows what might have happened?

He let himself into the garage and joined Eddie and Tim, who were reclining on green canvas deckchairs, listening to the recordings from Friday. Tim wound the reel back and handed Roy a tumbler of cider.

Eddie gave him a cigarette and light. 'How did it go? Bit too cold for a romantic stroll through the woods today.'

'It wasn't so bad,' Roy said, remembering Sammy's kissable lips on his, and the way she'd responded wildly to his touch. 'There's something really sexy about rolling in the mud and snow with a fit-looking bird, and at least she wants to see me again.' He drew on his cigarette and exhaled a perfect smoke ring. 'Yes,' he shouted. 'I did it, I fucking well did it!'

'You didn't?' Tim said. 'Not in this cold weather, surely?'

'No, you daft bugger. Not IT. I just blew a perfect smoke ring.' Roy shook his head. For all his clever ways Tim could be so dopey at times.

'Congratulations,' Eddie said. 'You're the first. And now things have changed between me and Angie, I bet you'll be the first to get a shag as well!'

'Maybe,' Roy said. Hopefully Sammy would be the one and very soon. 'Are we having a bet on whose first? Twenty fags for the winner. The losers buy them between them.'

Eddie and Tim nodded their agreement.

'We don't mention this to the girls,' Eddie said. 'I think Jane's the type who'd get upset if she thought there was a bet on her losing her virginity.'

'And Pat,' Tim said.

'If you want a contest, Ed, you could still take Angie out?' Roy suggested.

Eddie shrugged. 'I'm not sure. I like Jane. We'll see how it goes.'

'Fucking brilliant,' Roy said as they settled in the deckchairs and listened to the tape. 'If we carry on like this we'll be laughing. Get some more gigs lined up and they can stuff school and exams. Who needs 'em? We'll make it big one day, you'll see. We'll be up there with the best.'

## 6

'So, my folks'll be out Sunday afternoon,' Roy said to Sammy. 'Do you fancy coming over, and Eddie and Jane too?' It was Wednesday and the foursome were sitting in Mario's after school, drinking frothy coffee.

Eddie's eyes lit up and he looked at Jane. 'That okay with you?'

'Erm, yes. I'll say I'm going to Sammy's to do my homework.'

'And I'll say I'm going to Jane's,' Sammy said. 'What about Tim and Pat? We can't keep leaving them out.'

'Up to you,' Roy said. 'If you want to ask them, go ahead but you know what they're like. They don't seem to want to be alone. Think Tim's scared she'll want her wicked way with him.'

Sammy laughed. 'More like the other way round. I'll have to say something to her though, but I doubt she'll want to join us.'

'Any chance you can come to a party on Friday?' Eddie asked Jane.

'I doubt it... but I'll try,' she added as he frowned.

He shook his head. 'Time your parents gave you a bit more

freedom. Christ, you're sixteen. It's daft not being allowed a boyfriend at your age. Shit, you're old enough to be married.'

'I'm sorry.' Jane's eyes filled with tears.

He took her hand. 'No, *I'm* sorry. It's not your fault. Don't cry. But you need to stand up for yourself a bit more, Jane.'

Roy stared at Sammy for a long moment. The jukebox was quiet, the only sound the gurgling and spluttering of the coffee machine and the low murmur of student conversation from the table in the corner. 'What about you? Can you get out?'

'Yes,' she said with an air of determination. 'Course I can. Where shall I meet you?'

'Mersey Square at seven, near the four phone boxes.'

'I'll be there. Finish your coffee, Jane. We'd better get off home now and keep the parents sweet.'

* * *

'Right,' Sammy said, as she and Jane sat on the bus going home, 'this is the plan. You know I occasionally babysit for a woman on the estate? Well, I'll tell Mum I bumped into her and she asked me to help her out on Friday night. You can tell your mum you're sitting with me. Bring your going-out clothes in a bag and we can get changed in the toilets in Mersey Square.'

Jane smiled. 'Will it work?'

'Yes. I'm bloody determined I'm going out with Roy on Friday, no matter what. If I'm not with him, he might get off with somebody else and so might Eddie. We're going and that's the end of it.'

* * *

Eddie and Roy, wearing leather jackets and tight jeans, were waiting for them as the girls emerged from the public toilets in their best dresses and shoes and ran across the square to the four phone boxes. 'Where is this party?' Sammy asked as Roy caught her in his arms and kissed her.

'Wilmslow,' he said. 'We need to get a move on, the train goes in ten minutes.'

'Blimey, Wilmslow's a bit fancy,' Sammy said as they hurried along the main road and up the station approach. 'Who do you know that lives there?'

'A friend of Stuart's is going out with a girl from the new houses. He's a mate of ours as well. Dark-haired lad, Mac. He was at the gig last week. His girlfriend Jackie is fifteen today. Her folks have gone out and said she can have a party.'

'You okay?' Sammy asked as they jumped on the train. Jane was glancing nervously at every passenger.

'Just making sure no one's about who might know us.'

'There won't be. Wilmslow's far too posh, Jane. Nobody who lives up there will know the likes of us.'

* * *

Jane gazed at her surroundings, mouth agape. The house, on a cul-de-sac of six, was detached and modern with cream painted walls all the way through. There was even a toilet downstairs as well as a bathroom upstairs. How nice to have such luxury and everywhere felt so warm. The pretty blonde girl, whose party it was, took their coats upstairs and her boyfriend showed them into the spacious lounge where music played loudly on a polished wooden radiogram in the corner of the room. Her dad would be so envious of that, Jane thought. He was always going on about buying one, but her mum said they were far too expensive and they'd have to wait until they won on Littlewoods. Jane wondered if Jackie's parents had won the pools to afford a house like this. The furniture was huge and when Eddie pulled her over to sit on the sofa she was worried they'd crush the red velvet cushions.

'Isn't it lovely in here?' she whispered as they cuddled up together in front of a roaring fire.

'Yep,' he said. 'When I'm rich from the group, I'll buy us a place like this.'

She stared at him and he laughed. 'I will, I promise you. We'll have it all; money, fancy cars and a house as big as this.'

She smiled. 'Nice dreams, Ed, but people like us don't get things like this. Anyway, we might not be seeing one another then.'

He frowned. 'What makes you say that? Don't you like me?'

'Of course I do, but we're very young.'

'Well, it won't be this year,' he said with a laugh. 'I mean in a few years when I've made the money.'

Jackie's boyfriend came into the room and changed the record.

'Let's have a dance,' Eddie said and pulled Jane to her feet.

'Err, foods in the dining room and drinks are in the kitchen,' Mac announced. 'Help yourselves.' He turned round at the door. 'I've got some dope,' he mouthed behind Jane's back.

Eddie stuck his thumb up and pulled Jane close. She snuggled up to him, loving the feeling of smooching in his arms. She wondered where Roy and Sammy were.

'They went upstairs. Let's go and get a drink.' Eddie took her hand, led her into the kitchen and poured two glasses of cider. Jane wrinkled her nose as she took a sip.

'I'm not sure I should have this,' she said. 'I've never had alcohol before.'

'Really? You don't have to drink it if you don't like it.' He held her close and kissed her. 'But just try a bit. It might relax you. I'm really looking forward to being alone with you on Sunday.'

'We won't be alone. Roy and Sammy will be there.'

He raised an eyebrow and smiled. 'I think we will be. Do you want something to eat?'

'Please.' They made their way into the dining room, where a cold buffet was laid out on the table. There were a few groups of people standing around, talking and smoking. Jane spotted John Grey and his girlfriend, Margaret. Stuart was talking to Mac, who had his arms around Jackie.

'Hi, Jane,' John greeted her. 'Sammy and Roy not with you?'

'Erm, yes.' She could feel her cheeks heating as she thought about what Roy and Sammy might be getting up to.

'They're upstairs,' Eddie said.

'Ah, right.' John laughed. 'Didn't waste much time, did he?'

Jane was aware of Stuart listening to their conversation and he didn't look too happy. He came over and stood beside them. 'Okay, Jane. Ed?'

Jane nodded, but couldn't look him in the eye. She went to the table and helped herself to some food. 'Ed, I'm going back into the lounge to eat this.'

'Okay, be with you in a minute.'

* * *

As Jane left the room, Eddie took the fat roll-up Mac offered and took a long drag. He exhaled slowly and smiled. 'Nice. Thanks.' He handed it back and Mac passed it to Stuart.

'Have another drag, Ed, while you can,' Stuart said. 'Don't think Jane will approve so now's your chance.'

Eddie took another couple of drags and thanked Stuart. He leant against the wall, loving the mellow feeling as the dope took hold. It was only the second time he'd shared a joint. It was something he'd like to get used to, if only he had the money to buy his own. 'I'd better go back to Jane.' He grabbed a plate, piled it up with sausage rolls and sandwiches and went back into the lounge. Jane was sitting alone and he felt a bit guilty for that. She looked happy enough though. The fire had given her cheeks a rosy glow and her brown eyes were sparkling, probably because she'd drunk half of the cider. She looked really pretty and he fancied the arse off her. He closed the door, sat down next to her and put his plate on the coffee table.

'You okay?'

She nodded, kicked her shoes off and tucked her feet up underneath her bottom. Eddie took her in his arms and kissed her, running his hands over her thighs. He could feel the little bumps of her suspenders through the fabric of her dress and thought about the soft flesh that waited between her stocking tops and knickers. He stroked her knees and his hand crept slowly up her skirt. She pulled away from him, a look of panic on her face.

'It's okay, I won't do anything you don't want to do,' he reassured her as the doorbell rang and then rang again continuously. 'Latecomers,' he tutted as she swung her legs down and looked expectantly at the lounge door. He kissed her again and pushed her back against the cushions.

Raised voices in the hallway and someone shouting 'Get out!' had them jumping to their feet. 'What the fuck's going on?' Eddie said, hurrying to the door. He stepped into the hall to see a fat Teddy Boy with his arms around Jackie, who was trying to fight him off and screaming for Mac to help her. But Mac was being held captive by two more interlopers and he struggled to get free, kicking out.

'Get the fuck out of here,' he yelled. 'This is a private party, you weren't invited.'

Eddie tried to push Jane back into the lounge but she refused to leave his side.

'He's got a knife,' she whispered as one of the Teddy Boys holding Mac produced a flick knife and held it near Mac's face. She could see John and Stuart standing over near the dining room and Stuart was whispering something to John, who was pointing at the kitchen door.

The fat boy who had hold of Jackie had her pushed up

against the wall and attempted to kiss her, pawing at her breasts, but she spat at him and tried to knee him between the legs. He laughed. 'Come on, darlin', I love a bit of a challenge.'

'Get your filthy hands off my girl,' Mac yelled but he was no match for his captors and screamed in pain as they twisted his arms up his back.

Eddie heard a crack as one of Mac's arms broke.

'Shit!' he said as Mac collapsed to his knees, crying in agony as the men let go. Jackie screamed as the one with the knife drew it across her boyfriend's cheek and blood dripped onto the carpet.

He waved the knife in the air. 'Anybody else?'

Eddie stared at Stuart, who snuck into the kitchen. 'He's going for help,' he whispered to Jane, who was shaking in his arms. Roy and Sammy appeared on the stairs, wearing worried expressions and very little else. Roy pushed Sammy back up as one of the men looked in his direction, leering at Sammy's semi-naked state.

'Where's the booze and food?' the fat one demanded and Jackie pointed to the dining room. He dragged Jackie with him as the other two left Mac in a heap and followed them. Eddie ran to open the door at a quiet knock and let in Stuart and a grey-haired man wearing a silk dressing gown, carrying a black doctor's bag.

'The police are on their way,' Stuart whispered, leaving the front door ajar. 'This is Doctor Longson from next door. Where's Jackie?'

'They've taken her in the dining room,' Eddie said. 'They're after booze.' He stopped as lights shone through the glass door and two cars pulled up on the drive. Four policemen hurried into the hall.

'They're in the dining room,' Stuart said, pointing to the door. 'They've got a flick knife.'

After making sure the doctor was okay attending to Mac,

three of the policemen rushed into the dining room and the fourth beckoned everyone else into the lounge as Roy and Sammy hurried downstairs with their coats on, ready to go. Jackie ran back to Mac and dropped to her knees crying as he tried to put an arm around her.

'I'll take him to the infirmary to get his arm X-rayed,' Doctor Longson said to Stuart. 'He'll need a couple of stitches in that cut as well. You're very lucky that it missed your eye, young man.'

'Thank you,' Jackie said, sobbing. 'We should ring my parents. They're at friends in Ashlea Village.'

'I'll do that, my dear,' the doctor said. 'Write down the number and then go and sit with the others. No doubt you'll need to give a statement.'

The Teddy Boys were led, handcuffed and swearing, out of the dining room and into the waiting police cars.

The fourth policeman took the names, addresses and brief statements from Stuart, Eddie and John Grey. Roy told him he didn't really see anything and neither did Sammy and Eddie breathed a sigh of relief that they didn't ask Jane for her details and tried to reassure her that it would be okay when the policeman said that if the case went to court, she might be asked to give evidence. She was crying and terrified her parents would find out that she'd lied to them. He thanked God that the dope had all been smoked and any evidence got rid of, too.

Jackie's parents arrived home and were given a briefing from the fourth policeman.

'They look quite normal,' Jane whispered to Eddie.

'What were you expecting, royalty?' he teased, trying to cheer her up.

'Well no, but I thought they'd be all, well, you know, really posh and stuck-up.'

'What, tiaras and stuff?' He smiled and ruffled her hair.

'And do you think we'll be really posh and stuck-up when we're rich enough to live in Wilmslow?'

'Don't suppose we will,' she said, relaxing with a cup of tea that Jackie's mum had insisted she have extra sugar in for shock.

It was a very subdued foursome that made their way back to Stockport on the train.

'You wouldn't think things like that could happen in a place like Wilmslow, would you?' Jane said. 'I still feel really shaky and sick. I was so scared they were going to kill Mac. Hope he'll be okay. It was horrible when his arm cracked, the pain must have been awful.'

'I know,' Eddie said, putting his arm around her. 'Try and put it out of your head now. We've got the gig tomorrow night and then on Sunday we'll have a nice afternoon at Roy's place.'

Jane sighed and looked across at Roy and Sammy, who were snogging the faces off each other. They hadn't even come up for air since they got on the train. She wondered if they'd done it at Jackie's place. They'd been upstairs long enough. Well, no doubt Sammy would say something on the bus home.

## 7

Sunday afternoon and carrying bulging satchels, Jane and Sammy hurried along to the rec, where they'd arranged to meet Eddie and Roy.

'God knows when I'm going to get this work done,' Jane said, trying to keep up with Sammy's long strides.

'Yeah,' Sammy said. 'I feel like chucking the bloody bag over the bridge into the Mersey. Still, it'll be worth having to do it tonight. I'm looking forward to spending a whole afternoon with Roy. We nearly did it at that party, you know. If those Teddy Boys hadn't arrived...'

Jane stopped and frowned. 'I wondered if you had, but you didn't say anything so I assumed you hadn't. I didn't like to ask.'

'I think we will today.'

'Sammy, you shouldn't. Aren't you scared? You're underage. What if he gets you into trouble? Remember that girl at school last year? Her boyfriend left her and she went to a mother and baby home and...' Jane stopped, realising she was babbling, but it was only because she was worried for Sammy.

'For God's sake, Jane, stop it! Roy's got something to use. Just don't say anything to Pat. There they are.' She waved as

Eddie and Roy swaggered towards them, jacket collars turned up against the biting wind.

'All right, girls?' Roy blew on his cold fingers. 'Come on then, let's get to my place. It's bloody brass monkeys today.' He wrapped his arms around Sammy. 'You look good enough to eat.'

'Brass monkeys?' Jane frowned.

Eddie slipped an arm around her shoulders and smiled. He explained what Roy meant and she felt her cheeks heating. She'd heard her dad say it often enough but no one had told her the meaning. But then they wouldn't. Things below the waist were never discussed at home. When she'd started her periods, her mum had told her to keep away from boys, but she didn't say why. Biology lessons at school were all about reproduction in plants and frogs. It was no wonder she felt in such a spin over things.

Eddie took her satchel. 'Bloody hell, this weighs a ton! Hope you've no plans to open it.' He gave her the look that made her legs go wobbly and her tummy turn somersaults.

'Of course not,' she said, slipping her arm around his waist as they hurried along.

As Roy unlocked the front door of the smart semi-detached house a fat, black and white Springer Spaniel hurtled down the hall and flung itself against his legs, whimpering and panting with excitement. 'This is Monty,' he said as the dog squirmed with delight. 'Tickle his tummy, he loves it.'

Jane and Sammy bent to tickle the delighted dog, who grunted and wriggled on his back, paws in the air, leaving clumps of moulting hair all over the dark-red carpet.

'He's lovely. I always wanted a dog but Mum said they smell,' Jane said.

'Sammy, come and tickle my tummy, please. I like it even more than Monty does!' Roy laughed as he pulled her to her feet and down the hallway.

She blushed. 'You are naughty sometimes, Roy.'

'I know.' He led the way into the cosy sitting room, where a coal fire blazed in the grate. 'But you like it, don't you?'

She laughed and smacked his arm.

'It's nice and warm in here,' Jane said, taking her coat and scarf off. She flopped down on a big floral sofa in front of the fire. Eddie sat beside her and pulled her into his arms. He kissed her and gently pushed her back onto the soft cushions. She was vaguely aware of music playing as Roy put on a record and was soon lost in Eddie's kisses and caresses. Twenty minutes later, she emerged breathless from his embrace, warning bells ringing in her head. She was fast getting out of her depth; his hands were everywhere.

'Eddie, stop.' She sat up and pushed him away, straightened her skirt and pulled her unbuttoned blouse around her. She looked for Roy and Sammy, but they'd disappeared.

'C'mon, Jane, it's okay. There's no one to see us.' Eddie pulled her back down. His hands crept up her skirt again. 'They've gone up to Roy's bedroom.'

'Oh no, have they?' Jane pushed his hands away again.

'I didn't hear Sammy being dragged off kicking and screaming, so I presume she went willingly.'

'I hope she knows what she's doing.' Jane pulled her skirt back down, wishing they'd gone for a walk instead of coming to Roy's house. She felt she was fighting a losing battle – Eddie's fumbling was so hard to resist.

'Roy knows what he's doing, he'll be careful. So will I.' He lovingly nuzzled her neck, his mouth moving over her body. 'Jane, c'mon, please,' he said and opened her blouse again.

'But Sammy's underage,' Jane said.

He looked up. 'She's sixteen. Stop worrying about her, I bet she's not worrying about you.'

'She's only fourteen, and so am I,' Jane blurted out before she could stop herself. Sammy would go mad with her now.

Eddie jerked away from her, shock registering on his flushed face. 'What? Why the hell did you tell me you were sixteen?'

'Because I didn't think you'd want me if you knew I was just a kid.' Jane felt tears welling. 'I'm not even fifteen 'till November, Sammy's fifteen soon.'

'You should have told me the truth. It wouldn't have made any difference to the way I feel, but it would to the way I've acted with you.'

Her shoulders shook. She felt sure he'd finish with her right there and then. She straightened her clothes, feeling her cheeks heating as she realised how close she'd come to losing her virginity and all because of her stupid lies.

'I wouldn't have done what I did if I'd known. I can't relax now, I need a ciggie.' He flicked his fringe from his eyes, lit up and inhaled deeply.

Jane chewed her lip as he gazed silently at her. He looked angry and she wondered what he was thinking. Probably working out how to tell her to go away – it was over. He threw the butt into the fire, fastened his shirt and tucked it into his jeans, his hands shaking as he zipped himself up.

Jane felt guilty when she saw his shaking hands. She was so naïve. She must have given him signals that she was willing or he wouldn't have gone so far. 'I'm sorry, Ed, really. I didn't mean to lead you on. Don't treat me like a kid, please. I don't feel like a kid when I'm with you. I want to be close and kiss and cuddle, but I'm scared of getting into trouble. I'm just not ready to go all the way.'

Eddie took her hands. 'It's okay. Let's just enjoy what's left of the afternoon. We won't go any further than we already have done, not yet. But don't lie to me again. Look at the problems it'll cause. Roy will hit the bloody roof when he finds out how young Sammy really is. It's probably too late now anyway, because he was planning to go all the way with her, if she'd let him, and he was quite sure she would.'

'It was my stupid idea to say we were older. I feel really bad. I've teased you and let you down.'

Eddie shook his head. 'It's all right. It doesn't change how I feel about you. Anyway, Sammy herself told Roy that she was sixteen.' He stood up and ran his hands through his hair. 'I'll make a coffee. Do you want one?'

She wiped her eyes on the sleeve of her blouse. He looked less angry now. 'Please, Ed.'

\* \* \*

In the kitchen Eddie filled the kettle. He needed a few minutes away from her to collect his scrambled thoughts. She was beautiful; he wanted her badly, but fourteen, Jesus Christ, talk about cradle-snatching. Thank God they'd stopped when they had. He vowed there and then that their first time would be special and if that meant waiting 'till she turned sixteen, then wait they would. Meantime, it was his responsibility to make sure that when they were alone together, they didn't get too carried away.

He lit another cigarette as he searched the cupboards for coffee and mugs and found a bottle of Camp Coffee Essence. He tipped a measure into the mugs and put some milk on the stove to boil. He leant against the worktop and blew a wobbly smoke ring, his mind racing, not only for himself and Jane, but also for Roy and Sammy and what they'd probably already done. Roy wouldn't be very happy, if Eddie knew his mate. He was crazy about Sammy, there was no doubt about it, but Eddie was sure the fact that she was so young would horrify him.

The milk boiled and he poured it into the mugs, topped them up with hot water and spooned in sugar. He carried the mugs through to the lounge, his cigarette dangling from his lips. Jane was on the rug with her arms around Monty, sobbing into his silky ears. The dog was licking the salty tears off her face and whimpering in sympathy. Eddie placed the mugs on the hearth, threw the remains of his cigarette on the fire and drew Jane into his arms. 'Do you still want to keep on seeing me or would you rather we packed it in? It's up to you. I love being with you, but I know that lying to get out to be with me causes you problems with your parents. Now you've told me how old you really are, I can understand it.'

Jane smiled through her tears. 'I still want to see you, I don't want us to finish. You'll just have to be patient if I can't get out sometimes, or if I fight you off.'

'I will be. Now drink your coffee while it's still hot. By the way, how old's Pat? Not that it matters – Tim's a good boy, not like Roy and me. He wouldn't make the first move.'

'She's fifteen in May. Pat wouldn't make the first move either, so she and Tim will be quite safe.'

As Eddie and Jane were sitting on the rug in companionable silence, drinking their coffee, Monty lying contentedly beside them, the living room door flew open. Roy and Sammy, arms around one another, flushed and beaming from ear to ear, walked into the room. Sammy's cool blue eyes were sparkling and Roy was grinning like a Cheshire cat.

'You owe me a packet of fags,' he mouthed in Eddie's direction. 'Ah, coffee – would you like one, Sam?'

'Please.' She sat down on the sofa and looked closely at Jane. 'What's up? Have you been crying?'

Jane nodded, looking at Eddie, who squeezed her hand reassuringly.

'Tell her,' he urged.

'Eddie knows we're only fourteen. You have to tell Roy.'

Sammy's face paled and she stared silently at the fire. Roy came back in the room with the coffees and handed her a mug.

'What's up with you three?' He sat down beside Sammy and accepted the cigarette Eddie offered him.

'Tell him, Sam. It's only fair,' Eddie said, putting his arm around Jane's shoulders when the tears started again.

'Tell me what?' Roy looked from Eddie to Sammy.

Sammy shook her head.

'Tell me what?' Roy repeated, looking at Eddie.

'The girls have been lying about their ages. They're actually only fourteen,' Eddie said, raising an eyebrow at Roy.

'Shit!' Roy's dark eyes widened and he banged his mug down on the coffee table, slopping the liquid over a newspaper. 'Fucking hell, Sam! I thought you were sixteen.' He turned to face her, running his hands through his hair.

Sammy looked at him, defiance written all over her face. She tossed her long hair back. 'And if you'd known that I was just a kid, would it have made any difference?'

He looked at her in amazement. 'Of course it would, you stupid girl. You're way underage. I could be fucking prosecuted and banged away for what I've done. Jesus, if your parents find out, they'll kill me.'

Sammy slammed her mug down beside Roy's and stood up, eyes blazing. 'But you wanted to do it, Roy, nothing was gonna stop you. I told you at the party that we should wait a bit until we'd been together longer, but oh no, you wouldn't listen, telling me everybody does it.' She grabbed her coat, scarf and satchel and stormed out of the room, leaving the other three staring after her.

Roy gathered his wits as the front door banged shut and he grabbed his jacket and ran after her. 'Sammy, wait, please, don't go like this,' he pleaded, catching her up on the corner.

'Just get lost, you creep! You got what you wanted, now leave me alone.' She pushed him away and ran off down the road.

* * *

Angry tears fell down Sammy's cheeks. What had she done? Her mum was always issuing warnings about not getting involved with boys until she was older but she was so sure she could handle things with Roy. Today he'd been even more persuasive than before and had worn down her resistance, even though deep down she knew it was against the law. Well, it was too late now, she'd done it and it wasn't something she could change.

* * *

Roy stood on the corner, wondering what to do. Underage or not, what they'd done this afternoon had been wonderful. He couldn't just let her walk out of his life. He ran after her, catching her up on the main road, and stood in front of her, blocking her path.

'Sammy, please.'

'Get out of the bloody way, you swine!' Sammy swung her heavy satchel at him and caught him on the chin.

He reeled backwards. Regaining his balance, he grabbed her arm and took the satchel from her. He dropped it on the pavement and looked deep into her angry eyes. He knew then, without a doubt in the world, that he wanted to be with her forever. She was amazing, feisty, sexy, and those endless legs, everything he'd ever wanted in one complete package. Life would always be a challenge with Sammy, he was sure of that, but it was one he wanted to take on.

'Sammy, love, please listen to me. I'm sorry. It was such a shock, can't you see that? I know you're not a kid, you certainly didn't act like one. I wasn't blaming you, it was my fault. I really like you, in fact... well, I think I'm falling in love with you, and I don't care how young you are. Please don't think I was only after one thing – it was my first time as well.'

'Really?' Sammy looked up through her tears. 'I would never have guessed. Especially the second time!' she said and her eyes twinkled. 'I think I love you too.' She touched his face 'Your chin's bleeding all down the front of your shirt. We'd better go back to your place and get you cleaned up.'

'Well, that's definitely round one to you!' Roy put his arms around her and breathed a sigh of relief. Young though she was, he couldn't lose her now; he wanted her for life.

## 8

School dragged on for an eternity on Monday. Jane had a banging head that she knew was caused by worry and all she wanted to do was go home and lie down. But before the end of the afternoon break Pat cornered her and Sammy as they strolled around the playground, heads together, discussing Sunday afternoon.

'Say nothing,' Jane muttered as Pat stood in front of them with her arms folded.

'You two have hardly said a word to me since yesterday. What happened, why are you being so secretive?'

'Nothing happened,' Sammy said. A blush crept up her neck as she averted her eyes from Pat's searching gaze.

'Well, something must have, you're never usually this quiet. Have you done something you shouldn't with Roy and Eddie?'

'Of course not,' Jane said. Sammy stayed silent, looking down at the floor.

'Sammy?' Pat lowered her voice as a group of girls hurried by. 'You didn't?'

'Don't you dare tell Mum and Tom.'

'Oh God, how could you?'

'Easy.' Sammy shrugged.

'But it's against the law. What if you have a baby? And what if Molly and Dad find out?'

'I won't have a baby, Roy used something. And they won't find out if you keep your mouth shut.'

'I'll keep quiet as long as you don't do it again,' Pat said, looking pious. 'Tim and me are waiting until we get serious. You should too.'

'We *are* serious.'

'But you won't do it again, will you?'

The end-of-break bell rang out. As they hurried back into school, Sammy whispered to Jane, 'Talk about saved by the bell! I'm making her no promises. What me and Roy do is our own business.'

Jane sighed. 'Don't tell her how close Ed and I got. I don't want to wait forever, but I'll try and hang on until I'm sixteen.'

'Yeah,' Sammy said, raising an eyebrow. 'If you can.'

\* \* \*

Much to Jane's surprise, Eddie was waiting outside school. He lounged against the wall opposite the school gates, cigarette dangling. Her stomach lurched. Maybe he'd had second thoughts and had come to finish with her. But his smile was reassuring. 'I'll see you two later,' she said to Sammy and Pat. She ran across the road to Eddie as he waved.

'Hi,' he said. 'Thought we could walk into town.' He put his arms around her and kissed her in full view of half the girls from her form. Her legs turned to jelly and she enjoyed the looks of envy the others gave her as they strolled by. Eddie took her satchel and pulled her closer. Jane smiled, proud as punch to be his girl, even though he was a bit of a handful.

'Are we going to the record shop?'

'Yep.'

As they walked down the road she told him about Pat's reaction to Sammy and Roy.

'Fuck! Hope she keeps her mouth shut. Does she know what happened between us?'

Jane shook her head. 'Haven't you been to school today?' She frowned, taking in his leather jacket, jeans, and distinct lack of school uniform.

'Nope.'

'Ed, you'll be in even more trouble. You've only got a few more months now.'

He shrugged. 'Had toothache earlier. I've been trying to write songs. Music's my future, I've gotta make it work. Anyway, stop nagging. You sound like my mum.' He looked into her eyes and stole another lingering kiss.

She felt the familiar warm tummy-tugging. Resisting him was going to be so hard. She didn't know if she had the strength.

\* \* \*

'Mum, is there enough hot water for a bath?' Jane popped her head around the lounge door. Homework done, headache miraculously gone, she felt better than she'd felt all day, thanks to Eddie's reassuring hugs and kisses, and was looking forward to a soak with the scented bath cubes Sammy had given her for Christmas.

Her mum, sitting quietly on the sofa watching TV with her dad, said, 'There's plenty, love. Have you done your homework?'

'Yes.'

'Enjoy your bath. Shout me when you're finished and I'll make some cocoa.'

\* \* \*

Enid got up to turn the television off and heard a blood-curdling scream.

'What the hell was that?' Ben said and rushed out of the room and up the stairs two at a time. Peter, and Harry-from-next-door, dressed up in their Lone Ranger and Tonto outfits, rolled on the landing carpet, convulsed with laughter.

'What the bloody hell have you done?' Ben demanded.

Jane stood by the bathroom door, hysterical and pointing fearfully at the sink. Ben peered inside. The biggest spider he'd ever seen was trying unsuccessfully to climb up the slippery surface on very wobbly legs.

'Peter, where did this come from?' Ben bellowed as Enid appeared beside him.

Jane fell into her mum's arms, shaking from head to toe.

'Harry brought it round in a toffee tin, Dad. It's called Fred. He's saving it to put in his sister's bed. We thought we'd try it out on our Jane,' Peter said.

Ben felt his mouth twitch as he looked at the worried little faces. Then he looked at Jane's stricken face. She was terrified of spiders and he wasn't that keen on them himself.

'Don't you ever do anything like this again. You know your sister doesn't like spiders, it's not funny.'

'I won't, Dad.' Peter hung his head. 'Sorry, honestly.'

'Right, my lad, you can go straight to your room and Harry can go home. Take that spider with you and, Harry, if you want to see your next birthday, don't even think about putting it in your Debbie's bed.'

* * *

After her bath, Jane lay on the bed, thumping headache back, feeling drained. Her mum had brought her up a mug of cocoa and two aspirins. She shuddered as the image of the spider lurked behind her eyelids every time she closed them. The last couple of days had taken their toll, what with the trouble at Jackie's party and then yesterday at Roy's. When she and Eddie had met up with everyone in the record shop earlier Pat had been embarrassed, so much so that she wouldn't even look Roy in the eye or speak to Sammy. As they waited at Mersey Square for the bus home Jane had tried her best to smooth Pat's ruffled feathers, telling her that everyone was entitled to make their own decisions about how far to go and when.

She wondered how on earth she'd be able to hang on to her virginity as well as her boyfriend in the next few months. It was all very well magazine problem pages giving out advice from well-meaning agony aunts, that you should wait until your wedding day or lose the boy's respect. The women who penned the smug replies mustn't have had boyfriends as persistent and persuasive as Eddie and Roy. Even though Eddie had reassured her again that they would wait until she was older, Jane felt certain that as soon as they were alone, he'd try again. Was it all worth it? The best thing would be to stop seeing him. But she didn't want to. She turned on her side, switched off her bedside lamp and closed her weary eyes.

Angie peered through the steamed-up windows of Mario's and spotted Eddie talking to Roy and Tim. She'd called at his house to see him. His mum said he'd be in the coffee shop if he wasn't at Roy's place. She smoothed down her black flared skirt, checked her stocking seams were straight, then took a compact from her bag, touched up her lipstick and re-knotted her red spotty neckerchief. She undid the top three buttons of her white fitted blouse, looked down and smiled. She could see her cleavage and the lacy top of her new bra. Perfect. A lad at school had told her today that she looked like the actress Tuesday Weld except for her hair. She fluffed out her curls. She might even go blonde when she left school. She looked at Eddie as he glanced up when the bell jangled. He half-smiled as she clicked across the tiled floor on red stilettos and then turned his attention back to whatever Roy was saying. She felt annoyed: after all her effort to look good for him, he'd hardly even looked at her. Well, he was going to have to talk to her whether he liked it or not. She sat down on the vacant chair next to him and crossed her silky-clad legs, making sure her skirt rode up slightly. Tim smiled at her and Roy got to his feet.

'Coffee, Angie?'

'Thank you, Roy.' She slid her handbag under the chair and touched Eddie's arm. 'Good job one of you cares. Aren't you even going to say hello? I haven't seen you properly for nearly two weeks.'

'Yeah, er, hi. Sorry. Been really busy with the group.'

'And how's it going?'

His face lit up. 'Great. Mario's given us a regular spot here now on Saturdays.'

'Right.' Damn, that meant he'd be spending even more rehearsal time with Roy and Tim. 'I'll come and see you play. Maybe this Saturday, if Cathy can make it.'

Eddie frowned. 'Why would you wanna do that? You're not interested. Well, you never used to be. Always trying to stop me practising 'cos you wanted to do something.'

Roy brought her coffee over and she took a sip. If she wanted Eddie to date her again she'd better start showing some enthusiasm for the group.

'I am interested but you always shut me out,' she said, pouting.

Eddie shrugged. 'Whatever. Anyway, why are you here?'

'I wanted to see you, why else? And also, I wondered if you're doing anything on Friday night.' She lowered her voice, put her hand on his thigh and leant across to whisper, 'My sister is definitely going out and I'm babysitting.'

Her lips brushed his cheek. He looked surprised and pulled away. She stared at him. His indifference was beginning to piss her off. Were they still going out together or what? She sat back as Roy offered her a cigarette and light, she took a long drag and blew a perfect smoke ring above their heads. She smirked as Eddie's jaw dropped.

Roy laughed. 'Not just a pretty face – you should get her to teach you, Ed.'

'So, are you alright for Friday?' she persisted.

'I've got plans.'

'Oh... really? What are you doing?'

'Nothing to do with you. I'm going for a pee.' He got to his feet, scraping back his chair with such force, it tipped over. Roy caught and righted it. He looked at Angie with raised eyebrows.

'Think that might be a no, love.'

She sighed and picked up her coffee. 'I don't know what's wrong with him lately. He ignores me in school. He hasn't phoned and I hear him telling his mum to say he's out when I ring him.'

She drained her cup as Roy patted her arm. 'Think he needs a break. He's in trouble at home because of truancy. I'd leave him alone for a while if I were you while he sorts himself out.'

She got to her feet and picked up her handbag. Eddie was taking his time having a pee. No doubt waiting until she'd gone. Well, she wasn't hanging around just to be ignored. She'd have to try and catch him tomorrow if he was in school. After all the mithering he'd done about going all the way, why would he turn down the chance of babysitting with her now? It didn't make sense. She said goodbye to Roy and Tim and left Mario's with a lingering glance back over her shoulder, but there was still no sign of him.

\* \* \*

Eddie slipped out of the gents' when he saw Angie leaving. He went back to Tim and Roy and sat down. He hoped his reason for dashing to the toilet had gone unnoticed. As soon as she'd leant across and put her hand on his thigh he'd felt a rush of heat to his groin. She'd looked and smelled nice too and he'd caught a glimpse of white lace down the open front of her blouse.

'Told her to leave you alone for a bit,' Roy said. 'If you don't want to see her again, you should tell her.'

'Yeah, and I will. Just can't be doing with her crying all over the place like she did last year when I tried to finish it.'

Roy shook his head. 'Don't mess her about. If you're serious with Jane then dump her. You can't have two girls, it's not fair on either of them.'

'Like I said, I will.' Eddie handed around cigarettes. 'I'll have this fag then I'm off home.'

'So are we,' Roy said.

* * *

Angie went to Cathy's house straight from Mario's. She burst into tears as Cathy let her in.

'Oh, you look lovely, but I take it things didn't go well?' Cathy said, giving her a hug.

'He's not interested,' Angie sobbed. 'I don't know what to do. I love him, Cath. How can I get him back?'

'To be honest, I don't know why you want him back but chasing him won't get you anywhere. In fact, if you ignore him and go out with other lads he might get jealous. But you have to do it under his nose.'

'The group is playing at Mario's on Saturday. Will you come with me? I'll get myself dolled up and ask Richard to do my hair. Think I'll buy a new dress too.'

'Don't go mad. He's not worth it. But I can't come this weekend, it'll have to be next week.'

'Thanks, Cath. I don't care how long it takes. I'll dance with and kiss every lad in the coffee shop if it gets his attention. One way or another I'm gonna get him back. I wouldn't mind if it was another girl that was making him act weird with me but I've not seen him with anyone and surely he'd tell me if it was over between us, instead of just avoiding me. I think it's that bloody group, he's obsessed with it.'

'Who knows?' Cathy sighed. 'He's a law unto himself, that one.'

* * *

Eddie kicked off his shoes in the hall and cocked an ear. The house was quiet except for the distant rumble of his dad's snores. In the front parlour he poured himself a whisky from his dad's drinks cupboard and sat down on the sofa in front of the dying embers. He sipped his drink and thought about Angie and how she'd turned him on so easily. He sighed. He was tempted, but he couldn't let her know that or she'd never leave him alone. When he was kissing and cuddling Jane he never gave her a second thought.

He'd arranged to see Jane on Friday if she could get out and they were going to the pictures. Like Roy said, he should tell Angie it was over, but something was stopping him and it wasn't just the thought of her crying all over the place. He fancied her still, but he really liked Jane. He knocked back the rest of his drink and helped himself to another. Why was it all so bloody confusing? He couldn't really have two girls, could he? How would he keep them apart? He finished his drink, topped up the whisky bottle with water, rinsed the glass and put everything back in the cupboard. He felt quite mellow now, but along with that feeling came the need to do stuff with Angie. His head in a spin, he made his way up to bed, wishing he'd not been so bloody stupid. He shouldn't have ignored her. They could have gone round to the recess at the back of the coffee shop. She wouldn't have refused him and there was no Cathy to disturb them tonight. Now all he'd got to look forward to was a lonesome night on his own.

## 9

## TUESDAY, 3 FEBRUARY 1959

'You're not gonna believe this,' Tim said as he let Eddie and Roy in for a day of rehearsals. They'd planned to start as soon as Tim's mum left for work and had been waiting around the corner until she got on the bus. He thrust a copy of the *Daily Mirror* at them, his hands shaking. The headline read 'Top "Rock" Stars Die in Crash!'

'Fucking hell!' Eddie sat down on the bottom stair. 'How? When?'

'Last night, after a show. Plane crash. I can't take it in. It's not quite a year since we saw him play in Liverpool.'

'Bloody hell! Ritchie Valens and The Big Bopper as well.' Roy sat down on the stair behind Eddie and read over his shoulder. 'Buddy was so young, only twenty-two.'

'Ritchie was just seventeen,' Eddie said. 'Just a bit older than us lot.'

'Makes you think.' Tim shook his head. 'Like my mum's always saying, you don't know what's around the corner.' He joined Eddie on the bottom stair and the three sat in silence for a while, staring at the headline.

'Let's take this as a sign.' Eddie got to his feet and handed the paper back to Tim. 'We all pull our weight and make sure Roy and The Raiders gets off the ground this year.'

'We'll do it for Buddy's memory,' Tim said. 'If it wasn't for him...' He ran his hands through his hair and sighed. 'I'll make us a coffee and then we'll go down to Flanagan and Grey's and see if John knows anything other than what's in the paper.'

\* \* \*

Jane and Sammy were in Flanagan and Grey's as the boys ran down the stairs. Eddie grabbed hold of Jane and kissed her.

'How come you're not at school?' He gently wiped his fingers over her tear-stained cheeks.

'Couldn't face it.' She sobbed against his shoulder. 'Saw my dad's paper before he left for work. I can't believe it.'

'Neither can we,' Roy said, his arms around Sammy.

'Where's Pat?' Tim asked.

'School,' Sammy said. 'She wouldn't take the day off. We knew you lot would come down here eventually.'

'We came to see if John knows anything more than us,' Eddie said.

John shook his head. 'Only what's in the papers, Ed, and I bought them all. The Crickets weren't touring with him. One newspaper said that Buddy apparently chartered a small plane because the tour bus kept breaking down in freezing temperatures. The plane must have taken off in really bad weather. It came down soon after.'

'That's awful,' Jane said. 'You'll never get me on a plane. Look what happened to Manchester United in Munich last year. Almost to the day, too and that was bad weather.'

'It does put you off a bit,' Eddie agreed. 'But it's supposed to be one of the safest forms of transport. They were just unlucky.'

'I don't care. You'd have to knock me out to get me on a plane.'

'Right, well, what we gonna do for the rest of the day?' Roy said, looking at his watch.

'It's only half ten. We can't hang about in here all day. John's got work to do. Let's go and see Mario, get a coffee and ask if he'll let us do a bit of a tribute night on Saturday. Then we can go to my place until school finishing time.'

'I'm up for that,' Eddie said. 'Jane?'

'Err, well... okay. I don't suppose there's much else we can do.'

Sammy smiled and snuggled up to Roy. 'I'm okay with that.'

'I'll go home,' Tim said. 'I'm not playing gooseberry to you lot. I'll meet Pat from school and catch up with you back here.'

\* \* \*

Mario's windows were steamed up as usual and the place was heaving with a different type of customer to the ones Eddie was used to seeing. Gossiping housewives, laden shopping bags by their feet and headscarves tied around their hair, were seated at every table, their loud voices competing with the noise of the spluttering coffee machine and the jukebox. He remembered it was Tuesday market day and hoped his mum wasn't in town with Aunty Minnie.

'Two toasted teacakes, one Eccles cake and three coffees,' Mario yelled as Rosa dashed by with a tray. 'Hello, boys – and girls,' he greeted them. 'Come through into the back.' He led them into a spacious room that did triple duty as a sitting room, staffroom, and office and was furnished with a sofa, two big armchairs, a coffee table and a large desk, piled high with papers. The wall-mounted gas fire was lit and the room felt warm and cosy. 'Make yourselves comfortable and I'll send someone through with coffee and toast.' He dashed back out and Eddie could hear him shouting for Rosa to get a move on.

Mario's son Vincento popped his head around the door and

grinned at them. 'Be with you as soon as I can. He's a right slave-driver today as you can hear.'

'Okay, Vinnie,' Eddie said. He sat down on a chair and pulled Jane onto his knee. Roy and Sammy took the opposite chair. 'Well, this is good of Mario. Saves rubbing shoulders with the housewives.'

'Fishwives, more like,' Roy said, throwing him a cigarette. 'Did you hear the gob on that one near the door? Imagine coming home to her after a hard day's graft?'

'No, thanks,' Eddie said, lighting his cigarette and chucking the box of matches across to Roy. 'Hope you don't turn out like that,' he teased as Jane smacked him on the arm.

'Cheeky sod!' She laughed as he blew a wonky smoke ring above her head.

'Told you, you'll have to get Angie to teach you that,' Roy said, then stopped as though realising what he'd said.

'Who's Angie?' Sammy asked. 'And teach him what?'

'Err, she's a girl at school.' Eddie glared at Roy. 'She can blow perfect smoke rings. Ah, here's the coffee.' He shook his head in Roy's direction as the girls got up to help Vinnie with the tray. 'Thanks, Vinnie. We'll settle up on the way out.'

'S'okay, Ed. Dad says no charge. He knows you'll be upset today because of what's happened with Buddy Holly. He's coming in to talk to you when he gets a minute, he's got an idea.'

'So have we,' Roy said. He mouthed sorry at Eddie as Vinnie left the room.

Sammy and Jane handed them coffees and plates of toast.

'Wonder if Mario's got the same idea as us,' Eddie mused.

'What idea's that?' Jane took a sip of coffee and sat down on the rug by his feet. She leant against his legs and helped herself to a piece of toast.

'We'd like to do a tribute on Saturday night,' Roy said. 'All the Buddy Holly songs we know, plus we can learn another couple this week if we miss a bit more school.'

'Why don't you learn Ritchie's "Donna"?' Sammy suggested.

'Hmm, maybe,' Eddie said. 'Perhaps Tim could do that one. His voice is probably more suited.'

'Well, if you do "Donna", you're going to have to learn "Chantilly Lace" as well,' Jane said. 'You can't leave The Bopper out.'

'I've been thinking about that.' Roy looked pleased with himself. 'We could finish with it and get everyone to sing along with us. That way, if we fluff anything, it won't matter. Half of 'em won't know the right words anyway.' He stopped as Mario came into the room and flopped down on the sofa.

'Oh, those women, they'll be the death of me. Some of them still have their curlers in under those headscarves. Italian women are so much smarter, the way they present themselves and do their hair. My wife, she wouldn't dream of setting foot outside the door dressed like that.'

Roy laughed. 'Not the smartest birds in the world, are they?'

'And their voices,' Mario continued. 'You can hear them a mile down the road.' He mopped his sweaty face with a hanky. 'Anyway, boys, I have an idea for Saturday.'

Eddie smiled at Roy as Mario outlined the same plan they were about to suggest. 'I'll get Rosa to make a few posters. We should have a good night and I'll pay you extra money, of course.'

'Leave it with us, Mario,' Roy said.

'I'll help Rosa with the posters,' Sammy said. 'I love designing stuff. We can do them later at my house. I'll have a chat with her before we go.'

'I'll leave you to finish your coffees then and see you soon,' Mario said as he went back to work.

'Right, well, let's get to my place,' Roy said, giving Sammy a squeeze, his dark eyes twinkling. 'We've got work to do – later.'

Eddie looked at Jane, who was eyeing him shyly from under

her fringe. 'S'okay,' he whispered reassuringly. 'C'mon, let's just enjoy a kiss and a cuddle. I made you a promise, remember?'

She smiled and he pulled her to her feet and hugged her and hoped he could keep his promise as she felt so good in his arms.

* * *

Angie looked at the poster on the door of Mario's. She hadn't seen Eddie and Roy in school since Monday and wondered why. She could understand them taking Tuesday off, but all week? So... a special tribute tonight, that should be good. She glanced at her watch. If she was quick, she could get to Susan Smarts and back before her lunch break was over. The red dress she'd had her eye on was still hanging at the back of the window. She'd seen it again this morning on her way to the salon. Richard said he'd put her hair up for her later when they got a quiet moment. She felt a little thrill go through her at the thought of him doing her hair, standing close to her, putting his hands on her shoulders, and then shook herself. She shouldn't be having thoughts like that. The hairdo was for Eddie's benefit, to help win him back.

She hurried on her way and dashed into the dress shop. The dark-haired assistant looked up as she almost fell through the door in her haste. The carpet was thick and spongy and Angie felt her stilettos sink into the depth of the pile, making her walk a bit clumsily. She almost wished she'd put her boots on, but they wouldn't have looked right with the dress and she needed to be sure it was perfect.

'That red dress in the window, may I try it on, please?'

'Of course, madam.' The assistant lifted the dress out and hung it on the door of the fitting room. 'Call me if you need help with the zip.'

'Thank you.' Angie locked herself in the small mirrored

room and slipped out of her clothes. She popped the dress over her head and the slinky fabric slid down over her body, clinging in all the right places, just as she'd imagined it would. She managed the zip by herself and turned this way and that to check it looked okay from all angles. It was perfect. There was no way Eddie would ignore her tonight. The price tag of sixty-nine and eleven was a bit heart-stopping but her mum had given her a pound towards it and she'd saved the rest from her Saturday and babysitting jobs. She deserved it. She quickly got dressed and went back into the sales area.

'I'll take it.'

'Did it look nice?' The assistant folded the dress, wrapped it in layers of tissue paper and placed it in a box.

'Very nice,' Angie said as the box was put in a green and gold carrier bag. She handed over her hard-earned money, pocketed the handwritten receipt and swanned out of the shop, swinging her fancy bag with pride.

\* \* \*

Jane, followed by Sammy and Pat, made her way across the crowded room to a table at the side of the makeshift stage. Stuart and John had waved them over. The group was in the middle of a soundcheck but Eddie raised his hand to her in the middle of a beat. Jane smiled and waved back. The girls sat down and John went to get them a drink.

'The place is heaving,' Jane said, shrugging out of her coat. 'Think Mario could do with bigger premises for his live music nights.'

'He's got his eye on the building next door,' Stuart said. 'The old printer keeps threatening to retire. As soon as he does, Mario will be in with an offer. He keeps talking about opening a proper licensed club.'

'If he does that we'll have to up our ages again, girls,' Sammy said, taking the glass of Coke John handed her.

The soundcheck finished, they were joined by the boys. Roy went to get drinks for them and Stuart looked around for two more chairs as Mac and Jackie arrived.

'How's your arm?' Jane asked. Mac wore a sling, his arm in a cast.

'Getting there,' Mac said. 'Got a couple of pins in it, but it's doing okay.'

'And your face?'

Mac ran his fingers over his cheek. 'Just a little scar now. That'll fade in time.'

'He was lucky,' Jackie said. 'If luck's the right word.'

Mac smiled. 'I was. I need a word with Roy,' he said and went to join Roy at the counter.

Eddie slid his arm around Jane's shoulders and dropped a kiss on her lips. 'You look lovely,' he whispered.

'Thank you.' She looked down at her simple black and white shift dress and wished she had the money to buy nice clothes. Jackie looked gorgeous in her silky, green and black top and full skirt, but then again, she had a rich mum and dad to treat her. Jane made a mental note to ask John about a Saturday job. She kept forgetting to do it.

'Come and dance with me.' Eddie pulled her to her feet and led her onto the small dance floor as The Platters' 'Smoke Gets in Your Eyes' played on the jukebox.

In his arms it didn't matter what she was wearing because smooching with him made her feel like a million dollars. On Tuesday at Roy's he'd told her that he loved her. She wasn't sure if he'd said it just to get her to go a bit further, which they did. He'd shown her how to please him by touching him and at first, she'd been shocked and called him a mucky devil, but then afterwards, lying close together, he told her he loved her again so she told him she loved him too. Because she was really sure that she did. She still wouldn't let him go any further with her, even though he said they didn't need to go all the way for him to give her pleasure too. He said it was called heavy petting and that everybody did it, but she'd stood her ground and he'd seemed happy enough – for now.

'I need a pee,' he said as the song came to an end. 'Go back to the others. Won't be a minute.' He gave her a kiss and dashed away.

Roy was tipping something from a bottle into glasses of Coke as Jane sat down. 'Want a drop?' He gestured the bottle towards her. 'Vodka?'

'No, thanks. I'll stick to my Coke.'

'Very wise, Jane.' He laughed as Sammy pushed her glass forward. 'Not like this one.'

'You'd better be able to walk to Mersey Square later,' Pat said, frowning.

Sammy rolled her eyes and took a sip of her drink. Jane smiled. The pair were chalk and cheese and more so since meeting Tim and Roy. Well matched, she thought.

Eddie came back and sat down. He took a sip of the drink that Roy had laced with the vodka. His eyes lit up. 'Nice.'

'Even nicer.' Roy patted his jeans pocket. 'Dressing room for a minute.'

'Keep my seat warm,' Eddie said to Jane and followed Roy to the room at the back of the stage.

Jane stared after them, wondering what they were up to and why they hadn't asked Tim, who was leading Pat onto the floor to dance.

* * *

'You got some then?' Eddie asked, following Roy into the small room and shutting the door.

'I did. Good old Mac.' Roy took a package from his pocket

and proceeded to prepare a joint, first heating the small piece of cannabis in the silver paper it was wrapped in.

They sat down on two rickety chairs and Roy lit up. He passed the joint to Eddie, who took a long drag and closed his eyes. 'Bliss!' He gave it back to Roy. They had a couple more drags each and then Roy stubbed out the joint and put the remains on the windowsill. 'That'll do us for the final set. Do you feel okay, Ed? Don't want you falling off your bloody drum stool out there.'

'I feel great,' Eddie said, grinning lopsidedly. 'Could take on the world. That voddy in the Coke helped too.'

Roy laughed and looked at his watch. 'Half an hour then we need to get changed. A dance with the girls first, I think.'

As they walked across the stage Eddie grabbed Roy's arm. 'Fuck, Angie's talking to John and Stuart. Shit, hope she doesn't say anything to Jane.' Since spending Tuesday afternoon in Jane's arms, he hadn't given a thought to Angie, even though she'd been on his mind on Monday night. 'How do I get out of this?'

'Told you to tell her it was over,' Roy said as they got to the table.

'Eddie, I wondered where you were,' Angie gushed and flung her arms around him. She almost knocked him flying and he steadied himself and tried to push her away. But she clung to him and tried to kiss him. Bloody hell, she'd been drinking. That's all he needed. She was tarted up to the eyeballs and the combination of her strong perfume and Cherry B turned his stomach. He looked at Cathy, who was standing behind Stuart's chair. 'Think your friend needs to sit down,' he said pointedly. 'Why don't you take her to sit by the door and get her a coffee?'

Cathy glared at him. 'Why don't *you* take her to sit by the door and get her a coffee? She's your girlfriend.'

Eddie looked at Jane, whose face had gone pale. 'You've got it wrong, Cathy, this is my girlfriend.' He unhooked Angie's arms from around his neck, sat down, took Jane's hand and squeezed it reassuringly.

Angie stared at him, her eyes slightly glazed. 'She's your girlfriend? She's the reason you stopped seeing me?' She threw her head back and laughed. 'Ed, you've gotta be kidding me. She looks about twelve.' She turned to Jane. 'Sorry, love, he's my boyfriend, not yours. We've been together ages.'

'Cathy, get her out of here,' Vincento said, coming to the table to collect empty glasses. 'She's pissed and we don't serve alcohol. It's a special night. We don't want any trouble.'

Cathy grabbed Angie by the arm. 'You should try giving this lot the alcohol lecture, Vinnie. She's had one drink, that's all, and we've got tickets for tonight. You can't just throw us out.'

'Well, go and get her sobered up then. Take her near the door and get some fresh air. And if she starts again, you're both out.'

Jane was near to tears as Cathy led Angie away. Eddie put his arms around her and gave her a kiss. 'Sorry about that.'

'She used to be your girlfriend?'

'Yeah, but not for a while now. Not since I met you.'

'She looks so grown-up. How old is she?'

'Sixteen, nearly seventeen.'

'And did you... with her?' Jane whispered.

'No. We were close, but no... we didn't.'

'Do you want to go back to her? She seems to think she's still with you.' Tears were tumbling down her cheeks now and Eddie wiped them away with his hanky. He pulled her to her feet and took her into the dressing room, away from everyone's curious stares.

'I don't want to be with her. I told you how I feel about you on Tuesday. I know people will say it's puppy love, but it's how I feel. I should have told her it was over but I didn't. I think she knows now though.' He kissed her and held her close, silently cursing Angie for ruining his mellow mood.

'Let's get you back to the others. The group needs to get changed, ready to go on.'

\* \* \*

Angie sipped her coffee, staring over the rim of the cup as Eddie and the girl came out of the dressing room. He had his arm around her shoulders and was whispering in her ear. She smiled up at him and the look she gave him made Angie's stomach lurch. She'd looked at Eddie like that too; like he was the best thing on two legs, when really, he was just a cheating swine. She wondered how far he'd got with her. Not very, she'd bet her life on it. Well, he'd soon get fed up of that and she was blowed if she was going to hang around waiting. She'd been aware of eyes on her as she walked into the coffee bar tonight and knew there'd be no shortage of dance partners once the group started playing. She'd make sure she danced as close to the stage as she could. Let him see she didn't care, but also reminding him of what he'd miss. She knew she looked good and wished she'd not had that drink now. It had gone straight to her head on an empty stomach as she'd been too nervous to eat. But then again, she hadn't been anticipating Eddie being here with his little playmate. She took a cigarette from her bag, and although she had the lighter Eddie gave her ages ago, she went to ask Roy for a light, ignoring Eddie and the girl. She stood behind Roy's chair, her hands on his shoulders, even though Roy's girl was giving her the evil eye as he lit her cigarette.

'Right,' Roy said, jumping to his feet. 'Come on, let's get the show on the road.'

Angie watched as Eddie gave the girl a lingering kiss and then walked away without a backward glance at her. 'You just wait, Eddie Mellor,' she muttered as she walked back to Cathy. 'You'll be mine one day.'

## 10

Jane smiled as Eddie sang 'Heartbeat' and didn't take his eyes off her. The words of the song were so how she felt about him and she could see he meant them for her too. He flicked his floppy fringe from his eyes with each drum beat. No matter what he did to his hair, it was too soft to get the perfect, unmovable quiffs like Roy and Tim wore.

That Angie girl was draped all over a lad, dancing near the stage, snogging the face off him. His hands were all over her, but Eddie didn't seem to be bothered and hadn't glanced in her direction once. Jane was glad; after the earlier fiasco it would have spoiled the night for her and she felt so happy, she could burst.

'Just look at her,' Sammy said, lips curled in a sneer. 'What a tart! Can't believe Ed was seeing her.'

'Nice dress though,' Pat said. 'That'll have cost her a bit.'

As 'Heartbeat' finished, Roy played the opening to 'Rave On' and Sammy dragged Jane to her feet – 'Jive, come on.' They took to the floor. Stuart asked Pat to dance and Mac pulled Jackie up.

Jane couldn't remember having such a great time, ever. She

was looking forward to a kiss and cuddle after the gig finished and then tomorrow afternoon she was seeing Eddie at Roy's place again. Dad had given her permission to take a taxi home because it was a special night and he'd even handed over the fare and told her to make sure Pat and Sammy shared the journey. Jane could see Mario standing by the side of the stage, a happy smile on his face. He waved as he caught her eye. She waved back. The night had been a great success. She hoped he'd get his new premises soon.

As Roy announced the final song and told them that he wanted everyone to join in, the crowd surged as close to the makeshift stage as it could. Mario had lent the group some props and a cheer rang out as Vinnie lifted a small table and telephone onto the stage. 'Call for you,' he said to Roy.

'For me?' Roy picked up the phone and imitated Big Bopper's deep voice asking what his baby wanted and telling her that she knew what he liked.

The crowd went wild, singing 'Chantilly Lace' along with him. Someone had opened the door and teenagers spilled out onto the pavement, singing and dancing.

'Good job there's no houses nearby,' Sammy yelled. 'Aren't they just fabulous? And they're all ours.'

Jane laughed. 'They're great. I feel so proud of them. This is the best night ever.'

'It is. And we're only just beginning. You'll see, we're gonna have the time of our lives with these boys, Jane.'

* * *

Molly sorted laundry into colour groups and dropped the first lot of clothes into the twin tub. She shook her head as she looked at Sammy's pleated school skirt. 'What the devil has that girl been doing?' Dried mud coated the back. Pat's was still clean by comparison, hardly even needed to go through the machine. She hated doing the washing on a Sunday, but there was no time on a Monday now she was working. Traditional laundry days had long gone.

Her late mother would have had a fit; washing on a Sunday was unheard of in Molly's childhood home. But then again, her mother had had fits at everything Molly did. She'd not been the most understanding woman in the world. Molly had shamed the family, according to her mother, when she got pregnant and gave birth to Sammy at the age of sixteen. But she and Samuel Hardy had been really happy with their baby girl and they'd got married and had Susan four years later. Then she'd been widowed when the girls were six and two. Samuel's motorbike had skidded; he'd gone over the handlebars and died instantly from his injuries. She'd been alone for seven years with her girls until a friend had introduced her to widower Tom Mason, whose daughter Pat was Sammy's age. Tom had asked her out and they'd married almost a year ago. Molly didn't think she could be any happier than she was at the moment, but she'd never take her happiness for granted again.

Tom came into the kitchen and gave her a hug. He was followed by Sammy, who was dressed ready to go out, her satchel on her back.

'Mum, have you got that knitting pattern for Jane's mum? She was asking about it yesterday.'

'Yes, somewhere. I was going to drop it off later. I haven't seen Enid for a week or two so I'll catch up with her over a cuppa.'

'No need to go out,' Sammy said. 'You're busy here. I'll take it, save your legs.'

'For crying out loud, Sammy, I don't need my legs saving. I'm not even thirty-one yet!'

'Yeah, but like you say, you get tired, and you've got the dinner to cook as well as doing the washing. Just thought I'd save you some time, that's all.'

'I'll take it after dinner. I need to look for it first anyway.'
She glanced at Sammy, who was looking shifty, not meeting her
eye. 'By the way, what the devil happened to your school skirt?
It's covered in mud.'

'Is it? Don't know.' Sammy shrugged. 'Oh, maybe it's from
when I ran onto the hockey pitch and slipped. Anyway, I'm off
out now to Jane's to do homework and then we're going for a
walk.' She dashed out of the kitchen, leaving Molly staring
after her.

'What was all that?' Tom said. 'Has she left Pat on her own
again?'

'No, Pat went out ages ago. Said she was going to see a girl
from school about something or other. Peel the spuds for me,
Tom, while I root that pattern out.'

Susan, sitting at the kitchen table cutting out dressing-up
dolls from a book, looked up and sniffed.

'Susan, use your hanky,' Molly scolded, lifting a pile of knitting patterns onto the table. 'I won't tell you again.'

'Our Sammy's got a boyfriend.'

'What?'

'Sammy's got a boyfriend,' Susan repeated, pushing her hair
out of her eyes. 'He's called Roy. I heard her telling Pat where
she goes with him after school.'

'Susan, stop telling fibs,' Molly said.

'I'm not telling fibs.' Susan looked indignant. 'Pat's got one
as well. So has Jane.'

Molly pulled a chair out and sat down, facing Susan. 'Are
you sure? You'd better not be telling stories and making
things up?'

'I'm sure.' Susan nodded, dark brown curls, just like her
mother's, bouncing on her shoulders. 'Jane's boyfriend's name is
Eddie, Pat's is Tim. But you're not to tell them I told you.
They're horrible to me as it is. They won't let me in their
bedroom when they're talking.'

Molly rolled her eyes. The last thing teenage girls need is a younger sister ear-wigging conversations about boyfriends. She'd had all that with her own sister, telling tales about her to their mother. Susan had obviously done her share of ear-wigging at the door though. She tried a gentler approach: 'Right, love, these boyfriends, do the girls know them from school?'

Susan sniffed again and shook her head.

'Hanky!' Molly waited while Susan blew her nose.

Tom, eyebrows raised, sat down opposite Molly.

'Problem?'

'Err, not sure. Susan's just in the middle of telling me a very interesting tale. Carry on, Susan,' Molly encouraged. 'Where do they know these boys from then?'

'Record shop and Mario's. That's what I heard them say. They play guitars and drums and things.'

'Do they now?' Molly pursed her lips as the back door opened and Pat came in, bringing a blast of cold air with her.

'Pat, over here a minute,' Tom said as she kicked off her boots.

She took off her coat and scarf and joined them at the table. 'Yeah, what's up?'

'Susan tells us that you, Sammy and Jane have got boyfriends. Is this true?' Molly could tell from the blush creeping up Pat's neck and the way she glared at Susan that it was.

'Little snitch! Sammy'll go mad.'

'Don't speak to Susan like that,' Tom said. 'She did the right thing. Why didn't you tell us about these boys? How old are they?'

'I'm saying nothing until Sammy's here,' Pat said and leant back in her chair.

'Then go to your room.' Tom folded his arms. 'When Sammy gets back, we'll talk some more.'

'I'll go over to Jane's and bring Sammy back here.' Molly jumped to her feet. 'And I'll drop this pattern in for Enid.'

'Sammy isn't at Jane's,' Pat said. 'They've gone out.'

'Gone out where?' Molly asked.

Pat stared up at the ceiling. 'I'm saying nothing until Sammy's here,' she repeated, her eyes filling with tears.

'Fair enough.' Tom stood up. 'Room, now.'

'I had a feeling something was going on,' Molly said as Pat left the kitchen, slamming the door behind her. 'Sammy's been secretive lately and so has Pat, to a point.'

'Why didn't you say something?' Tom said. 'They're growing up though, love. It was bound to happen. Not a lot you can do without starting World War Three and I for one don't fancy being stuck in the middle of that.'

'I suppose so,' Molly said. 'But it's the secrecy that bothers me. Why won't Pat say anything? What doesn't she want us to know?' She pulled on her coat and picked up her keys. 'Won't be long. Keep your eye on that leg of lamb in the oven.'

'Why, what's it going to do, run away?' Tom laughed at his own joke as Molly left the house.

* * *

Molly hammered on the front door and Enid's face registered surprise when she opened it.

'I wasn't expecting to see you. Sammy said you weren't feeling too good when I said I'd pop over for that pattern, save you coming here. She said you'd gone to bed with a headache. Come through to the kitchen, I'm just washing up.'

'Lying little minx,' Molly muttered, following Enid.

'Who is?'

'Sammy, and she's not the only one.'

'Why, whatever have they been up to?'

'It's not just Sammy and Pat, it's your Jane as well. Has

Sammy been doing her homework here with Jane the last few Sundays?'

'No, our Jane's been at yours doing hers, hasn't she?'

Molly shook her head. 'They've been off meeting lads. God knows what they've been getting up to, but I've a pretty good idea. I'll skin that Sammy alive when I get my hands on her.'

A look of shock on her face, Enid sat down on a kitchen chair and gestured for Molly to do the same. 'So, what you're saying is that Jane hasn't been at your house at all. What about at night in the week, she often pops out for an hour or two, saying she's going to talk to Pat and Sammy?'

'She hasn't been round to our house for ages. She's obviously off meeting this lad called Eddie, whoever he is. Pat's seeing one called Tim, but she doesn't go missing as often as Sammy does. That little madam's been late home from school two or three nights a week, supposedly having extra tuition. I dread to think what this Roy is teaching her.'

'But they're together when they go out, aren't they?'

'Who knows?' Molly sighed. 'Sammy's on her own after school and I presume Jane's alone when she goes out.'

Enid drew a worried breath. 'So, what you're saying is that they're pretending to be at one another's houses when they're not. Well, the daft pair. They must have known that couldn't go on forever. Where are they now?'

'I don't know. Pat saw them earlier but she won't say anything until Sammy comes home. And it's obvious that Sammy didn't want us two to get together today in case we sussed them out.'

Enid chewed her lip. 'Do you know anything about these lads? Who they are, where they live? I mean, they might be nice boys from the grammar school and we might be worrying over nothing,' she said, optimistically.

'Well, if that's the case, why all the sneaking around and

lying?' Molly said. 'If they've nothing to hide, why haven't we met them?'

Enid sighed. 'I don't know what to think. I mean, they're sensible girls.'

'Most of the time, yes. But you know what young lads are like, only after one thing, and if you remember they can be very persuasive. Well, at least my Samuel was.'

'Oh, Jane's far too sensible to fall for any, err, sweet talk,' Enid said, blushing slightly. 'And your two know right from wrong. Maybe we should insist on meeting these lads. If we don't like them, we can stop the girls from seeing them.'

'I don't mind meeting them. What I object to is lies. Tom and I give those two ample freedom, there's no need for it.' Molly stood up. 'I'd better get back. I've left the washer on and Tom keeping a watch on the dinner.'

Molly hurried home, deep in thought. Maybe Enid was right, perhaps Roy, Eddie and Tim were nice lads and there was nothing to worry about. She wasn't totally convinced though. She'd not been much older than Sammy when she'd met Samuel and fallen for his sweet talking and had a baby. She didn't relish history repeating itself for her daughter.

* * *

Pat lay on her bed, staring up at the ceiling. She wished there was some way she could warn Sammy and Jane that the cat was out of the bag. She'd just come back from Tim's house after spending a couple of hours with him while his mum was out playing the organ at the local church. Not that they'd got up to anything much, but it was just nice to have him all to herself for a while and she didn't want her dad and Molly putting an end to that anytime soon. She heard the front door open and close and Molly calling that it was only her and then silence as the door to the kitchen banged shut. Dare she sneak out the front door and go to Roy's to warn them? Her coat and boots were in the kitchen. Damn. She jumped up and opened the wardrobe. Sammy's old red duffle coat hung forlornly on a hanger. It was waiting for Susan to grow into it. Pat pulled it on. A bit short in the sleeves and halfway up her backside but the day was too cold to go out without a coat so it would have to do. She pulled up the hood and tied a scarf around her neck, pushed her feet into her school shoes and opened the bedroom door. Silence! She sneaked down the stairs and out of the front door, closing it quietly behind her.

\* \* \*

The loud rat-tat-tatting on the front door had Eddie and Jane shooting upright from their passionate clinch on the sofa. Roy and Sammy were upstairs.

'Who's that?' Jane gasped, pulling her sweater down.

'God knows,' Eddie groaned. He went to answer the door and let in an agitated Pat. She followed him into the sitting room, where Jane was straightening her long hair with her fingers.

'Pat, what's wrong?' Jane said as Pat burst into tears. 'And why are you wearing Sammy's old coat?'

'They know,' Pat wailed. 'Dad and Molly, they know about the boys. Molly's been to your mum's, Jane, so she'll know too.' She flopped onto the sofa next to Jane and told her and Eddie what had happened. As she finished, the door opened and Roy and Sammy came in.

'We heard the door. What's wrong?' Roy asked as Sammy went to sit next to Pat and Jane. Pat repeated her tale.

'The little snitch!' Sammy exclaimed. 'Just wait till I get my bloody hands on her.'

Eddie sat down on the floor next to Jane's feet. 'Might be the best thing,' he said. 'Get it sorted out with the parents and then you can come and go as you please. No more lying and sneaking about.'

Sammy sighed. 'While that might work with your mum and dad, Ed, it won't work with ours.'

'Mine'll kill me,' Jane said, tears starting. 'They'll make me stop seeing you, Ed. I can't bear it.'

'They won't. Not if I've got anything to do with it,' he said. 'I'll come back with you now, tell them I want to take you out and stuff.'

'God, no, you can't do that,' Jane cried. 'Let me talk to them first. See what happens. I'll meet you tomorrow in the shop after school, if I can.'

'And I'll see you there, too,' Sammy said to Roy. 'You'd better tell Tim what's happened. Did you see him earlier, Pat?'

Pat nodded tearfully.

'We'll walk you home as far as we can,' Eddie said. 'To the rec at least, and hopefully see you tomorrow.'

## 11

Heart sinking to her boots when she was met by an ominous silence instead of a cheery greeting, Jane slunk into the kitchen. Her dad had his back to her, buttering bread on the worktop, and her mum was forking salmon from a tin into a dish. It was always the same tea on a Sunday: salmon sandwiches on Hovis, Madeira cake, followed by tinned pears in syrup, topped with Carnation milk. She hoped she wouldn't be as predictable at mealtimes when she got married. She'd bet Jackie's mum and dad weren't as boring when they sat down to eat and Jackie called puddings, desserts. That must be the posh word for it. She'd need to learn posh words for things if Eddie wanted to live in Wilmslow. She shook her head and tried to stop her mind flitting all over the place as her dad finished his bread-buttering and turned, his mouth stretched in a tight line. He had red spots on his cheeks that he always got when he was angry. Jane felt sick – she wished she'd let Eddie come back with her now.

'Where've you been?'

'Out with Sammy. I told you where I was going.'

Her mum finished fiddling with the salmon, rinsed her

hands at the sink and came straight to the point: 'Who's this Eddie that Molly's told us about?'

Jane could feel her cheeks heating and she looked down at the floor. Bluff her way out or tell the truth? God, she couldn't bear to lose Eddie just because her parents were so against her having a boyfriend. She could feel her eyes welling up and blinked rapidly. She had to be strong here and fight for herself. Being with Eddie had given her confidence, she felt more grown-up lately and not only that, if she wasn't allowed out to see him, he might get back with that Angie girl and she couldn't bear the thought of that either. Here goes. She took a deep breath and stuttered, 'Eddie... err, he's... err, m-my boyfriend.'

'And how long's this been going on?' her dad asked.

'Only a few weeks.'

'And you never thought to mention it?' her mum said.

'No, because you would have said I was too young, and that I couldn't see him and I really like him and it's not fair that you should stop me going out. Everybody at school has boyfriends. I'm not a little girl anymore and you can't tell me what to do...' Her words tumbled over each other.

She fell quiet as her dad held up his hand and said, 'Enough!' She'd gone too far. Well, that was it. She'd be confined to her room for good now. They'd probably even meet her from school so she couldn't slope off with Eddie.

'All we ask from you and our Peter is that you behave yourselves and tell us the truth about where you're going and who you're with,' her dad said.

Her mum sighed heavily. 'Like your dad says, you should always tell us where you're going and who with. It's for your own safety. You're only fourteen. We don't know this lad from Adam and that's what's worrying us. Anyway,' she drew a breath and continued, 'we've had a talk and if you're that struck on him, we'd better meet him. Ask him to come to tea next Sunday and we'll judge for ourselves if we think he's suitable enough for you to go out with. Meantime, no sneaking out at night. If you say you're going to Sammy's, you go to Sammy's. Understood?'

Jane chewed her lip. She'd got off lightly, but dare she chance her arm? They hadn't actually said she couldn't see Eddie, but... 'What about next Saturday night? Eddie's a musician. He's in a group. He plays drums and sings and we go to watch them at Mario's Coffee Bar.'

'A musician?' Her mum's eyebrows shot up her forehead, already creased with worry lines. 'Oh my God, they're all wild, if what you read in the papers is true. I don't like the sound of that at all. Is that what he does for a job? How old is he?' She fired questions at Jane, while her dad lit a cigarette and frowned.

'He's still at school until July,' Jane said. 'It's what he'd like to do for a job but his parents say he has to get a proper one and he's, err, he's sixteen.'

'Sixteen and he's in a group?' Her mum shook her head. 'Oh, Jane, you can do better than that for yourself.'

'Mum, that's an awful thing to say. You can't judge him before you meet him. It's not fair. He's a really nice boy and I... I love him.' She burst into tears and ran to the door. 'I'm going up to my room.'

'Hang on a minute,' her mum said. 'Next Sunday. Tea,' she repeated. 'And until then, you just behave yourself.'

'But what about Saturday night?'

'If your father says you can go, then you can. At least we know you're not on your own with him while you're at the coffee bar.'

'Dad?' Jane fixed him with the most pleading look she could muster.

'Oh, I suppose so,' he said, stubbing out his half-smoked cigarette. 'Safety in numbers and all that.'

\* \* \*

'What do you think?' Enid said as Ben sat at the kitchen table staring into space. 'I know she's your little girl and you're worried about her, but she seems quite smitten. She's far too young to know her own mind though. It'll all fizzle out in a few weeks.'

'It might not. We didn't,' Ben reminded her. 'You were only fifteen when I met you at that dance and I was sixteen. Similar age difference and your mother kicked up a right stink about me taking you out.'

'I remember,' Enid said with a nostalgic smile. 'Our first courting days were done in secret.'

'So, Jane's no different, just a bit younger.'

Enid nodded. 'We had the war to contend with as well.'

'We did, but the blackout came in handy at times!' Ben smirked as Enid felt her cheeks heating and smacked his arm.

'Stop it. You'll have me worried to death now about what they've been getting up to.'

'That's what's bothering me.'

'Oh, Ben. Well, what can we do?'

'Nothing for the minute. We'll meet the lad and take it from there.'

\* \* \*

'Did you get the Spanish Inquisition too?' Jane asked as she joined Sammy and Pat in their room after tea.

'We certainly did,' Sammy said, and then making Jane and Pat jump, yelled, 'I'll kill that little brat if she comes near me again.'

They heard a scuffle outside and Pat flung open the door to see Susan hurrying off down the stairs.

'I knew she was there,' Sammy said. 'She'll have followed you up, Jane. Nosy little cow!'

'Well, I haven't been banned from seeing Eddie,' Jane said, flopping down on Sammy's bed. 'They want him to come for tea next Sunday.'

'Same with us,' Sammy said. 'They want to meet Roy and Tim next Sunday, too. Bloody Susan, always ear-wigging everything we say. I just hope to God she didn't hear me telling Pat what Roy and I did in Norman's Woods the other night after school. I've already had earache from Mum about the mud on the back of my skirt.'

'Susan might not have understood what you meant,' Jane said.

'No, but Mum would. If Susan repeated what she heard, Mum would be down on me like a ton of bricks. She's already asked me in a roundabout sort of way if we've done it. I denied it, of course, but she didn't ask Pat if she had. I must have looked guilty or something. Oh God, if she finds out, Roy'll be prosecuted and I'll be locked up in this room and fed bread and water for the rest of my life, or even worse, sent away to a nunnery, or whatever they call it.'

'Stop being dramatic,' Pat said, laughing. 'Anyway, bit too late in the day for you to be a nun.'

'I'm not being dramatic; it's all right for you, you and Tim have been really good and he looks like an angel. Roy's hardly every mother's dream of a suitable boyfriend for their daughter. He always looks as though he's been up to mischief, even when he hasn't. Mum will take one look at him and she'll just know. Anyway, whatever they say, I'll run away before I stop seeing him!' Sammy finished, a mutinous look on her face.

\* \* \*

On Monday, while they waited for the boys in Flanagan and Grey's, Jane asked John if he'd consider her for a job as a Saturday girl.

'We're refurbishing the shop next month,' he said. 'Once it's finished, I'll be in touch. I could definitely use another pair of hands. How does that sound?'

'Oh great,' Jane said, already planning her new wardrobe in her head. 'I can work in the school holidays as well if you ever need me.'

'That'll be handy. Ah, here are the lads. Oh dear, glum faces. What's up with you three?'

'School,' Eddie said, taking his tie off and stuffing it in his blazer pocket. 'Me and Roy, we've been kicked out.'

'For good?' John said. 'No surprise really.'

Roy shrugged. 'It's not, but we're gonna get hell from the parents.'

'My dad'll go fucking mad,' Eddie said. 'I don't even wanna go home. He'll go on and on about how they should bring back National Service and how we don't know we're born today and that he had to fight in the war and stuff.'

Jane put her arms around him and gave him a hug. He hugged her back and dropped a kiss on her lips. 'So what reasons did they give for expelling you, other than truant? They can't just chuck you out for that, surely?'

'Truant,' Eddie began, 'not handing homework in on time, not doing homework, smoking behind the bike sheds, swearing... Do you want me to go on?'

She raised an eyebrow. 'Err, I guess that's enough to get anybody expelled.'

'Yep. Anyway, enough about all that, how did it go yesterday? You're here, so I presume we're not banned from seeing each other?'

She shook her head. 'Not as such, but we do need to talk. Let's all go to Mario's and we can fill you in on our news.'

* * *

'If it makes them feel better then I'll come for tea,' Eddie said, after Jane finished explaining Sunday's happenings. He took a swig from his bottle of Coke. 'And if I get to see you more often then that's okay.'

'Same here,' Roy said. 'Meeting girlfriends' parents is a new thing for me.'

'Well, as long as you behave it should be all right,' Sammy said. 'No rude jokes or anything and I'm sure they'll like you.'

'I'll even wear a suit,' Roy said with a grin. 'We'll do you proud, won't we, Tim?'

'There's no need to go mad,' Pat said, laughing. 'Just be yourselves. On second thoughts, that doesn't include you, Roy,' she finished as he raised an amused eyebrow.

'What are you going to say to your parents about school?' Jane said.

Eddie handed round cigarettes and sighed. 'God knows. I bet the head's called home already, although I've got a letter in my bag to give to Mum. I'll have to get a job to keep her happy, just something to be going on with until the group makes it big.'

'Are you allowed back in to take your GCEs?' Sammy asked.

'Yeah, we are,' Roy said. 'Can't see the point though. We'll fail them anyway. Have to see what Mum and Dad say. I suppose I could help them out in the shop for now. Might keep 'em off my back. Ed and I can do some rehearsing. Pity Tim didn't get chucked out too!'

'Just one thing,' Jane said. 'Don't mention you've been expelled on Sunday. It won't go down well and we need all the help we can get.'

* * *

Eddie strolled into the kitchen and handed his mother the letter from school. His dad was still at work, thank God. At least she'd have a bit of time to get over the shock and she might take his side if he persuaded her it was for the best and he'd look for a job.

'Is this what I think it is?' She put on her reading glasses and opened the envelope.

Eddie chewed his lip. 'Err, yeah. 'Fraid so. Sorry, Mum. I'll look for a job right away.'

'Oh, Eddie. Your dad'll go mad.'

'I know, but it can't be helped, Mum. I don't need exams and stuff for what I want to do. I know enough to get me through life. I'll be fine. I'm going out in a minute before he gets back. I can't face a big row and the same arguments again and again. Tell him I'll look for a job and that's it.'

'What about your tea?'

'I'll get fish and chips. Got a bit of money left over from the gig. See, I'm paying my way already.'

'There's no need for that. Here,' she said, opening her purse and pushing a half crown into his hand. 'I can't say I'm not disappointed. I had such high hopes for you, son; a good job, getting married to a nice girl and being able to buy a little house of your own in time.'

He smiled. 'Mum, forget it, all that's a long way off in the future. Married? God, I'm only sixteen. We're going to make it big with the group. You should have seen the crowd at the gig on Saturday, they went wild. Oh, and by the way, I've got a nice girl.'

His mum pulled a face. 'You know what I think of her. She's too forward for her own good, that one. I don't like you going out with her, Ed.'

'Not Angie. That's over. This one's called Jane. She's lovely. I'll bring her round one day.'

Her face brightened. 'That'll be nice. Go and get yourself

ready before your dad gets home, otherwise you'll not get out of the door in one piece.'

In his room Eddie changed into his usual jeans and T-shirt and thought about earlier when Angie had come up to him at the bus stop after school to commiserate about his expulsion. She'd seemed genuinely concerned about what his parents would say but told him she was envious in a way as she'd love to be able to leave school and start her hair-dressing apprentice-ship right now. She'd wished him luck and then pulled him into her arms and kissed him full on the lips in front of a crowd who'd cheered loudly and told him to get in there. For a split second he'd responded and then jerked away when he felt the familiar tingling begin. Shit, why did she still have that effect on him when it was Jane he was certain he loved?

* * *

The coffee bar was heaving again on Saturday night and as the group got changed in between spots, Mario knocked and came into the dressing room.

'You okay, Mario?' Eddie asked, tucking his shirt into black leather jeans that Roy's dad had lent them the money to buy.

'I'm good, Eddie. Busy again out there. I'm going to do a midweek music night starting next Wednesday. Do you boys want the first gig? I have another group who are interested in working too.'

'Brilliant,' Roy said. 'We'll take the first one. Who's the other group?'

'They call themselves The Scorpions,' Mario said. 'A group of lads who work at the bank down the road. They play music occasionally and are looking for a bit more work. Two of them are in tonight. I took them to your table and they're talking to John and Stu and your good ladies. Right, back to work. See you later.' Mario closed the door as he left the room.

'Well, that's good. Give us a bit more money anyway,' Eddie said. 'Next week, me and Roy could go round pubs and clubs and see if we can get anything else lined up.'

'Don't forget I've still got to go to school,' Tim said. 'Can't do too many late nights for now.'

\* \* \*

Jane was talking animatedly to a lad with brown hair who'd taken the seat Eddie had vacated. He stood behind her chair and put his hands on her shoulders, staring at the lad, who looked up at him with cool grey eyes.

'You gonna introduce me to your friend, Jane?'

'Oh, er, this is Mark Fisher and that's his friend Tony talking to John,' Jane said. 'Mario brought them to meet us. They're in a group called The Scorpions. They're going to be playing here soon. Mark, this is Eddie.'

'Her boyfriend,' Eddie said pointedly. He didn't like the way Mark was looking at Jane, as though he had the hots for her.

Mark got to his feet. 'I believe I'm sitting in your seat. Sorry.'

'Thanks.' Eddie sat down, grabbed Jane and kissed her and then rested one hand possessively on her knee. 'So, what instrument do you play?'

'Bass,' Mark replied and offered Eddie a cigarette.

'Ta.' Eddie took the ciggie and Mark flicked his lighter in his direction. 'Double?'

'No. Four-string electric; Fender Precision. I just got it the other week from the Music Exchange.'

'Very nice.' He must have some money, Eddie thought. Mind you, if he worked at the bank he'd be loaded. 'What sort of music do you play?'

'Similar to you. We were in here last Saturday for the

tribute night. The Raiders have a great sound, fabulous harmonies.'

'Thanks.' Eddie nodded and took a long drag on his cigarette. He glanced at his watch. 'We're back on in ten, Jane. Fancy a quick dance?' He led her on to the floor and took her in his arms as Mario's current favourite Platters song, 'Twilight Time', played on the jukebox.

'You okay, Ed?' Jane asked. 'You looked a bit annoyed with Mark.'

He shrugged. 'Didn't like the way he was ogling you.'

She pulled away from him, frowning. 'He wasn't. He was just being friendly.'

'Yeah, well, don't get *too* friendly.'

'Are you jealous? There's no need to be. That's the first time I've ever set eyes on him. Anyway, I love you.'

'Sorry. I love you too. I'm just feeling a bit edgy. Not been a good week. Dad's not speaking to me over school and I'm not exactly looking forward to tomorrow either.'

She smiled. 'Why? My parents aren't ogres, you know. I'm sure they'll like you.'

He shrugged again. 'They might not.'

Vinnie came over as Eddie led Jane back to her seat. 'Dad said you can leave your gear overnight. Save Roy's dad having to come out to pick it up.'

'Oh, fantastic,' Roy said. 'I'll let him know. Can I use the phone?'

'Of course. We'll be here from twelve tomorrow,' Vinnie said. 'Collect it anytime after that.'

'See you in a bit,' Eddie said and kissed Jane. He looked across at Mark, who was talking to Stuart and John. There was something about him that he didn't like, apart from the way he'd looked at Jane, but he couldn't quite fathom what.

In the middle of 'Johnny B. Goode' Eddie spotted Angie and Cathy on the dance floor. He hadn't even realised they were here tonight. Angie waved at him and he nodded and smiled. A couple of lads went up to them and Angie jived with the one who grabbed her around the waist. Eddie recognised him as a boy from their school who'd left last year. As he twirled Angie under his arm, her full dance skirt flared out and from his raised vantage point behind the drum kit, Eddie caught a glimpse of stocking tops and black lace. The familiar tingling started and he really had to concentrate not to miss a beat. Then he saw Jane dancing with Mark. She caught his eye and he saw her anxious expression. She said something to Mark and went to sit down. Mark looked at Eddie and shook his head slightly as if to say it was only a dance.

Roy announced the last song and turned to look at Eddie. 'What's wrong?' he mouthed.

'Nothing.'

'You were out of beat on that last one.'

'I know. Sorry.' Eddie counted in 'That'll Be the Day' and tried to concentrate. His head felt full of stuff going round and round. He shouldn't have had a drink tonight or shared a joint. It hadn't made him feel good like it usually did.

* * *

Eddie made his way back to Mario's after seeing Jane on the bus at Mersey Square and promising not to be late tomorrow for tea. They'd had a few cross words about her dancing with Mark and he felt bad about upsetting her when he knew damn well there was no need. Roy and Tim had got the last bus home, but he'd made the excuse that he'd left his wallet in the dressing room. He hadn't, it was in his jacket pocket. He was hoping to catch Angie before she left to go home. Cathy would be with her though. That was the problem.

He stood in a shop doorway opposite the coffee bar and lit a cigarette. He saw the pair coming out and was about to holler

Angie's name when a sleek black car pulled up and a tall, smartly dressed young man with a mop of dark curls jumped out.

Angie saw the man and Eddie at the same time. Eddie raised his hand but she ignored him and he heard her say, 'Richard, what are you doing here?' He detected the excitement in her voice.

'Hiya, doll,' the man said, flinging his arms around her. 'Just passing, so I thought I'd see if you and your friend would like a lift home.'

'Err, I'll walk, thanks,' Cathy said, glaring at Eddie.

Eddie glared back.

'I'll have a lift. Thanks, Richard.' Angie allowed him to take her arm and help her into the front passenger seat.

Eddie watched as the vehicle sped away. Cathy came across to him, as he knew she would. She had a smirk on her face and he felt like smacking her one across it.

'Who was that?' he asked.

'Angie's friend from work.'

'Well, why's he picked her up?'

'I don't know. He fancies her, I think. She fancies him.'

'Does she?'

'Yeah. You jealous?'

'No.' He turned and made to walk away. Cathy grabbed his arm.

'I think you are. It's your own fault. You treated her like shit, she deserves better.'

'And what would you know?' He shook her off and hurried away down the road, seething inside.

* * *

Back home, Eddie helped himself to his dad's whisky. He knocked the drink back in one and poured another, not caring if his dad discovered he'd been helping himself. It was a new bottle anyway so he could get away with watering it down a couple of times. That guy who picked Angie up had looked a lot older than her, in his twenties at least. What if he tried it on? Would she let him? If she'd been drinking tonight, she might well be feeling up for it. She'd be putty in his hands. He'd probably already got her on the back seat with her knickers off.

He took the glass into the kitchen and rinsed it. Tormented by the thoughts that the guy was shagging Angie right now, he punched the kitchen door so hard, he heard his knuckles crunch. He howled in pain and sank to the floor, clutching his right hand.

## 12

Lillian awoke with a jump, disturbed by a noise from downstairs. She looked at the bedside clock. Almost one, no doubt Eddie coming in late and banging about. Might as well go and pay a visit now she was awake. She slid out of bed, trying not to disturb Fred, who let out a succession of snores and turned over onto his side. She pulled on her dressing gown, pushed her feet into fluffy slippers and went out onto the landing. The hall light was on and she leant over the balustrade. 'Ed, is that you?' she called softly.

There was no reply so she hurried into the bathroom. As she came out she heard a faint moan. 'Ed,' she called again. 'You alright, son?' She made her way down the stairs and stopped as she caught sight of him sitting on the floor by the kitchen door, holding his hand, face as white as the gloss paintwork. 'What's wrong?' She helped him to his feet.

He held out his swollen right hand that was turning shades of purple around the knuckles.

'How've you done that?' She led him into the kitchen, turned on the cold water and held his hand underneath the tap for a short time, then patted it dry with a towel. He remained

silent and she sat him down at the kitchen table and rummaged
in a cupboard for her first-aid tin. 'There's a bottle of arnica in
here somewhere, it might stop it bruising any further. Although
looking at it, it wouldn't surprise me if you haven't broken
something.'

She found the bottle and sprinkled the arnica onto a piece
of lint and then wrapped it around his hand with a bandage.
'So,' she said once she'd secured the bandage with a pin, 'cat got
your tongue? How did it happen?'

'I punched the kitchen door,' Eddie mumbled.

'What? Why on earth did you do that, you silly lad?'

'I was angry.'

She frowned. 'Have you had a falling-out with someone?'

He shook his head.

She pushed his floppy fringe from his eyes and could see he
was close to tears. She gave him a minute or two to compose
himself and tried again. 'Are you worrying about your dad's
reaction to what happened at school? He'll get over it, love. You
might have a job lined up soon and it'll soften the blow a bit.'

Eddie half-smiled. 'Yeah, maybe. I promise I'll start looking
next week. There was an advert in Jerome's Outfitters' window
for an assistant. Might pop in and see if they'll give me an
interview.'

'That'd be nice.' She got him a glass of water and two
aspirins. 'They'll ease the pain. Now I know you too well; it's
not just school and your dad's reaction that's upsetting you.
There's something else.'

Eddie crunched the aspirins and grimaced. He took a long
swig of water. 'It'll sound daft, Mum, but I'm feeling confused. I
told you about my new girl, Jane, and... well, I really like her.
She's pretty and a nice person. I'm invited to tea tomorrow to
meet her parents.'

'And you're worried about it?' Lillian sat back down again.
'Oh, it'll be fine, Ed. Just wear something smart and be polite.

How could they not like you?' She smiled at her handsome boy.
Any girl would be proud to be seen out with him.

He sighed. 'Yeah, I suppose it'll be okay.'

'So why are you feeling confused? I don't understand.'

'I saw Angie tonight with another lad. I felt jealous. Don't
know why, I don't wanna go out with her anymore; well, I don't
think I do anyway. I want to be with Jane. But seeing her with
him made me feel really angry.'

'Feelings can jump about all over the show at your age, Ed. I
daresay you'll have many girlfriends before you settle down. As
far as I'm concerned, you did the right thing, finishing with
Angie.'

'I suppose so. Think I'd better go up to bed. Night, Mum.
Thanks for listening and seeing to my hand.'

'I think you should go to the infirmary in the morning and
get it looked at. Your dad will take you. But go on, get off to bed
for now.'

Eddie left the room and Lillian stayed at the table with her
thoughts. She tried her best to understand him; he wasn't a bad
lad really, just restless at times. Kids today expected so much
more than she and Fred had done when they were Eddie's age.
And there'd been no such thing as teenagers then either. The
word had only come into use in the last few years because of all
this American music youngsters played all the time. Bloody
jungle music, Fred called it. She hoped tomorrow's visit to
Jane's would go well. The last thing she wanted was Eddie
getting mixed up with that Turner girl again.

* * *

Eddie sat with his dad in the hospital waiting room. He'd had an
X-ray and been told no bones were broken. At least his dad was
speaking to him now, albeit only when he had to, burying his
head in the *Sunday People* newspaper in between conversa-

tions. But he'd shown sympathy earlier when his mum had removed the bandage and he'd seen the swollen and bruised state of Eddie's knuckles. His mum had told his dad that he'd tripped and banged his hand as he'd fallen against the door. His dad agreed a visit to the infirmary was a must and they'd been here since nine o'clock. He looked at his watch: just gone eleven. He wished they'd get a move on. He didn't want to be late for Jane's and he needed to go home and get changed. His mum said she'd iron him a nice shirt to go with his clean jeans. She also said he should wear smart trousers but he drew the line at that. It wasn't a job interview, a nice shirt would do fine. He looked up as his name was called and a young nurse beckoned him into a cubicle.

He sat down as she examined his hand. 'Looks sore,' she sympathised. 'But luckily you've not broken anything. I'll strap you up and then we'll see you again. You'll need to rest it until you come back. No lifting or anything strenuous.'

Eddie felt his heart sink. The gig at Mario's on Wednesday. Roy would go mad, especially when he told him how it had happened and why. 'Err, so I won't be able to play my drums?'

'I'm afraid not.' She looked closely at him. 'I thought I recognised you. You're in Roy Cantello's group. I saw you play at Mario's the other week.'

'That's me.' He smiled.

Fancy being recognised already, and by a good-looking bird, too.

'My younger sister went out with Roy last year,' she said, deftly wrapping a crepe bandage around his knuckles and securing it around his wrist with two strips of sticking plaster. 'It didn't last, of course. Sue said he had a problem with his hands!'

He smirked. 'Sounds like Roy.'

She fastened a sling around his neck and positioned his hand in it. 'Keep that on for a couple of days.' She gave him a card with an appointment for a week on Monday.

He thanked her, said goodbye and went back to the waiting room.

His dad looked up from his newspaper: 'Okay, lad?'

Eddie nodded; glad the real reason for his injury had been kept secret. His dad would never have understood.

On Sunday afternoon, on the dot of five, and with Susan safely dispatched to her friend's, Sammy answered the front door to two young men she scarcely recognised. Dressed in smart navy suits, white shirts, navy and white striped ties, and not a hair out of place, Tim carried a box of Cadbury's Milk Tray and Roy a bunch of slightly wilting spring flowers.

'Bloody hell!' Sammy exclaimed. 'You look like dummies from Jerome's Outfitters' shop window!' She stepped back and invited them inside.

'This little performance better be worth something,' Roy whispered. He dropped a chaste kiss on her cheek as Molly appeared behind them.

'This is my mum, Molly, and this is Roy and Tim,' Sammy introduced them, trying hard not to giggle. 'You can call her Molly, she prefers it.'

Roy held out his hand and the wilting flowers and Tim shyly handed over the chocolates and shook Molly by the hand.

'Thanks, boys,' she said, accepting their gifts. 'Go through to the sitting room, we're just putting the finishing touches to tea. You keep them company – Sammy, Tom and I can manage. I'll send Pat through.'

Sammy closed the sitting room door and motioned to two chairs either side of the fireplace. 'Park yourselves there and then Tom and Mum can sit on the sofa and give you the third degree,' she said. 'What do you look like, and where on earth did the suits come from?'

'We were ushers at my cousin's wedding last year,' Tim said. 'We think we look smart.'

'Oh, you do, very! You just don't look like Roy and Tim.'

Pat slipped into the room and clapped a hand to her mouth. 'My, oh my, don't we look posh!'

'Don't you start,' Roy said. 'We didn't want to look like young daughter seducers in jeans and leathers, not for the first meeting anyway.'

'Well, Tim's not a daughter seducer,' Sammy said. 'He looks angelic, but you, Roy...' She shook her head. 'You're a lost cause. Try and avoid eye contact with me if you can.'

'Okay. Anything else I should do? This is all new to me, you know.' Roy tugged at his neatly knotted tie. 'I'm being bloody strangled here.'

Sammy patted his hand. For all his joking around, Roy could be a sensitive soul and she knew that he was as nervous as she was. 'You'll be fine, honestly. Just be yourself, only not too naughty, please.'

He nodded and took a deep breath. The sitting room door opened and Molly carried in a tray of rose-patterned cups and saucers complete with matching teapot.

'Best china,' Sammy muttered. 'You are honoured.'

Roy grimaced. 'Is that wise?'

'Pat, bring that little folding table over from the corner and put it in front of the fire. We can eat off our knees. It's much more relaxing, don't you think, boys?' She sat down on the sofa.

They nodded as Sammy poured the tea and handed them a cup each.

Tom carried in a tray laden with sandwiches and cakes and put it on the table. He introduced himself. 'Help yourselves, boys. There's salmon, cheese and potted beef. Sammy tells us you're in a group.' He sat down next to Molly. 'What instruments do you play?'

Tim's face lit up. 'Roy plays lead guitar and sings and I play a stand-up bass.'

'Jane's boyfriend Ed's their drummer,' Sammy chipped in. 'Mum and Tom like music, especially Elvis and Buddy Holly.'

'Eddie sings a lot of our songs,' Roy said. 'He's got a great voice, his harmonies are brilliant – I expect that's because he used to be a choirboy.' He stretched out his long legs towards Sammy, who was sitting on the rug in front of him.

She leant back lightly against him and frowned. Ed, a choirboy? First she'd heard about it. 'You should hear Ed sing "Heartbeat", Mum.' Sammy knew that 'Heartbeat' was a particular favourite of her mum's.

'So, what'll you do for work when you finish school?' Tom asked, reaching for a sandwich.

'Not sure yet,' Roy replied. 'Tim fancies doing a motor mechanics apprenticeship and my mother will expect me to join one of our family businesses.'

'Oh, what trade is the family in?' Molly asked.

'Fruit and veg and undertaking,' Roy said. 'My mother's brother runs a funeral parlour.'

Sammy's eyebrows shot up and disappeared under her fringe as she choked on the cake she was eating. She looked closely at Roy but he was avoiding her gaze as she'd told him to do. He'd never spoken of a family undertaker. His mum and dad ran the fruit and vegetable shop. Was he taking the mickey here? You never quite knew with Roy.

'Well, there's plenty of work in that field, son,' Tom said. 'I mean, it's hardly a dying trade.'

Tom sniggered at his own joke as Roy looked at him with a deadpan expression. 'That's right, Tom. I'd be guaranteed a job for life. I mean, let's face it, there's not much money in rock 'n' roll. I'd be better off learning how to lay out and embalm!'

Sammy leapt up and brushed the crumbs from her dress.

She grabbed the empty teapot, turned to Roy and smiled sweetly. 'Come and help me make more tea, please.'

'Of course, Sammy.' Roy excused himself and followed her out of the room. In the kitchen she shut the door. He took the teapot from her, put it on the worktop and pulled her into his arms. He pressed her up against the door, kissing her slowly and passionately. He hitched up the full skirt of her blue striped dress and ground his hips against hers.

'Roy, stop it, you randy sod,' she gasped. 'Mum might come in.'

'Just something to keep me going,' he said, grinning wickedly.

She smoothed her skirt down and filled the kettle. 'What was all that rubbish about undertakers and Eddie being a choirboy?'

'Sounds good, doesn't it?' he said. 'I mean, somebody who lays out bodies for a living and an ex-choirboy are hardly likely to be the life and soul of the party, are they?' He looped her long hair behind her ear and nibbled her neck as she tried to spoon tea into the pot.

She shook her head and laughed. What would he think of next? 'Well, don't say anything else. Get them talking music. They're interested. It's a safe enough subject. Hopefully after one more cup, we can make our escape.'

'You coming back to mine? Mum and Dad are out and I need you. It's been a long week.'

She looked into his dark, broody eyes and couldn't resist him when he gave her that sultry look. 'Yes, I am, but Pat and Tim will have to come with us.'

'That's okay. Ed and Jane will be coming along too, later. Thought we could all go to Mario's tonight.' The kettle whistled and he filled the teapot. 'After you,' he said, opening the door as Sammy carried the pot.

* * *

After the young couples left, Tom and Molly tidied up and relaxed together on the sofa. Tom took her hand. 'Were you taken in by that little lot?'

'Of course not. The boys looked uncomfortable in those suits – I'm sure they're more at home in jeans and leather jackets,' Molly said, laughing.

'Tim seems a nice enough lad, but I reckon Roy, for all the spiel he gave us about the funeral parlour, is a right handful. Odd that he hardly looked at Sammy all the time he was here.'

'I think he was trying to avoid eye contact. It would have been a dead giveaway of his feelings for her.'

'Do you still feel they're up to no good?'

'Not sure. Sammy denied it when I questioned her and without proof...' Molly shrugged. 'All we can do is hope they're being sensible and that's something only time will tell.'

'Yeah,' Tom said. He stood up and stretched. 'I'll go and collect Susan. Do you want to walk round with me, or would you rather stay here with your thoughts?'

'I'll come with you,' Molly said.

* * *

Eddie knocked on the front door and stood back as he waited. He could hear someone yelling, 'Will somebody answer the door?' and then Jane was opening it, a big smile on her face. It vanished as soon as she saw his sling.

'It looks worse than it is...' he began as her brown eyes clouded with concern.

'What happened?' she said, pulling him inside.

'Argument with the kitchen door. I, err, tripped and banged my hand as I fell.' He hoped his cheeks weren't going red. He hated lying, but could hardly tell her the truth. 'It's just badly bruised, nothing broken. Trouble is, I've not spoken to Roy yet and we've got that gig at Mario's on Wednesday.'

'Oh no,' she said, leading him into the lounge. 'Sit down.' She gestured to the sofa and sat beside him. 'What will you do?'

He shrugged. 'Not sure. Maybe Roy can get a stand-in drummer for the night. I should be okay for Saturday if I rest it.'

'Perhaps those lads that were in Mario's could loan their drummer.'

'We'll see.' The less they had to do with that other group, the better. He didn't want to encourage them and borrowing their drummer would mean Mark might come to the gig. Mind you, Jane would be with him if he wasn't playing himself. He looked up as the door opened and a blonde-haired woman came in, pushing a laden tea trolley.

Jane got to her feet. 'This is my mum. Mum, this is Eddie.'

Eddie jumped up and offered his left hand.

'Have you had an accident?' Jane's mum eyed him up and down. She didn't take his hand and he let it fall down by his side.

He saw her mouth purse slightly as she took in his jeans and leather jacket.

'Err, yes,' he said as Jane related the tale he'd told her.

'You're lucky nothing's broken then. Go and tell your dad to bring the teapot in, Jane.' She nodded to the sofa. 'Sit yourself back down.'

Eddie sat down and focused on the television in the corner. It was the same set as the one his parents had at home. 'Same telly as ours,' he said, struggling to think of something to say. *Come on, Jane, how long does it take to give your dad a message about a teapot?* There was something in the way Jane's mum was looking at him that told him she wasn't that keen and it was making him break out in a sweat. His shirt felt scratchy around his neck. His mum had told him she'd starched it to make the collar nice and crisp. He wished she hadn't bothered – he'd end up with a rash at this rate.

'Right, here we are,' Jane said, coming back into the room with her dad. 'This is my dad. That's Eddie, Dad.'

'Pleased to meet you, son.' Jane's dad shook his left hand and smiled.

Eddie felt himself relaxing as Jane sat down beside him. Her parents sat in opposite chairs and made a fuss of pouring tea and handing out the food. They ate in silence for a while. Jane helped him as he struggled with his cup and saucer and the plate balanced on his knee. Eddie felt his every move was being watched by her mother. She was younger than his own mum and quite a looker for her age; smartly dressed in a red dress with shiny stockings, and red high heels like Angie wore. Shit, why had Angie popped into his head just then? He tried to concentrate on what Jane's parents were saying before he got the vision of Angie's stocking tops and black lacy knickers. Something about what he planned to do after finishing school.

'Erm, I intend to take up music as a profession,' he said. No point in lying. If they didn't like it, they could lump it. Jane's mum's lips pursed tighter still. What did she expect him to say? That he wanted to be a brain surgeon or something? That sneaky slug of whisky he'd had for Dutch courage before leaving home was playing havoc with his mind.

'More tea, Ed?' Jane asked. She held out a fancy plate. 'Have a cake.'

'No tea, thanks. I, err, I need to pay a visit.'

'Oh yes, it's upstairs. I'll show you.'

Out in the hall she said, 'You okay, Ed? You look a bit flushed. Are you in pain?'

'Yes, a bit. I'll be okay, but can we go to Roy's soon? I could do with some fresh air.'

'You've only been here half an hour. Can we stretch it out a bit longer, please? For me.'

He sighed. 'Okay. I can't do my zip with one hand, will you help me?'

She blushed. 'I'd love to, but I'd better not. I'll get Dad to help you. He'll understand; he broke his arm last year. Go on up, it's the first door on your right.'

* * *

'Dad?' Jane popped her head around the lounge door. 'Can you help Eddie, please? He can't unzip his jeans properly. And he'll need them doing up again after.'

Her dad jumped up. 'Of course, love. It's a bloody struggle with one hand.'

Jane sat back down on the sofa, pulling her skirt down over her knees. 'Well, Mum, what do you think of him?' She chewed her lip as her mum looked her directly in the eye.

'I'll be honest, Jane. I don't think he's the one for you. He's a good-looking boy, but he's got his heart set on being a musician and that's not a job to provide for a secure future. You'll never have two halfpennies to rub together if you get involved with him.'

Jane swallowed hard. 'So you don't like him then?'

'I'm not saying I don't like him, or that you can't see him. I just don't think he's right for you. I mean, he could have made a bit more effort with his appearance for one thing. Fancy coming round in jeans and black leather. Not really the way to make an impression on your new girlfriend's parents.' She stopped as the lounge door opened and Eddie came back in, followed by Ben. 'More tea now, Eddie?'

'Err, no thanks.' He looked at his watch and then at Jane, who picked up a piece of cake.

'In a minute,' she mouthed. 'Err, Mum, we're meeting up with Sammy and the others so we'll be leaving soon.'

'I don't want you in late tonight,' her mum said. 'Quick word in the kitchen before you leave.'

'Won't be a minute, Ed.'

Jane followed her out of the room, her heart sinking.

\* \* \*

'Right, a few ground rules,' Enid began as Jane folded her arms in a defiant manner and leant back against the worktop. 'I'm not stopping you seeing him, but I think you need to concentrate a bit more at school. You've been distracted for weeks now and we don't want you falling behind. Your dad and I, well, we'd like you to have all the chances we never got. A good job and to be able to buy nice things when you get your own home. I can tell you now you won't have any of that with him. Life will be one long struggle.' Enid stopped, Jane was filling up. Maybe she was being a bit hard. The lad had been polite, he was clean, but there was something she couldn't put her finger on and she felt in her bones that her daughter was in for a lot of heartache if they got serious. 'Anyway, you can go out now, but be home by ten thirty. Saturdays and Wednesdays are fine but the rest of the week, you stay in.'

'Okay,' Jane said, 'but you're wrong about Eddie and we'll prove you wrong. I love him, he loves me. You'll say now that we're too young to know what love's all about.'

'No, I won't. I wasn't much older than you when I met your father, but I will say this: you just be careful. He's older than you. I know what lads his age are like. Now you'd better go back to him and get on your way.'

## 13

Angie breezed into Mario's on Sunday night and joined Cathy at their usual table. She removed her jacket, smoothed her black pencil skirt over her hips and sat down. 'Cheers, Cath.' She picked up the waiting glass of Coke. 'I'll get the next round.'

'Is that new?' Cathy said, gesturing her drink towards Angie's neat, white cap-sleeved blouse.

'Yes.' Angie smiled and popped open the top two buttons. 'I treated myself.'

'Don't know how you afford it. You're always buying something new.'

'I save my tips. You should treat yourself sometime. That pleated skirt and twin-set are a bit square, my mum wears stuff like that.' She stopped as Eddie and Roy, with Jane and Sammy in tow, came into the coffee bar and went to speak to Vincento. She saw that Eddie had his arm in a sling. 'Wonder what he's done?'

'Probably been fighting,' Cathy said. 'Anyway, never mind him, how did it go with Richard last night? And why did he come looking for you?'

'He'd dropped his fiancée off and was passing, that's all,'

Angie said. 'He remembered me telling him I was going to see the group play. He thought he'd offer me a lift.'

'Did you go straight home?'

'No, we went for a little drive first,' Angie said, feeling her cheeks heating. She looked at her hands and studied her red-painted fingernails.

'And?'

'And nothing, well, apart from a quick kiss and a cuddle. Did Eddie say anything? He gave me a funny look.' She hurriedly changed the subject. There was no way she was telling Cathy that she and Richard had parked up last night for a petting session in the back of his car. They'd had a snog in the staffroom at lunchtime and she'd half-expected him to turn up last night. They'd almost gone all the way but Richard had stopped in time and told her he couldn't cheat on his fiancée. She was glad in a way, because she wanted Eddie to be her first, but she'd felt a bit let down and wasn't quite sure how she'd look Richard in the eye next week at work.

'He asked who Richard was,' Cathy was saying, breaking her scattered thoughts.

'Oh, right, and what did you tell him?'

'That he worked with you and that you fancied him. I think he was jealous.'

'Good. Serves him right. He's insensitive for kissing her last week in front of me.'

'Well, that's Eddie all over. I don't know why you want him back, you must be crazy.'

'I love him, Cathy.'

'No, you don't. It's infatuation. If you loved him, you wouldn't be kissing and cuddling Richard, who's bloody well engaged. You don't half pick 'em.'

'What do you know? You've never had a boyfriend. I like Richard, but Ed and I were good together, till she came on the scene.' Angie looked over to where Eddie was now sitting with Roy. Sammy and Jane were making their way to the ladies'.

'Back in a minute.' Angie fixed on a friendly smile and went over to Eddie.

'So, what happened to you?' she asked. 'Get into a fight on the way home?'

'I fell,' he said.

'Oh, really?' She raised a disbelieving eyebrow. 'How are you going to play your drums?'

'I can't, not for a few days.' He looked at her, holding her gaze. 'Did you get home okay last night? Saw you got a lift.'

'Yes, thank you. Richard made sure I was alright.'

'I bet he did,' Eddie muttered.

'Sorry, did you say something?'

'Ed, that's enough.' Roy nodded in the direction of Jane and Sammy, who were on their way back, but had stopped to talk to Rosa.

'Bye then, I'll leave you to your little girlfriends,' Angie said and walked away. Eddie had a glint in his eye but she wasn't giving him the chance to say anything else. The fact that he was jealous would do for now.

* * *

Eddie stared after Angie's wiggling arse in her tight black skirt and fought the familiar feelings. He forced his attention back to Jane and Sammy as they came to the table.

'What did she want?' Sammy frowned.

'Just wondered what had happened to Ed, that's all,' Roy said.

'I don't trust her.'

'Leave it, Sam. Come and dance.' Roy pulled her onto the floor as the jukebox burst into life.

'What did she want, Ed?' Jane stroked his arm.

'Nothing, she was concerned, just like Roy said.' Eddie felt weary. He wanted to go home and lie down. His hand was hurting bad; he could do with something for the pain. Roy hadn't been too happy when he'd explained what had happened and that he couldn't drum at Wednesday's gig. Roy said he knew a guy who might stand in. He also said he needed his head examined, feeling the way he did about Angie when he had a nice girl like Jane. Eddie knew Roy was right but he couldn't get Angie and that Richard fellow out of his mind.

\* \* \*

'What's the matter with Eddie?' Sammy asked as Roy held her close while they smooched to Elvis's 'Don't'. 'He's really tetchy tonight.'

'He's a bit on edge after meeting Jane's parents and he's in pain with his hand,' Roy said.

'How did he really hurt it? I mean, falling over and banging it on the door sounds a bit of a lame excuse. Surely it wouldn't have warranted all that strapping up and a sling? Was he in a fight and doesn't want Jane to know?'

'Only with himself. He punched the kitchen door in a fit of temper last night. Now don't you dare tell Jane that or I'll be really angry with you.'

'Why did he do that? He's usually so placid.'

'I'm not saying any more, Sammy. Please don't ask me.'

'I bet it's got something to do with her, hasn't it?' Sammy shot Angie a frosty look.

'Stop it or I'll take you home,' Roy said and planted a kiss on her lips. 'Now shut up and dance.'

\* \* \*

Jane took Eddie's uninjured hand in hers. 'What's wrong? You've been quiet for hours. Is it my parents? Or is it something to do with her over there? You keep looking at her and she keeps staring at us.'

'I don't keep looking at her, it's just been a bad day. I didn't get much sleep and was up early for the hospital. I don't think your mother likes me either,' he finished, looking sulky.

Jane chewed her lip. She hadn't seen him in a mood before. 'Why do you think my mum doesn't like you?'

'Just a feeling,' he grunted.

'You're being over-sensitive. She didn't say anything to you to make you think she didn't like you, did she?' The mood he was in, she couldn't tell him what her mother really thought, because he'd probably say 'that's it, it's over' and walk away. 'You'll get to know her in time and she'll get to know you.'

'Yeah, I'm sorry, you're right. I think I should go home. I'm tired. Do you want to stay here with Roy and Sammy, or would you like me to walk you to Mersey Square?'

'I'll stay. See you tomorrow after school. Are you going to Jerome's to ask about that job you told me about?'

'Yeah, I will if I feel up to it. I'll meet you in the record shop.' He kissed Jane goodnight, said goodbye to Sammy and Roy and left.

\* \* \*

Eddie stood outside Mario's and lit a cigarette, his head spinning. He needed some time on his own. He took in the cool night air, enjoying the solitude and his ciggie. Someone called his name and he spotted Mark Fisher and his friend Tony walking towards him. Shit, maybe he should stay after all in case Mark tried to chat Jane up but then again, he really couldn't be bothered and, anyway, he was sure he could trust Jane.

'Evening, Eddie. What happened to you then?' Tony said with a grin. 'Push you out of bed, did she?'

'Argument with a door.'

'You going back inside?' Mark asked.

'No, I'm off home. Roy's in there with Sammy and my girl. Roy might need to use your drummer on Wednesday if he can't get fixed up.'

'Okay,' Mark said. 'We'll go in and see him. Take care, Ed.'

Eddie waved goodbye and went on his way, wondering now if he should have hung around. Could he trust Mark? He was about to walk down Broadgate when he heard someone else calling his name. Thinking it was Jane and that she'd changed her mind, he turned to see Angie running towards him. He waited until she caught up.

'Can I walk to Mersey Square with you?' she gasped.

'Why? Not getting a lift tonight?' he sneered.

'No, I don't think so. Would it bother you if I did?'

'Why would it do that?' Eddie looked at her, his head on one side.

Angie shrugged. 'Don't know, you tell me.'

'It wouldn't.' He turned and carried on walking.

'Well, I think it would, more than you're willing to admit.'

He stopped abruptly and Angie bumped into the back of him. Turning, he grabbed her arm and pulled her into the nearest shop doorway. 'Oh, you do, do you?'

'Don't be so rough,' she said, trying to pull away from him, but he wasn't letting go.

'Shut up and kiss me,' he demanded. He released his hold on her, pushed her up against the shop door and draped his uninjured arm around her shoulders. Shocked into silence by his irrational behaviour, Angie kissed him. He kissed her back; a long, slow, lingering kiss that left her breathless and he more confused than ever. He breathed in the fresh clean scent of her hair, and her perfume, which was new and lighter than she usually wore. He felt the familiar tingling to the point where he thought his balls might explode. He looked down into her shocked eyes.

'Did that guy shag you last night?'

'Eddie! No.'

'You sure?' He shook her by the shoulder.

'Of course I'm sure, but why would it bother you if he had? You finished with me.'

He took a deep breath. 'I don't know why, but it does. Come home with me.'

'What about Jane?'

'She's going home with Roy and Sammy.'

She hesitated. 'Your parents, won't they be in?'

'No, they'll be at my aunt's till eleven.'

'Are you sure it's what you want?' she said, looking into his eyes.

'I'm sure.'

'Okay.'

He took her hand as they ran down the hill and jumped on a bus for the short journey. He opened the front door and went into the parlour to make sure his parents were still out, beckoning Angie to follow.

He slid his good arm out of his jacket and tossed it on a chair. 'I'm having a drink. Do you want one?' He poured two large whiskies and handed one over. 'Knock it back, it'll relax you.' His own drink warmed his churning stomach as he tried to push the image of Jane's trusting face from his mind.

Angie took a few sips and handed the rest to him. He drained her glass, grabbed her hand and led her upstairs to his bedroom. He kicked the door shut, drew the curtains and turned on the lamp. 'Can you do something with this sling for me, please?'

Angie gently slid his arm out of the sling and pulled it over his head. She sat down on the bed and he sat down beside her.

He kissed her and unbuttoned her top, slipping it back over her shoulders. 'It's going to be a bit of a struggle, you'll have to help me,' he murmured.

'We'll manage,' Angie said, helping him out of his shirt and jeans and dropping them onto the floor. She unzipped her skirt, slipped out of it and lay back against the pillows.

Eddie looked at her lying there in her white lacy underwear and felt ready to burst. He unhooked her bra with one hand and kissed her breasts properly for the first time without the confines of clothes, while stroking the soft flesh of her inner thighs above her stocking tops. 'You sure you want to go all the way?' he said, slipping his hand into her knickers.

'I'm really sure,' she said as his fingers explored her. She pushed his pants down and stroked his erection. He moaned with pleasure and peeled off her knickers, terrified of coming too soon as she caressed him. He rolled on top and between her legs, trying to get inside her.

She arched her back and cried out as he pushed hard. 'I'm sorry,' he whispered. 'I feel so clumsy with one hand.'

'It's okay, it's okay. It hurt just then.' She bit her lip as he thrust into her again. 'Ed, you'll have to be careful,' she reminded him, 'we're not taking precautions.'

'I will be,' he said, looking into her eyes. She groaned and moved her hips in time as he moved slowly, trying to support his weight on one hand, his confidence growing with each stroke. His lips were on hers again, as the most wonderful feelings of pleasure grew in him and guilt flew out of the window as he tried to keep control for as long as he could. All those fumbles and night-time wanks were paying off now as he got beyond the point of needing to come right away and concentrated on the rhythm. He looked down at Angie. Her eyes closed, face flushed, curls fanned halo-like around her head. She gave a low moan and began to writhe and he quickened his pace. She cried his name and he felt her nails digging into his arse as she pulled him deep inside and sent him crashing to his own climax, forgetting to withdraw as he'd planned to.

'Angie,' he yelled, collapsing on top of her. 'Oh God!' He lay with his face buried in her neck until his breathing returned to normal. She stroked his hair and caressed his back.

He rolled off and lay by her side, kissing her again. 'That was brilliant. The lads at school say the first time's not all it's cracked up to be, but that was fucking amazing. I really needed it after the shitty day I've had.' He fell quiet and looked at her. Tears were running down her cheeks. 'What's wrong? Didn't you like it?'

'Nothing's wrong,' she muttered.

'There is, tell me. I hurt you, didn't I? It's 'cos it's the first time. It won't hurt again.'

'Do you love me, Eddie?'

He rolled his eyes heavenward. 'Oh please, not the love thing again.' He lay back on his pillow. 'Why do you always have to spoil things and ask me that?' He sat up, lit a cigarette and offered her one. She shook her head and sat up beside him, wiping her eyes with the corner of the sheet.

'We shouldn't have done it,' she said tearfully.

'Why not? I thought you wanted to as much as I did, and it was good. You enjoyed it, didn't you?'

Surely she wasn't disappointed after all the time they'd waited.

'I don't mean we shouldn't have done it at all. I mean, we shouldn't have done it without using something, or without you being careful. What if I have a baby now?' She chewed her lip. 'My mum would kill me. We'd have to get married.'

'You'll be okay, honestly. They say you can't get pregnant the first time,' Eddie re-assured her with more confidence than he felt. Doubts were starting to crowd his mind now. He was beginning to feel guilty and a little ashamed. He'd been unfaithful to Jane. She must never find out, she'd be so upset.

Angie wanted him to love her and he didn't. And God, horror of horrors, what if he really had just given her a baby? The thought filled him with terror. His own parents would go crazy and her mother would come baying for his blood.

'I will have that cigarette,' she said, taking his from him and sharing.

'Listen, don't worry.' He tried his best to sound reassuring. 'When do you next, umm, you know?'

'This week sometime. Tuesday or Wednesday I'm due.'

Eddie sighed, feeling slightly relieved. 'Well, that's okay then. Roy told me that the beginning and end of the month is supposed to be safe.'

'And since when did Roy Cantello become a family planning expert?'

'It's what Sammy told him. She read it in something.'

Angie sighed and stubbed out the cigarette end in the old tobacco tin that Eddie used as an ashtray. 'Well, let's hope she's right. I'm going before your mum and dad come home. I'll help you get dressed.' She slid out of bed and picked up his clothes.

'You've got a fit body, Angie.' He smiled, looking through half-closed eyes. 'I do fancy you.' He hoped the compliment was better than nothing, because he just couldn't tell her that he loved her.

'Thank you.' She buttoned up his shirt and zipped him into his jeans. She dressed herself and brushed her hair, fluffed out her curls with her fingers and checked her appearance in the dressing table mirror. 'Can you tell?' She turned to face him. 'I mean, do I look different? Do you think my mum will guess?'

'Guess what?' Eddie asked, struggling to pull on his socks with one hand. He stood up and opened his bedroom window to let out the smell of smoke and tipped the contents of the makeshift ashtray onto the garden below.

'Guess that I've done it?'

'Yeah, it's written all over your face.'

'I don't want Cathy to find out. She'll go mad with me.'

'Well, I won't be telling her, or anyone else for that matter,' he said. 'I, err, I don't want Jane to find out either. I'll take you to Mersey Square to get your bus. Come on, hurry up. And, Angie, thanks. I wanted to be your first!'

She kissed him. 'I wanted you to be my first, Eddie, because I love you. I promise I won't say anything to Jane.'

As they approached Mersey Square, Eddie nervously checked his watch: Jane and Sammy would have left for home on their bus five minutes ago, so it should be safe to wait with Angie for hers. He felt terrible now; totally consumed with guilt and he just wanted her to go. She draped herself all over him and he kissed her goodnight as the bus pulled up. He was so preoccupied with his guilty thoughts that he didn't see his every move being observed. As he turned the corner, Roy stepped out of the shadows directly in front of him.

'You said you were going home.'

Eddie jumped. 'I was, I did,' he faltered. 'Fuck, you scared the life out of me.'

'Where's your sling?'

'Shit, I forgot to put it back on.'

'Where've you been? I saw you putting Angie on the bus. She disappeared from the coffee bar not long after you. I put two and two together, but I was really hoping I was wrong.'

'We went to my place,' Eddie muttered.

'And did you?' Roy asked.

'Did I what?' Eddie looked away, feeling embarrassed.

'Did you shag her?'

'Yeah, and I wish to God I hadn't, so don't go on at me for fuck's sake. I've had a hell of a day. From the minute I got up, it's been shit!'

Roy seemed taken aback by this outburst. 'So you didn't enjoy it then?' He raised an incredulous eyebrow.

'Of course I did, it was brilliant. But I shouldn't have done it. I should have waited to do it with Jane. I feel terrible, guilty as hell, and I don't know how I'll keep it from her. I wanted us to be the first for each other and for it to be special. I've ruined all that now. Angie asked me if I loved her and I snapped at her. I feel awful about that, too. And there's another thing, we didn't take precautions, and I wasn't careful either!'

'Oh shit, Ed, you stupid fool! You should have got something from me.'

'I didn't think I'd need anything. I was going home because I felt rough and wanted time alone. Ending up in bed with Angie was the last thing I thought I'd be doing tonight. I could hardly have come back into Mario's and asked you for something in front of Sammy and Jane. Anyway, I think it was a safe time.'

Roy blew out his cheeks. 'Well, I hope for your sake it was, or you're in big trouble, mate. Old Mother Turner would castrate you on the spot.'

## 14

Eddie stared at Mr Jerome, who looked over his thick glasses and tapped his nicotine-stained teeth with a pen. The red-faced old man, with thick silver hair and matching moustache, had been running the tailor's, along with his brother, since the year dot. Eddie's dad had bought suits from here all his life and Eddie's one and only smart jacket, which he was wearing for the interview, had been made here, along with the pair of black trousers his mum had tried to get him to wear for tea at Jane's. He fidgeted nervously under Mr Jerome's scrutiny, certain that the old man was going to say he didn't want young ruffians like Eddie working in his establishment. The windowless office was airless and stuffy and smelt of Uncle Joe's Mint Balls and his mum had starched the collar of his white shirt again. What with that and his tie, Eddie felt like he was being strangled.

'How long will you be incapacitated with the hand, Mr Mellor?' Mr Jerome asked, ceasing his teeth tapping for a minute.

'Er, I should be okay by the end of the week,' Eddie replied.

'Well, what if I give you a trial run of a month, starting next Monday? I'll place you in the position of junior sales assistant for now and if things work out, maybe train you in the tailoring side of the business at a later date.'

Eddie let out a breath. It was better than nothing and would do for a few weeks until he and Roy got some more gigs lined up. It'd make his mum happy and keep his dad off his back for a while. The rest of the sales staff looked as old as Mr Jerome, so the sooner he was out of there, the better.

'Thank you, sir. That's very kind of you.'

Mr Jerome stood up and Eddie got to his feet. They shook hands and Eddie left the shop and hurried to Flanagan and Grey's to meet Jane and the others. He ran down the stairs and was met by loud whistles from a grinning Roy, Tim and John Grey.

'Who's posh then?' Roy teased. 'How did it go?'

'Got it. Well, I start a month's trial next week.' He pulled off his tie, shoved it in his pocket and undid the top two buttons on his shirt. 'We gotta get some gigs soon. Doubt whether I'll be able to stand more than a few weeks in there.'

'I'm working on it,' Roy said.

'Listen, Roy,' John began, 'if you get gigs out of the area and your dad doesn't mind me using his van, I can drive you, perhaps even manage the group. Try and get you some gigs lined up. Stu will do a bit of roadying for you too. We had a chat about it on Saturday night.'

'Really? That'd be great. We'd like to try and get gigs in Manchester, but it's getting the gear there that's the problem. Dad doesn't mind driving locally, but he's tired after working all day. I'll start driving lessons next month when I'm seventeen.'

'Well, it'll help you out for the time being. Here are your girls,' John said as Jane, Sammy and Pat came into the shop.

'Oh, you look nice,' Jane said as Eddie gave her a hug.

'Don't get too used to it,' he said. 'Mind you, it'll be suits all the way when I start the new job.'

'You got it then? Oh, I'm so proud of you.' She kissed him.

He rested his chin on top of her head and the guilty feelings surged through him again.

'Shall we go to Mario's?' Roy suggested. 'Celebrate Ed's new job with a Coke.'

* * *

Every time the door opened, Eddie felt his eyes stray across the crowded coffee bar. He was dreading Angie coming in. It'd be hard to hide his guilt from Jane if she came over to talk to him and he'd no doubts she'd do just that.

'Have you finished your drink?' he said, more sharply than he meant to.

'No.' Jane looked at him, frowning. 'What's up with you?'

'Nothing. I just wanna go home and get out of these clothes. Hurry up and I'll walk you to Mersey Square.' He drummed the fingers of his uninjured hand on the table as Jane finished her Coke.

'Aren't we waiting for the others?' she said as he retrieved her satchel from under the chair and pulled her to her feet.

'They'll be ages and like I said, I wanna get out of these clothes before anybody sees me. I'll be at yours later, Roy.'

They said their goodbyes and Eddie hurried Jane out of the door. She linked his arm as they walked down Broadgate.

'Will I see you after school tomorrow?' she said.

'Depends on where Roy and I get to. If we're in Manchester, we won't be back until late because of club opening times. Leave it tomorrow and I'll see you on Wednesday at the gig. Your mum said you can come out Wednesday, didn't she?'

'Yep. It'll be strange seeing someone else playing drums.'

He took her in his arms and kissed her as they reached the bus shelter. 'It means I get to spend more time with you and we can have a dance. I'll sing a few songs with Roy, but most of the time I'll be with you.'

'I'll look forward to it.'

The bus pulled up and he gave her one last kiss and waved her off.

'Dad's given permission for John to drive us to gigs in the van,' Roy said. He stretched out on his bed, hands behind his head, as Eddie sprawled on the bedroom floor, notebook on his knee. 'I called John just before you arrived and he's asking his uncle, who runs a pub in Cheadle, if we can use the upstairs function room a couple of nights a week to rehearse in. John said there's loads of space and we should get a good sound. Be better than Tim's mum's garage when it's cold and we won't have to worry about the neighbours and noise.'

'That'll be brilliant,' Eddie enthused. 'A driver, manager, roadie, and rehearsal room, all in one go. We need to make that list now of clubs to visit, we've only got this week free before I start work.'

'And me,' Roy said. 'Dad wants me in the shop. I don't mind, because he'll put petrol in the van and slip me a few bob, but it'll put paid to meeting the girls after school. Still, won't be for long, just until we start working the group properly. I was thinking earlier, how do you feel about getting another guitarist on board? Rhythm, you know. It'll fill out the sound a bit.' He threw a cigarette and box of matches over to Eddie.

Eddie plugged the ciggie in his mouth and wiggled it up and down. 'Can't do matches, you'll have to light it for me.'

'Oh, sorry, Ed, keep forgetting.' Roy got up and lit Eddie's cigarette and his own. 'So, what do you reckon, about another guitarist, I mean?'

'Well, yeah, if we can get a decent one. Anything to give the group strength.'

'We'll run it by Tim later and then ask John to put a postcard up in the shop and we can look in the Music Exchange too. There are often adverts in their window for people looking to join groups. Right, chuck me that pad and pen and I'll start the list, seeing as you can't write. By the way, have you heard from Angie yet, whether she's... erm, okay?'

Eddie shook his head. 'Tuesday or Wednesday,' she said. 'I'm just keeping my fingers crossed.'

'All you can do, mate.'

* * *

On Wednesday evening, as he was leaving for Mario's, Eddie got the call from Angie that he'd been praying for: he was off the hook. He let out a sigh of relief and felt the weight lifting from his shoulders. Angie asked him again not to say anything to Cathy. As if he would, anyway.

'Don't you dare say anything to Jane either,' he said.

'I won't.'

'I gotta go out now,' he said. 'Call you soon. Maybe we can get together again sometime?' He hung up before she had a chance to reply, said goodbye to his mum and left the house. Could he juggle two girls? Did he want to? It was good with Angie on Sunday. The guilt was receding now that he was pretty certain she wouldn't tell Jane in return for his silence.

* * *

Angie replaced the receiver and sat down on the bottom stair. Eddie wanted to see her again. She could hardly wait, but when he called, she was going to play hard to get and let him do the chasing. She was determined not to be at his beck and call, especially if he was still seeing Jane. The girls at the salon had told her that once you let a boy have his way, he wouldn't want to know. Well, that didn't seem to apply to Eddie.

When she next spoke to him, she planned to make him jealous by telling him that Richard had taken her out for a meal. And he had, on Monday night, to a nice restaurant in Wilmslow, not a fish and chip café like Eddie usually took her to. He'd treated her with respect, which was more than Eddie had ever done. After that first time Richard didn't ask for much more than a kiss and cuddle at the end of the night. It was nice to be treated like a lady for a change. She'd felt quite grown-up on his arm as he'd led her into the restaurant. He wasn't half the flirt the girls in the salon had made him out to be and while they were out, he seemed only to have eyes for her. But at the end of the day, he was engaged and planning to get married next year and she was certain that her real feelings and future lay with Eddie.

Over the next couple of weeks, Richard called regularly at Mario's for Angie. He never ventured inside, but waited in his car until she came out. Several times he'd been there as Eddie, Jane and the others had followed her out. She always smiled pointedly and waved goodbye to them as she got in the car and was whisked away.

She could tell from the way Eddie glared at her that he was jealous. It wouldn't be long now, she thought. During the group's spot tonight, he'd caught her eye several times. She knew that look. She'd bet a penny to a pound he'd call her tomorrow, and she was ready to see him again, of that she was sure.

* * *

Eddie bundled Jane past Richard's car as Angie got in. He was seething inside, knowing the smile and wave were all for his benefit.

'I wonder why Angie's friend doesn't come inside for her,' Jane said as he hurried her to Mersey Square.

'Why are you so bothered about what they do?'

'I'm not. Why are you so snappy? Every time I mention her name, you bite my head off. Anyone would think you still fancy her and that you're jealous.'

'Don't be so stupid,' he said and then felt guilty as her brown eyes clouded. He pulled her into his arms. They were losing the closeness they shared and it was his fault. He hated hurting Jane, but couldn't handle seeing Angie getting into Richard's car. He clapped his hand to his mouth and yawned. All the late nights rehearsing, the extra gigs they'd been playing, plus getting used to working full-time in Jerome's was taking it out of him and making him tetchy.

'Sorry, Jane,' he said and cuddled her close. 'Come over to Roy's house tomorrow afternoon if you're allowed, and we can have a bit of time together. I feel I've hardly seen you this week.'

'That'd be lovely, Ed. I'll see what I can do.' Jane pulled him into the bus shelter. 'Kiss me like you used to, please.'

'Hey, move over, you two,' Roy said, appearing behind them with Sammy, Tim and Pat. 'That's mine and Sammy's corner. Have a chip!' He pushed a greasy newspaper wrap under their noses.

'No, thanks,' Eddie said. 'Me and Jane will come over to yours tomorrow afternoon, is that okay?'

'Yeah, no problem. I thought your folks were away though. Why don't you go to yours?'

'Jane prefers safety in numbers,' he said, smiling at her as she blushed.

'Where are your mum and dad?' Sammy asked.

'Gone to Brighton, to see my Aunt Celia.'

'You could have a party tomorrow night.' Roy's eyes lit up. 'Empty house, no parents.'

'No chance, not after what happened at Jackie's place. I'm planning a peaceful evening, listening to records and drinking Dad's whisky.'

Eddie was hatching a plan. He was going to phone Angie when he got home and ask her to come over tomorrow night, if she wanted to. This evening, while the group was playing, he'd noticed that every time he looked in her direction, she'd been watching him. He was certain he'd not misread the signs. In spite of Richard and his flash suits and fancy car, she wanted to see him again. Fingers crossed that she'd spend the whole night with him. He was going to suggest that she tell her mother she was staying overnight at Cathy's house. Angie was daredevil enough to try and get away with that sort of thing.

'Hasn't your dad noticed you keep topping up his whisky bottle with water, yet?' Tim's voice broke Eddie's thoughts.

'I didn't last time. John got me a half-bottle of whisky – I topped it up with that.'

'He's a good manager is John, looking after our every need,' Tim said.

'Almost our every need.' Roy looked hungrily at Sammy, who was munching on the last of the chips.

'Sod off, Roy, you insatiable beast! You can wait until tomorrow.'

'Promise?' He planted a kiss on her greasy lips.

'Promise.' She kissed him back as the bus pulled up.

'See you tomorrow, Jane.' Eddie kissed her goodbye.

She jumped on the bus and blew him a kiss.

* * *

'Got a fag, Roy?' Eddie asked as they took a shortcut up the steps beside the Plaza Cinema that led onto Broadgate. Roy lit two cigarettes and handed one to Eddie. They were going back to Mario's to help John and Stuart pack their gear away. Tim had packed his bass ready for them and jumped on the bus to his home to save space in the van.

Eddie took a lengthy drag on his cigarette and said, 'You know the other week when you said I should have come to you to borrow something? Well, I need to now, for tomorrow.'

Roy looked at him and frowned. 'Thought Jane wanted to wait until she's older. So, you've managed to sweet-talk her round at last.'

'Err...' Eddie looked sheepishly down at the pavement. 'She does want to wait. I'm planning on asking Angie over tomorrow night.'

Roy raised an eyebrow. 'Thought that was supposed to be a one-night stand. Something you did on impulse and wouldn't do again.'

'Well, yeah, er, it was. But I want to see her again, can't get her out of my head.'

'What's happening with this Richard guy? Isn't she seeing him?'

'Not as far as I know. They're just friends at work. He takes her out occasionally and picks her up after her nights out. Angie said he's getting married next year.'

'So, meantime, he's using Angie as his bit on the side and so are you.'

'It's not like that. I'm sure she's not sleeping with him. I was her first. Anyway, I'm not using her – I like her.'

'And what about Jane? You felt dead guilty last time and it won't be any easier the next. You shouldn't two-time her, Ed. She's a really nice girl, you're bloody lucky to have her.'

Eddie threw his cigarette end down and stamped on it. 'You've no idea what it's like, have you? I'll be alone with Jane tomorrow afternoon. She still won't let me go all the way and it's driving me bloody crazy. I've got at least another year of this, I don't know if I can stand it. It's okay for you, you've got Sammy.'

'Can't you talk Jane round? Tell her you love her or something, she might let you then.'

Eddie shook his head. 'I do tell her I love her, all the bloody time. Makes no difference. She's got this thing about waiting till she's sixteen. I've tried everything I can think of. Miss Frigid Knickers isn't in it.'

Roy laughed. 'Okay, but if it's gonna be a regular occurrence you can buy your own.' He fished in his jacket pocket and handed Eddie a packet of Durex. 'There's two left in there. I need the other pack for me and Sam – I'm not riding bareback for you or anyone else, mate.'

Eddie smiled gratefully and pushed the packet into the pocket of his jeans. 'Thanks, Roy, you're a real pal. I tried to get some at lunchtime today, but the assistant in the chemist's near work's a right nosy cow. She lives on our street and I'm pretty sure she'd say something to Mum. I ended up buying some Old Spice and a glucose lolly. I felt a right fool, as though everyone in the shop knew what I really wanted. I'll go to the barber's on Monday and get you a replacement packet. I've got to go in there to get my hair cut anyway, the boss said it's too long for work. I already feel like a stupid mannequin in the poncey suit and tie without getting my hair cut. Still, it won't be forever.'

'Just till we're famous!' he chorused with Roy, bursting into laughter as they went back into Mario's.

## 15

Eddie sat down on the bottom stair and dialled Angie's number. He prayed her mother wouldn't pick up. It was very late and he hoped her parents would be in bed by now and that Richard had dropped her off. He drummed his fingers on his thigh in a single para-diddle exercise while he waited for someone to answer. When someone did, he almost dropped the receiver. Shit, it was the old witch. He cleared his throat. 'Can I speak to Angie, please?'

'At this time of night? She's just about to go to bed.'

Eddie heard Angie's voice in the background, asking who was calling. Next thing, she was saying hello.

'It's Eddie. Can you talk?'

'Err, depends what you want to talk about.'

'I meant, are you alone now?'

'Yes,' she lowered her voice. 'Mum's just gone upstairs. What do you want?'

'Any chance of seeing you tomorrow night?' He fell silent and waited for her reply, which seemed to take ages. 'You still there?'

'Yes, I am. But I'm not sure. Is it a good idea?'

'It's up to you.' He wasn't going to beg. 'My parents are away. Thought you might like to come here. In fact, I, er, I wondered if you'd stay over.'

'All night?' Her voice held an incredulous note.

'Yeah. Tell your mum you're staying at Cathy's.'

'I don't know if I dare. Hmm, leave it with me. I'm not promising, but what time do you have in mind?'

'About eight?' That would give him plenty of time to spend with Jane, walk her to Mersey Square and come back to get ready.

'Might see you tomorrow then.'

Angie took off her make-up, brushed her teeth and smothered her face with Nivea Cream. Dare she do it? Would her mum buy it? She'd spent the night at Cathy's a few times but had usually given her parents a bit more warning and Cathy had always been here when she'd asked if it was okay. A whole night with Eddie, though. It'd be worth it, even if she ended up grounded for the rest of the month. It might be the start of him wanting to get back with her. People didn't spend nights together unless they were serious. But what if Cathy called to speak to her while she was out? Could she risk telling her? Eddie wouldn't want her to know. Oh well, she had a few hours to come up with a plan.

* * *

'You smell nice,' Jane said, snuggling closer to Eddie on the sofa at Roy's place. She traced a finger around the deep dimple in his chin.

'Do I?' He grinned. 'It's Old Spice aftershave.'

'Oh, I nearly got you some for Valentine's last month,' Jane said. 'Wasn't sure if you liked it though.'

'I like what you gave me for Valentine's,' he said. 'It's nice and personal.'

Jane smiled. She'd made him a red felt heart, embroidered their names on it with gold thread and filled it with chocolates that he'd shared with her. He'd told her it was the nicest thing anyone had ever done for him and he'd given her a single red rose and her favourite In Love perfume. She sat up and straightened her clothes. 'I'd better be going soon, Ed. Mum said I had to be back by four to get my homework done before tea.'

He nodded. 'That's okay.'

A tap at the door made them jump and Roy and Sammy came in.

'Hi, you two,' Sammy said. 'Hope we're not interrupting anything?'

'Nope. We're getting ready to go home,' Jane replied.

'I'll come with you,' Sammy said. 'Are you two walking us across the rec?'

'Of course.' Roy picked up the jacket he'd flung over the back of a chair and Eddie jumped to his feet and hauled Jane to hers.

'You gonna show them?' Roy raised an eyebrow at Sammy.

'Can I?'

'Yeah. They won't blab to anyone.'

Sammy fished down the front of her sweater and pulled out a ring on a thin gold chain. 'We're secretly engaged. But you can't tell a soul, not even Pat.'

'Oh, Sammy, how romantic,' Jane gasped, admiring the gold ring with its solitaire diamond. 'It's so pretty.' She gave her a hug and squeezed Roy's hand, not quite knowing what to say to him.

'It's an early birthday present. I'll wear it on my finger when we're out,' Sammy said, dropping the chain back inside her sweater. 'But I'll have to hide it the rest of the time until I'm older.'

'Err, congratulations then.' Eddie frowned at Roy, who looked away.

'Right, let's get you two home,' Roy said, helping Sammy on with her jacket.

* * *

'Did you call her then?' Roy asked as he and Eddie walked back to Jackson's Heath.

'Yeah, far as I know, she's coming over later.'

'Don't know how you can do it.' Roy stopped on the corner of Paradise Road and looked at Eddie. 'Cheat on Jane, I mean. I wouldn't cheat on my Sammy for anything, I love the bones of her.'

Eddie shrugged. 'That why you bought her a ring?'

Roy nodded. 'Emptied my Post Office savings account. I wanted to make a commitment to her. We're gonna be doing a lot of work out of the area with the group if things pan out and I don't want her going out and meeting another lad. At least now she knows I'm serious about us.'

Eddie looked away from Roy's intense stare and was quiet for a moment. 'I'm not ready to get serious just yet. I love Jane. She knows it. But I can't help how I feel about Angie, I fancy the arse off her.'

'You always did.' Roy's laugh was hollow. 'She's a dirty girl, but I'm going to quote my mother here: it'll all end in tears.'

'Don't be daft, it's just a bit of fun. Angie'll think so too.'

* * *

Eddie rushed around chucking dirty clothes into the laundry basket and made his bed for the first time in three days. He took a quick bath, pulled on fresh pants, un-ironed jeans and T-shirt, combed his hair and splashed on more of the Old Spice he'd bought in the chemist. Jane said he smelt nice; Angie might like it too. He checked his watch, quarter to eight. Well, she hadn't called to say she wasn't coming so he assumed she was.

He slipped the packet of Durex Roy had given him into the drawer of the bedside table and went downstairs, drew the curtains and switched on the standard lamp near the window. He'd lit the fire when he came home and gave it a poke now and threw on more coal. Satisfied the room looked cosy and felt warm, he switched his dad's radiogram on and loaded it with records. Angie loved smoochy stuff so he chose carefully but added a couple of his favourites too. Rather than drag her off to bed right away, he thought she'd be more relaxed downstairs for a while.

He rooted in the drinks cupboard and found his mum's Advocaat. Angie liked a snowball and there was always lemonade in the kitchen as his mum enjoyed a tipple at the weekend too. He ran back upstairs and retrieved the bottle of cider he'd hidden in his dressing table before his parents left and there was a bit of left-over cannabis from last night's gig that Roy said he could have.

Just enough for a skinny joint, but it'd have to do. He didn't know if Angie had ever tried it, but he reckoned she'd be up for having a go. That was the thing with Angie; she was usually up for anything. So why did he only like her in small doses? He couldn't work it out. He'd spend forever with Jane if she was allowed to spend it with him, even though it would leave him frustrated. Life was so unfair at times. He wished it was Jane who was coming to stay over. He'd give anything to hold her all night and do it properly with her. The doorbell rang, interrupting his thoughts.

Angie's smile split her face as he opened the door and she

strolled in and dropped her overnight bag on the hall floor. She flung her arms around him and kissed him.

He kissed her back and then pulled away from her over-eager embrace and put her bag at the bottom of the stairs.

'Come into the sitting room.'

She followed him and flopped down on the sofa. 'It's nice and warm in here.' She took off her coat, threw it over the arm of the sofa and smoothed the creases from her full black skirt.

'You look nice.' She did, as always. 'Fancy a drink?'

She ignored his compliment and wrinkled her nose. 'Not if it's your dad's whisky.'

'I've got cider or you can have a snowball.'

Her face lit up. 'Snowball, please. Can we watch *Sunday Night at the London Palladium*?'

'Yeah, I suppose so.' Give him time to knock back a drink or two and try and relax. He felt jittery and knew it was because he kept thinking about Jane. 'Who's the star tonight?'

'Connie Francis. It's already started, it's ten past.'

Connie Francis! Christ! He pulled a face but switched on the TV. Keep her happy. Angie slipped her red stilettos off and tucked her feet up under her bottom. Her black boat-necked top slipped down over her right shoulder and he got a glimpse of black satin and felt a familiar tingle. Even the sight of her bra strap made him feel hard. While the set warmed up, he went to the kitchen for lemonade. When he came back, The Tiller Girls were strutting their stuff, legs kicking out as they twirled around, arms linked, in a circle. The sight made him think of his dad who, without fail, pointed his cigarette at the screen every week and said the same thing, 'They've got to be fit, you know, them girls,' while his mum shook her head and got on with her knitting.

He gave Angie her snowball and sat down next to her with a glass of cider. She snuggled up to him, slipped her arm through his and sighed. 'Isn't this cosy, Ed? We're just like an old married couple.'

He knocked his drink back, feeling his semi-erection receding at her words. Trust her, he hoped she wouldn't get any ideas. He jumped up and refilled his glass.

'Want a top-up?'

'No, thanks, I've hardly started this one.'

He sat back down and lit a cigarette. Bruce Forsyth was cracking his usual corny jokes. Beat the Clock was next. Eddie stared at the screen, bored, while Angie laughed at the couple who were trying to do an exchange of clothes within so many seconds. He slid his arm around her, stroking her naked shoulder. She kissed his cheek and nibbled his ear. He slipped his hand down the front of her top and gently squeezed her breast as Bruce called 'Stop the Clock!' Then she was kissing him and he took her glass, put it with his on the coffee table and laid her back against the cushions, sliding his hands under her top, tweaking her nipples under the soft band of her bra. He kissed her hard, entwining his tongue with hers and felt his erection returning. He pulled her skirt up and stroked her through the satin of her knickers, feeling her warmth. She groaned and squirmed beneath him, reaching to unzip his jeans.

'Let's go upstairs,' he whispered, remembering the packet of Durex in his room. He pulled her to her feet but she stopped in the doorway and looked back. Bruce was introducing Connie Francis – 'Oh, can we just watch her, please, Ed? We've got all night to do stuff.'

He rolled his eyes and sat back down. Fucking hell, what was she like? He was beginning to think this wasn't a good idea. She could turn him on easily enough, but she could also turn him off just as quickly. The phone rang and he jumped up to answer it, hoping it wasn't Jane or his mum.

'Hope I've not caught you on the job, mate,' Roy said. 'John Grey just called. He thinks he's found us a new guitarist. A guy called Phil Jackson. He's arranged for him to audition with us tomorrow night. He's pretty good apparently, sings as well. Can you make it?'

'Yeah, course I can. Sounds promising. And no, you didn't catch us on the job. She's watching bloody Connie Francis.'

'You're joking? Thought you'd have her pissed and laid by now. See you tomorrow, and Ed, if you do manage to get your leg over, don't leave it to chance again.'

'I won't.' Eddie smiled and hung up. He went back into the sitting room, where Angie was singing along to 'Who's Sorry Now?' He sat down again, offered her a cigarette and lit one for himself. Well, he was – sorry now, that is. He wished he hadn't asked her to stay. He should have planned a quickie and then taken her home. 'My Happiness' was next and as soon as it was over, he jumped up and turned the telly off, ignoring Angie's disapproving humph.

'I like to watch them all go round on the stage at the end,' she said, lips pouting.

'Well, I don't. You came here to see me, not watch the bloody telly.' He threw the end of his ciggy onto the fire. She stubbed hers out in the ashtray and got to her feet.

'Come on then, Mr Impatient.'

She led the way upstairs. Eddie grabbed her bag from the hall and followed.

Angie rummaged in her bag, told him she wouldn't be long and made for the bathroom, leaving him staring after her. He took off his jeans and T-shirt, got into bed, shivering, and pulled the blankets up to his neck. He didn't know whether he was cold, nervous, though God knew why when it wasn't the first time; or feeling guilty because he kept thinking about Jane. He lay there for what felt like ages.

What the fuck was she doing?

The door opened and she came in, smiling. He caught his breath as she walked towards him, wearing a short, black floaty top and matching knickers – well, if you could call them that, no more than a scrap of lace that covered her arse where it touched.

'Do you like them?' she said, twirling in front of him. 'They're baby-dolls. I've been saving them for a special occasion.'

He moved over and pulled back the covers and she slid in beside him. She was in his arms immediately, smelling of talcum powder and minty toothpaste. She kissed him and wrapped her legs around his. He had her top and the scrap of lace off in no time, kissing her neck and breasts and raining little kisses down her tummy. She tugged his pants off and whispered that she wanted him inside her now.

'In a minute,' he said. 'We've got all night.'

It'd be over before they started if it was up to her. He kissed her again and she got on top and tried to guide him in but he flipped her onto her back. He wasn't taking any chances and reached for the Durex, tore the top off a packet with his teeth and rolled the rubber on, hoping he was doing it right. It was the first time he'd used one and he hated the feel and the smell but the alternative wasn't an option. He knelt between her legs and looked down. She was sexy, nice breasts, tiny waist and hips you could grab hold of, and she was pretty too, with her kissable lips and cute freckly nose. He was lucky she was here. The lads from school would give their right arms to be kneeling where he was right now. He wished he could feel something other than wanting sex with her. She reached up and put her hands around his hips and she groaned and writhed.

'Please, Ed, now.'

She pulled him down and he slid inside her, moving slowly, hating the rubber and the way it took away the edge off his feelings. Angie moved in rhythm, clawing his back and arse like she did last time. If she left scratches, he'd have to make sure Jane didn't see them next Sunday at Roy's. Christ, why was he thinking about Jane right now? He blocked his mind and rolled

Angie on top so she could straddle him properly. He gripped her around the waist while she tossed her hair around and rode him, and then he flipped her back down again when he sensed she was nearly there as he was too. He cried out and held her tight but still couldn't say it even though he knew she was expecting him to. She'd be asking him in a minute. He felt distanced now, as though he wasn't really there, and it wasn't him that had just shagged her. He lay back and caught his breath. She didn't ask him but she was looking at him expectantly.

'You okay?'

She nodded; her green eyes bright as though fighting tears.

He reached for the joint he'd rolled earlier. 'Fancy sharing this?'

She frowned. 'Funny-looking ciggie.'

'It's a joint, dope, cannabis. Make you feel good.'

Her eyes widened. 'That's a drug.'

'It's not really, it's only like having a drink. It's harmless.'

'Okay.' She sat up, took a turn and coughed. She handed the joint over and stretched out beside him.

Eddie took another drag and handed it back. He slid out of bed and made for the bathroom, wondering what the heck he should do with the spent Durex. Would it block the lavvy? He couldn't leave it in the bin, his mum would find it. He wrapped it in toilet paper, ran downstairs and chucked it on the fire along with another shovel of coal. Back upstairs, Angie had a contented smile on her face. She reached for him as he climbed back into bed.

'Shall we go down and have another drink?' he said, moving away from her. 'I'll put some music on.'

'Yes, that'll be nice.' She slid out of bed, reached for her baby-dolls and handed him his pants and T-shirt.

\* \* \*

Angie curled up on the sofa as Eddie switched the radiogram on and mixed her another snowball. He hadn't said that he loved her but his actions showed that he did. She felt all warm and woozy inside and her head felt light, but she also felt happy. He'd probably finish with Jane next week, he had no need to be seeing her now. Tonight was so good, she was sure he'd want more. She wondered if she should tell him that Cathy knew she was here. She'd had no choice really. Cathy said she'd cover for her if her mother called but she'd also ranted on about how stupid Angie was and that Eddie was using her. She decided against telling him – he'd go nuts and it'd give him a reason to tell her to go.

He sat down beside her and took a sip from his glass of cider as Eddie Cochran sang 'Summertime Blues'.

'That was Roy who called earlier. Looks like we've got a new guitarist for the group. He's auditioning with us tomorrow night.'

'Oh, right.'

'Yeah. Hopefully he'll be good. We've got a lot of gigs booked in now so I'm hoping to pack the job at Jerome's in soon.'

'Why would you want to pack a proper job in?'

'You sound like my mother,' he said. 'The job was only to keep me going until the group takes off.'

'Well, that's not going to happen, is it?' She took a sip of her snowball. 'I mean, you'll never be really famous, not like a proper group. You'll not be able to afford to settle down on money from gigs.'

She stopped. He was staring at her as though he hated her, his lips in a tight line, his blue eyes cold. She should have kept her mouth shut.

'You'll never understand me in a million years,' he said. 'I've no intention of settling down, and yes, the group will make me enough money to pack the job in soon enough.'

The next record dropped down the spindle and Eddie pulled a face and told her this one was his mum's and he'd chosen it for her.

'I do understand you, more than you know,' she said, putting down her drink and pulling him to his feet. 'Dance with me.'

He put his drink down and took her in his arms as Perry Como warbled 'Magic Moments'.

'If the likes of him can get famous so can we,' he grumbled.

She laughed and pulled away, but he yanked her close, running his hands over her lace knickers. He ground his hips against her and she could feel him getting hard again and buried her head in his shoulder.

He'd be dragging her upstairs again before too long.

## 16

Eddie felt sick. He'd been clock-watching all afternoon and it was now five thirty. Mr Jerome signalled to him that it was okay to go and he grabbed his leather jacket, pulled it on over his suit and dashed out of the shop. He fully expected to see Sammy waiting outside for him, arms folded, ready to have a go, and breathed a sigh of relief when she wasn't.

That morning, when he and Angie had hurried hand in hand across Mersey Square for her to catch the school bus, he'd spotted Sammy, Jane and Pat waiting for theirs. He thought he'd timed it right and they'd be long gone, but it appeared their bus was running late. As it pulled up, Sammy had turned and stopped dead as she spotted them. He saw her mouth drop; she shook her head and then pushed Jane in front and onto the bus before she saw them too. Had she told Jane or kept it to herself? Whatever, he'd no doubt she'd be reading him the riot act as soon as they met up. Angie's parting shot had been that she loved him and would he call her later? He'd snapped at her, reminded her of tonight's plans with the group and said he'd call her soon.

As he sat in the kitchen having breakfast earlier, she'd sauntered in, wearing her school uniform, no make-up and her hair scraped into a ponytail. She sat down opposite him and as she buttered toast and sipped tea, it was hard to believe she was the same girl he'd spent a passionate night with. He couldn't wait to get her out of the house and out of sight and he felt bad about that too. Sighing, he flicked up his jacket collar, lit a cigarette and made his way home.

'Ed, Roy just called,' his mum shouted, making him jump when he entered the house. He thought his parents weren't back until tomorrow. Shit, he hoped it wasn't obvious that he'd let Angie stay. Apart from the unmade bed, he'd tidied up, washed the glasses from last night and made sure she'd left nothing in the bathroom.

He popped his head around the kitchen door and eyed his mum warily. 'Hi, you're back early. How was Aunt Celia?'

'Oh, she's fine. Sends her love and a bit of spending money to tide you over.' She handed him a brown envelope. Inside were two five-pound notes. 'Did you manage okay on your own?'

'Yeah.' He pushed the money into his pocket. He was rich. Ten quid was almost three weeks' wages. Good old Aunt Celia. He was her only nephew and she'd always spoiled him. He'd treat Jane with some of it. 'I was out most of the weekend,' he said. 'Where's Dad?'

'Gone to get a tyre fixed.'

'Okay. Right, well, I'll call Roy back.'

'Don't forget to ring Celia and thank her for the money while you're at it. Do you want any tea? I'm doing egg and chips.'

'Please.' He sat on the stairs, spoke to his aunt in Brighton and then called Roy's place. Roy's mum picked up and told him to wait a minute.

'Just wanted to warn you, Ed,' Roy began. 'You were seen this morning.'

'I know. Saw Sammy glaring at me. Has she told Jane?'

'No, and she won't. She says you have to tell her yourself if it's over.'

'But it's not. I'm not finishing with her.'

'Do I take it last night didn't go well then?'

'It was fine, but I'm not finishing with Jane.'

'Well, it's up to you but you know how I feel about having two girls. Oh, and by the way, Sammy and Pat are coming along tonight to the audition.'

'Shit! Is Jane going too?'

Christ, Sammy would be giving him the evils all night and Jane would want to know why.

'Jane's not allowed out, but I can't be responsible for what Sammy says to you though. See you later.'

Eddie sat cradling the receiver. If he lost Jane now, he'd only got himself to blame. He couldn't bear it and had the urge to speak to her, to tell her that he loved her. He spent the next ten minutes talking to her and told her he would take her to the pictures on Wednesday because the group had no midweek gig.

'You can choose the film,' he said. 'Jane, I love you. Really miss seeing you after school.'

'I love you and I miss seeing you too, Ed. But you'll soon be free once the gigs build up and you can pack the job in. We'll catch up when you're nearly famous.'

His mum shouted that his tea was ready. He said goodbye and thought how different Jane was to Angie and her attitude towards the group: Jane had faith in them, Angie didn't. He made up his mind there and then that he wouldn't see Angie again. All he could do now was pray that Sammy didn't say anything to Jane.

* * *

As the group set up and ran through a soundcheck in the function room above John's uncle's pub, Eddie was conscious of Sammy looking at him. He couldn't meet her eyes and she'd ignored him when Pat gave him a friendly greeting. John Grey created a welcome diversion when he came upstairs, carrying an amplifier. He was closely followed by a tall, leather-clad young man, whose mane of blond hair fell over his forehead into his sparkling blue eyes. He carried a battered guitar case and placed it on the floor in front of the stage.

'This is Phil Jackson, everyone,' John introduced him.

The young man grinned in a friendly fashion and nodded at Sammy and Pat, who were sitting on stools, clutching bottles of Coke.

'Wow.' Sammy nudged Pat, who'd reluctantly been dragged along to give her opinion on the new guitarist. 'Now that sight beats staying in to wash your hair.'

'Hmm, he's a bit of a hunk,' Pat said. 'But my hair still needs a wash. I'm going after a couple of songs, no matter what you say.'

'Fair enough. I'll come home later with Roy.'

Phil shook hands with Roy, Tim and Eddie and plugged his guitar into the amp. He tuned up, twiddling knobs and twanging strings until satisfied and then nodded at Roy.

'Ready when you are.'

The group ran through a couple of songs and then Roy asked Phil if he'd like to sing solo.

'I've just learned a new one,' Phil said, stepping up to the mic. 'Let's give it a go. I'll start and you can follow my lead. It's pretty easy, it's the new Billy Fury song.'

Phil played the opening bars of 'Maybe Tomorrow' and started to sing. Sammy dragged Pat off the bar stool and they danced a pretend smooch, singing along. They clapped when Phil finished and Sammy stuck her thumb up to Roy. In spite of himself Eddie smiled – Phil got the girls' vote.

The group took a break and John got drinks in for them all.

'So,' he said, bringing a laden tray across the room and setting it down on a table, 'is he in, or what?'

'Lads?' Roy looked at Tim and Eddie, who nodded their approval. 'He certainly is. Which groups have you played with before, Phil?'

'Only the Delphonics,' Phil said. 'We disbanded a month ago. I've been at a loose end since then.'

'So, we were just in time really,' Eddie said. 'You'd have been snapped up in the next week or two.'

'We've quite a bit of work on,' Roy said. 'Dance halls, clubs and we're building the gigs list as we go.'

'I've got contacts in various clubs and pubs,' Phil said. 'I'll let you have the details.'

'Great.' Roy took a swig of his Coke. 'Before I came out tonight, I was talking to my dad and he suggested we change the name of the group to The Raiders. Drop the Roy bit, he said it sounded better. The Crickets just use that name now Buddy's dead. How does everybody feel about it?'

'I'm okay with it.' Eddie raised his glass.

'Me too.' Tim nodded.

'Okay then, The Raiders it is. I'll let Mario know before Rosa does the next lot of posters.'

Phil fished a harmonica from his jeans pocket. 'I can play this too.' He blew a few notes and laughed.

'Brilliant,' Roy said. 'Not many of the local groups have a harmonica player. We can do a bit of blues. Oh, Ed, we've gotta give up work soon. We need to get this group as great as we can in the next few months.'

Eddie nodded. 'I've decided on the way over here that I'm gonna give my notice in next week. Aunt Celia sent me a bit of money and with the gigs and two weeks' wages to come, I can manage for a while until we get more money rolling in. I've had enough of selling suits, The Raiders have to come first.'

He caught Sammy staring at him and added, 'And it'll give me a chance to meet my girl from school most days.'

Sammy shook her head and mouthed, 'Which one?'

He glared at her and Roy jumped to his feet and took Sammy to one side. Eddie could hear him telling her to keep out of it, while Pat looked puzzled and stared at him.

'What's going on?' she asked.

Eddie shrugged. It was clear that Sammy hadn't told Pat and he certainly wasn't about to.

Roy and Sammy came back to the table. 'Right, Tim and I will walk these two to the bus stop,' he said, ignoring Sammy's protestations that she didn't want to go just yet.

Eddie breathed a sigh of relief and lit the cigarette John offered him. Then felt bad because he was the cause of an argument that shouldn't have happened.

'Do you have a girl, Phil?' he asked.

Phil laughed. 'One or two, but no one serious. I like to play the field a bit. Plenty of time for serious when I'm older.'

'I quite agree,' Eddie said.

Phil officially joined The Raiders the week following his audition. The talented eighteen-year-old proved an expert guitarist at rehearsals over the next few nights and impressed everyone with his superb harmonica playing. He had a roving eye, but brought his own harem to the first gig.

* * *

Jane began her Saturday job in the re-furbished Flanagan and Grey's. The new sound-proof listening booths were popular with the town's teenagers and by midday, the shop was packed out. Sammy and Pat were lounging against the counter while Roy and Tim were talking to John and Stuart.

Sammy chomped on gum and blew a bubble. Roy stuck out his finger and popped it. The gum stuck to her lips. She tutted and smacked his arm. 'Now look what you've done.' She scrubbed at her face with a hanky.

'Sorry,' Roy said, pulling her into his arms. 'What's up with you today? You're a right grumpy sod.'

'Nothing,' she snapped. 'Let's go and have a wander around the market, Pat. We'll come back down to meet you before you close, Jane.'

'Oh, it's okay, Ed's meeting me,' Jane said. 'You don't have to hang around. Can you get me some stockings from Ahmed's, please? Anything but American Tan will do.'

'Yep,' Sammy said, pocketing the half-crown Jane handed over. 'See you in a bit,' she said to Roy, giving him a quick peck on the cheek.

'Will you make the coffees, please, Jane?' John said. 'Make one for Roy and Tim too.'

'Are you coming to watch us tonight in Bolton, Stu?' Roy asked as Jane went off to the storeroom to brew up.

'You bet,' Stuart said. 'I'll be roadying for you anyway. The girls aren't coming – Jane said there's not enough room in the van.'

'No, there isn't. John promised his girl she can come with us tonight so we're pretty full up with you as well. I don't think Sammy's all that bothered, to be honest – she's got a right moody head on her today, there's no pleasing her. I'm better off out of her way for a few hours. The Scorpions are playing at Mario's tonight, so the girls will probably go and see them.'

'Those lads are not bad actually,' John said. 'I'm thinking about asking if they fancy me as manager. What do you reckon?'

'Give it a whirl,' Roy said. 'You've got us in shape. If we keep getting the gigs like we're doing, I can stop working for my dad and just concentrate on the group. It's Ed's last day at Jerome's. All we need now is for Tim to finish school and we'll be laughing.'

* * *

Eddie met Jane after work and walked her to Mersey Square.

'Thank God that's over,' he said. 'I'm free now to concentrate on the group.'

'Have you told your mum and dad you've packed the job in yet?'

'Err, no, thought I'd leave it for now. I'll tell 'em next week.'

'Bet you don't,' she said, snuggling close to him.

'I will. If I'd told them before I'd handed my notice in, they'd have kicked up a right fuss. This way it's done and I'm out of there. Not much they can do or say now.'

Jane shook her head. 'Not really. Are we going to Roy's tomorrow as usual?'

'Actually, I think it's about time you came to my place and met my folks,' he said. 'I'll see you here tomorrow about two. That okay?'

She looked at him, wide-eyed. 'Meet your mum and dad? Are you sure?'

'Course I am. Think it'll put Mum's mind at rest that I'm seeing a nice girl.'

'Okay.' Jane smiled. 'See you tomorrow then. Have a good gig.'

'We will. You enjoy yourself at Mario's, if you go.'

He kissed her as the bus pulled up and waved her off. He walked across Mersey Square to his own bus stop, lounged against the wall and lit a cigarette. He felt a great sense of relief that he'd left Jerome's and was ready to put more time and effort into making the group the best it could be. He'd ignored Angie for the last two weeks and avoided her phone calls, getting his mum to tell her he wasn't in. He just hoped that if she was at Mario's tonight, she wouldn't say anything to Jane or worse still, that Sammy didn't have a go at Angie and kick off World War Three.

\* \* \*

The girls were sitting at a table close to the stage and clapped as The Scorpions finished their first set.

'You feeling better, Sam?' Jane asked as Sammy popped a couple of aspirins into her mouth.

'A bit. Still got cramps. I hate this bloody time of the month. It turns me into such a moody sod. Poor Roy, I've done nothing but bite his head off the last few days.'

She looked up as Mark Fisher and Tony appeared by their table.

'Can we get you girls a drink?' Mark asked, staring at Jane, who looked away.

'Yeah, thanks, Mark. Same again, three Cokes,' Sammy said, moving her chair around to make room.

Tony grabbed two spare chairs from the table behind and Mark came back with the drinks and sat down next to Jane.

'Fancy a dance?' he said as Vincento switched the jukebox back on.

'Oh, I'm not sure I should,' Jane said. 'Eddie might not like it.'

'Jane, for God's sake, he's asking you to dance, not marry him,' Sammy said. 'Go and enjoy yourself. You don't know what Ed gets up to when he's not with you.'

'What do you mean?' Jane got to her feet, frowning. 'He doesn't get up to anything.'

'No, of course he doesn't. Ignore me, it's my mood swings. Dance, go on.'

Pat stared at Sammy as Mark led Jane onto the dance floor. 'When' by The Kalin Twins played and Mark swung Jane into his arms.

'What was all that about?' Pat asked.

'You don't wanna know,' Sammy said, taking a sip of her drink.

Tony excused himself, grabbed a girl from the table behind and pulled her up to dance.

'Yes, I do,' Pat said. 'What's going on? You've been funny with Ed for a while now. What's he done?'

Sammy looked across the coffee bar to where Angie was sitting with a crowd of girls; her eyes fixed on Jane as Mark swung her around and pulled her close. Sammy didn't like the look on Angie's face. The bitch would no doubt tell Ed that Jane had danced with Mark. Not that it should matter, when he'd been cheating anyway.

'It's her,' she said to Pat, nodding in Angie's direction. 'Ed's been seeing her again.'

'No!' Pat's jaw dropped. 'Jane doesn't know, obviously?'

'Not yet. Don't know if he's stopped, but he was holding hands with her the other week in Mersey Square first thing in the morning. It was the Monday his parents were away. I think she stayed with him on the Sunday night, but Roy won't tell me if she did. Keeps telling me not to ask again. That means she did, otherwise he would just say no and have done with.'

'I don't know what to say. Jane looks really happy dancing with Mark. He's making her laugh anyway.'

'He's a nice lad. Got a good job too. Bet he'd be fun to go out with. And he seems to really fancy Jane, never takes his eyes off her.'

'Hmm, Eddie wouldn't like that.'

'Well, he won't know, will he? Because we're not going to tell him.'

Sammy smiled as the song ended. Mark brought Jane back to the table, thanked her and pecked her on the cheek. He excused himself and made his way to the gents'.

Jane sat down, cheeks flushed, and fanned her face with her hand. 'I enjoyed that.'

'We could tell,' Sammy said. 'He likes you.'

'I like him, but I'm Eddie's girl.'

'Yes, you are,' Pat said, glaring at Sammy before she had a chance to open her mouth.

\* \* \*

Jane shook Eddie's mum and dad's outstretched hands as they stood on ceremony in the front parlour. His mum invited her to sit down while his dad took her coat. Eddie sat down next to her. His parents left the room, his mum calling that she'd bring the tea things through in a minute, as she closed the door. He raised his eyebrows and took the opportunity to pull Jane into his arms and planted a kiss on her lips.

'They're very nice, your mum and dad,' she said as he let her go. 'How was last night's gig? I forgot to ask.'

'It was great; they'd like us back and they've booked us for next month. We're playing tomorrow night as well. Youth club dance in Didsbury. Any chance you can come?'

Jane shook her head. Her mum was sticking to her guns about her going out. No point in arguing with her and she still hadn't invited Eddie back to the house yet. Jane was hoping her mum would agree to him coming for tea again soon and then she'd get to know him better. Every time she asked, there was always an excuse – her mum was busy, or it wasn't convenient. Not that anything riveting ever happened on a Sunday, just the same old boring tea-time routine.

'Anything on for Wednesday night?' she asked.

'We're doing Mario's,' Eddie said, 'so I'll see you then.' He lowered his voice. 'I'll meet you tomorrow from school and we can go for a little walk. I'll have to leave here as though I'm going to work and find something to do until Roy's dad lets him off after dinner. Phil Jackson said I could go to his mum's place if I'm stuck. He's home all day so we can run through some songs together.'

He stopped and squeezed her hand as the door opened and his parents came in with a laden tea trolley.

An hour later, and stuffed with more food than she'd normally eat, Jane refused another piece of cake and asked if she could use the toilet.

'I'll show you where it is.' Eddie jumped up and led the way into the hall.

'Top of the stairs, turn left and it's the door directly facing you.' He followed her halfway and tutted as the doorbell rang. 'I'll get that, see you in a minute.' He ran back down and Jane made her way to the bathroom.

* * *

Angie fidgeted on the polished red doorstep, glancing into the front bay window. Behind the sparkling white nets, she could see movement and then she heard Eddie's voice in the hall. She rang the bell before she lost her nerve and changed her mind.

Eddie flung open the door, his jaw dropping when he saw it was her. The angry look on his face nearly made her turn and run. But why should she? She'd done nothing wrong. He was the one who'd ignored her after their night together. She wanted to know if they were seeing each other – or not.

'What are you doing here?' he demanded, pulling the door to behind him. 'What do you want?'

'I need to know where I stand,' she said. 'You won't answer my calls and you ignore me when you see me. After what we did the other week, I think you owe me an explanation. I thought we were back together again.'

'I never said that,' Eddie began, looking behind him as Jane pulled the door open. 'Angie's just going,' he said. 'She popped round to borrow a record but I haven't got the one she wants.'

'Oh, right.' Jane took hold of his arm.

'Jane,' Angie said, putting on a smile, 'I thought you and Ed were finished. I mean, after last night, well, I presumed you were seeing that lad from The Scorpions, Mark what's-his-name?'

'Err, no,' Jane said, blushing, which Angie took to mean she hadn't told Eddie about her dance with Mark.

'Why would you think that?' Eddie demanded. 'Jane's my girl, always has been.'

'Pity she didn't remember that last night then. Talk about when the cat's away. They were all over one another like a rash; dancing, laughing, hugging and then kissing.' Angie held back a smirk as Eddie's jaw tightened and Jane went red as a beetroot. 'I left shortly after that,' she continued, 'so I didn't see what else they got up to. But you know what we used to get up to round the back of the coffee bar, Ed.'

She smiled and stepped back as Eddie clenched his fists and shook Jane's arm off his. 'Well, I've gotta go now. I'm meeting Cathy. Might see you later if you're going to Mario's.'

She turned with a swagger and walked briskly down the road. That'd put the cat amongst the pigeons. Good, serve him right for messing her about, and her too, the smug little cow, holding his arm as though she owned him. Bet he still hadn't done it with her. Angie reckoned that she had far more rights to be with Eddie than Jane had.

* * *

'Upstairs, to my room,' Eddie said, slamming the front door and pushing Jane down the hall.

'But your mum and dad...' she said, looking towards the closed parlour door.

Eddie popped his head inside. 'Thanks for tea, we're going up to listen to some records.' He grabbed Jane's hand and dragged her upstairs with him as his mother called after them, 'Just behave yourselves.'

'Right,' he began and pulled her down onto the bed. 'What was that all about? You dancing with Mark bloody Fisher, I mean?'

'It was just one dance,' Jane muttered, her cheeks still red. 'And he wasn't all over me. We were jiving so he had to catch me and twirl me around. He pecked my cheek when he walked me back to the table. If you'd rather believe her than me that's fine. All you have to do is ask Sammy and Pat. But anyway, what was she on about? You and her at the back of the coffee shop? Have you been seeing her again? Because if you have, we're finished. I'm not being messed about.'

Eddie swallowed hard. 'No, I haven't,' he lied. 'And the back of the coffee shop was before us. And it was only a kiss and a cuddle.' And the odd grope or two but he wasn't admitting to that. 'So, there's nothing going on between you and Mark?'

She shook her head and looked down at her hands folded on her knee.

Eddie hated himself for trying to shift the blame onto her. She was a pretty girl and lads were going to ask her to dance. He wouldn't be there all the time now that the group was moving on and he couldn't expect her not to enjoy herself on her rare nights out. But there was something about Mark Fisher that he didn't like and the thought of Jane in his arms twisted his guts. He was sure he could trust her, but could he trust Mark?

He stroked her hair from her face and could see that she was near to tears. 'I'm sorry, Jane. I love you. I felt jealous when Angie said that.'

'It's okay. No more so than I did when she said about the two of you.'

'She'll be thinking she's split us up now.' Eddie sighed into her hair as he took her in his arms. He kissed her and pushed her gently back against the pillows. 'It's okay,' he whispered as she looked worriedly at the door. 'They won't come in. And if they do, we're not going to be doing anything they'll disapprove of.'

Jane snuggled into him and kissed him back.

'We'll stay here for a while and cuddle and stuff and then go to Mario's later,' he said. 'We'll show Angie that she can't split us up.'

And if he saw Mark Fisher, he'd give him a little warning to keep his hands off Jane.

## 17

JULY 1959

Eddie, Roy and Tim met up with the girls on the rec after school. Roy had brought two bottles of cider to celebrate the end of term and Tim's final day. It was hot and sunny and they sprawled under a large, shady oak tree, sharing the cider. Jane took her tie off and undid the first three buttons on her blouse, blowing down inside to cool herself.

'Want me to do that?' Eddie offered as she blushed and smacked his arm.

'Thank God it's all over for a few weeks,' Sammy said. 'This time next year it'll be our turn for freedom.'

'Yeah, only one more year of this horrible uniform,' Jane said, looking down at the grey pleated skirt they all hated wearing.

'It's not that bad,' Roy said. 'Especially on you three. You pull the skirts up nice and short and we get the odd flash of navy blue.'

'You're a dirty letch, Cantello,' Sammy said, laughing as he rolled her onto her back and tickled her.

'How did the driving lesson go this morning?' Eddie asked, reaching for the cider and taking his turn at a swig. Roy had started the lessons a few weeks ago on his seventeenth birthday and was determined to pass first time.

'Great,' Roy said. 'All being well, and if I pass my test, Dad said he's getting a new van for the business and we can have the old one for the group. He's paying for extra lessons, so the instructor said he'll take me out in the van for the next few.'

'Oh, that's good,' Eddie said. 'Our own van and it'll save John having to drive every night. We're getting so busy now and it seems unfair after working all day that he has to sort us lot out when he should be seeing his girl or having a rest.'

'That's what I thought,' Roy said. 'He looked really tired on Saturday and he said Margaret's been giving him earache about never being around to take her out.'

'Don't blame her,' Sammy chipped in. 'I mean, we have no choice when you're playing out of the area, but it's not fair that Margaret doesn't get to see John at the weekend.'

'You girls will be able to come with us occasionally once I'm driving,' Roy said. 'You can squeeze in with the gear. Phil's got a car now so he can take Ed and Tim to the gigs. And,' he stopped, looking at Sammy with a glint in his eyes, 'the back of the van'll come in very handy for other things.'

She laughed. 'Randy git!'

Jane smiled and pulled Eddie close.

'You okay?' he asked, handing her the cider. Her cheeks were flushed and her brown eyes sparkled. 'There's only a bit left. You might as well finish it.'

'I'm fine,' she whispered. 'I want to go to your place, now.' She drained the bottle and hiccupped.

'Why?' He looked closely at her. 'Jane, are you pissed?'

'No. But I want us to be alone.'

'I don't think so,' he said, grinning. 'I wouldn't trust myself and you'd hate yourself after.'

'I wouldn't.' She nuzzled his ear. 'Please, Ed.'

'No.' He laughed and pulled her to her feet. 'Come on, we'll call in to Mario's and get some coffee down you. See you lot at seven.' He slung his arm around Jane and led her away.

They'd all arranged to go for a celebratory fish and chip tea at The Ritz, Stockport's poshest chip shop, before meeting at Mario's for tonight's gig. Jane had brought a change of clothes in her bag and was coming to his house to get ready. He wanted to spend as much time with her as he could before she went on holiday to Blackpool with her family next week. Maybe in a year or two they'd be allowed to go away together.

* * *

Roy passed his driving test while Jane was still on holiday. He and Eddie took the van out each day afterwards, driving aimlessly around Stockport, at his dad's insistence, to get the feel of it. In a couple of weeks he was driving the group to Bolton for their next out-of-the-area gig. On Wednesday night they picked up the gear from the pub in Cheadle, where they left it on a regular basis now, and transported everything to Mario's.

As the group ran through a soundcheck, Sammy and Pat arrived and bagged a table by the side of the stage. The coffee bar filled and Mario switched on the jukebox. Eddie went to the counter to get drinks and Phil pulled out the small bottle of vodka he'd been hiding in his jeans pocket. He gave it to Sammy to store in her handbag. Eddie came back with a tray of Cokes in tall glasses and Sammy tipped a bit of vodka into each one.

'Dream Lover' by Bobby Darin blasted out and Roy yanked Sammy to her feet and onto the dance floor.

Eddie took a sip of his drink and sighed.

'Are you missing Jane, Ed?' Pat asked, touching his arm.

'I am, yeah. Be glad when it's Saturday.'

'Not long now. And at least you've been keeping busy with the group.'

He nodded. His mum and dad had been okay about him packing his job in once they saw how much work the group had got booked in. They'd had a moan at first but soon let the matter drop. He looked up as Mark Fisher and Tony walked in. They took a seat on the opposite side of the stage. Tony waved and Eddie waved back. Mark ignored him and turned away. He hadn't spoken a word to Eddie since he'd warned him to stay away from Jane. Eddie shrugged. No skin off his nose if Mark chose to sulk. How would he like it if Eddie had asked his girl to dance in his absence? Not that he'd ever seen him with a girl.

Sammy and Roy came back to the table and Mario announced that The Raiders would be on stage in fifteen minutes and snacks would be served during the interval.

'Better get changed,' Roy said.

In the dressing room they pulled on red satin shirts, black leather waistcoats and jeans. Roy lit a ready-rolled joint and passed it around. Tim declined, saying he had a headache.

'Never mind,' Phil said, taking a lengthy drag. 'All the more for us.' He flicked back his heavy blond fringe and grinned.

'Right, come on.' Roy stubbed out the joint and left the remains on the windowsill for their break.

* * *

Halfway through the second set, Eddie looked across the crowded coffee shop and spotted Angie and her mates at their usual table by the door. As he watched, he saw Mark and Tony stop beside them and exchange words. He wondered what had been said as Mark looked back to the stage, a smirk on his face, but Angie shook her head and then he and Tony left.

Angie saw Eddie looking and smiled. She gave a little wave. Damn, now she'd be thinking he was looking at her. As Roy launched in to 'Great Balls of Fire', a lad pulled Angie to her feet and onto the dance floor. Eddie had to admit that she

looked good. Her red and white polka dot dress twirled out
above legs that were lightly tanned. Her long curly hair was
caught up in a neat ponytail with a red-spotted ribbon, and
she'd kicked off her sandals and was dancing in bare feet.

As the lad swung her around, Eddie tried not to look at the
flash of white knickers. He groaned and tried to concentrate on
the drum roll. Angie smiled in his direction as the song came to
an end and the crowd yelled for more. Roy slowed down the
tempo with a bottom-squeezer slow song and Eddie saw the lad
draw Angie close, his hands fondling her arse as he danced with
her to 'Love Me Tender'. Shit, he couldn't believe how jealous
and turned on he felt right now. That was the trouble with
smoking dope.

\* \* \*

Eddie lifted the last of his drums up into the van and Roy said,
'I'm going to walk Sammy to Mersey Square with Tim and Pat.
Can you stay here with the gear, Ed? I'll drop you off at yours
when I get back.'

As they left, Phil got into his car and drove off with a wave.
Eddie shut the van door and walked to the corner. Angie and
Cathy were still hanging around on the street, talking. Angie
saw him and came over.

'Hi,' he said, offering her a cigarette.

She shook her head. 'You were great tonight. I really
enjoyed myself.'

'Thanks.'

That was rare praise, coming from her.

She shivered and pulled her short jacket around her
shoulders.

'It's chilly now the sun's gone in.'

'Come and sit in the van,' he offered, knowing that he
shouldn't. 'I'm minding the gear.'

She hesitated, looked back at Cathy, who was engaged in animated conversation with two more girls, and took his outstretched hand. They slipped around the corner unseen and Eddie opened the passenger door and helped her up. He climbed into the driver's side. He could smell her perfume and his stomach lurched, remembering the time she'd been in his bed in her scrap of black lace and the passionate night that followed.

He lifted his hand to her face and stroked her cheek. She leant forward and kissed him lightly and then she was in his arms. He kissed her and ran his hands over her body and onto her bare knees, inching up her dress until he reached her knickers.

She groaned and pushed him away. 'No, Ed. Whenever we do anything, you don't want to know me afterwards.'

'I do,' he whispered. 'Please.'

'Roy'll be back soon,' she said. 'I saw him going off with Sammy to the bus stop. And where's Jane tonight?'

'On holiday.'

'So you thought you'd play away with me?'

He shook his head. 'Sorry.'

'So am I. You have no idea how much you hurt me. I want you, but my feelings mean nothing to you.'

He stared at the windscreen for a few seconds. He was so turned on at the moment he could burst, desperate for her to touch him. She did this to him all the time, so what the fuck was he supposed to do? He wanted her and she wanted him.

'Can I see you tomorrow night?'

She chewed her lip. 'I'm not sleeping with you but I'll go out with you.'

'Okay. The summer fair's on at Norman's Woods fields. Do you fancy it?'

She smiled. 'Yes, I do. We had a great time last year. Where shall I meet you?'

'Mersey Square at seven.' He stopped as he heard Cathy calling her name. He gave her a quick kiss and she clambered out of the van and ran around the corner.

He sat back and lit a cigarette. After the fair they could have a stroll through Norman's Woods and maybe a grope up against a tree. A picture of Jane's smiling face popped into his head and he blinked it away. She wouldn't know and Angie wouldn't tell. He'd forgotten to ask her what Fisher had said to her earlier. He'd do it tomorrow.

\* \* \*

Eddie flung his arm around Angie's shoulders as she was thrown against him when the Waltzer operator, riding the platform, jumped on the back of their car and spun them round and round. She clung to him, screaming and giggling, and Eddie laughed at her reactions while Gene Vincent belted out 'Be-Bop-A-Lula' in the background.

As the ride slowed and came to a stop, Eddie helped Angie out of the car and caught her as she wobbled. They'd shared a bottle of cider earlier so the wobbling was more pronounced. He put his arm round her waist as they walked around the fairground, looking at the side shows and breathing in the sickly-sweet smell of candyfloss and toffee apples that competed with the appetising aroma of fried onions. Eddie won a stuffed dog at the rifle range and presented it to her. They queued for the Ferris Wheel and Ghost Train and she snogged the face off him in the dark. He was dying to get her alone.

'Shall we, err, go for a walk in the woods now?' He tried to keep it casual, not sound so eager.

'Yeah, let's.'

She clung to his arm as he led her away from the fair and down a winding path and the slope that brought to them to a clearing with the old bench that had been there for years. There was no one around but in the background Eddie could still hear the noise of the fair and the Everly Brothers' 'Bye Bye Love' playing. He sat down on the bench and pulled Angie onto his knee. He wrapped his arms around her and kissed her, feeling his erection growing by the second.

Dressed for a hot summer's night, Angie wore a loose white sundress with narrow straps and a matching bolero. He slid the bolero off her shoulders and slipped the straps and the top of her dress down. She was bra-less and her breasts were begging to be played with. She gasped as he took a nipple in his mouth, twiddling the other between his finger and thumb.

He slid her off his knee and pulled her over to a patch of long grass under a tree. They lay side by side, holding, kissing and touching each another intimately until she was close and he couldn't hold back any longer. He pulled her white lacy knickers off and pushed inside her. He caught his breath and looked at her face. Eyes closed, cheeks flushed and a smile on her lips. God, she could turn him on like there was no tomorrow and he hammered away until she shuddered and cried his name, sending him over the edge. He pulled out just in time and cursed himself for not getting some Durex today. He knew they'd probably shag tonight so why he'd forgotten he didn't know. But still, he'd withdrawn in time, so it should be okay. He rolled onto his back and dug in his jeans' pocket for a hanky. He wiped her sticky tummy and chucked the hanky into the grass behind them.

Angie sat up, pulled on her knickers and straightened her clothes. She stared at him as he yanked up his pants and jeans and zipped himself up.

'You okay?' he muttered, rooting for cigarettes in his pocket and offering her one.

'Yeah. Are you?'

He nodded and they sat with their backs against a tree for a few minutes, enjoying the warmth of the night.

'What did Mark Fisher say to you last night?' he asked.

She frowned. 'When?'

'When he was on his way out of the coffee bar. He said something but you shook your head and he left.'

'Oh, he asked if I'd like to go for a drink with him sometime. But I said no. I wouldn't go out with him, he's not really my type.'

'What is your type?' He blew a wobbly smoke ring above his head and grinned.

'You are,' she said.

'What about Richard? Have you been out with him lately?'

'I have lunch with him every day. We're working together now. I started my apprenticeship the week after school finished.'

'Is lunch all you're having?'

'Eddie! God, you're worse than Cathy. Richard's a really nice guy and we're good friends. Anyway, you're still seeing Jane and I don't expect tonight will change that. When's she back from holiday?'

'Saturday.'

'So, tonight's a one-off, as usual?' She sighed and took a long drag on her cigarette.

He rolled onto his stomach and she brushed his floppy fringe from his eyes.

'Maybe,' he said. 'Let's see what happens. You know I fancy the arse off you.'

She laughed. 'I won't say anything to Jane, if you don't say anything to Cathy.'

'Thanks, and I won't.' He jumped to his feet and pulled her up. 'Better get you home if you've gotta get up for work tomorrow.'

## 18

NOVEMBER 1959

Jane picked up her handbag and made her way to the ladies'. Saturday night and the coffee bar was heaving as usual. The Scorpions were playing. She wondered when Mario would get the chance to buy the building next door and achieve his dream of a proper club. The Raiders were at a club in Altrincham and she'd arranged to see Eddie tomorrow afternoon at his parents' place. She was looking forward to it as this week he'd been so busy, they'd been like ships that pass in the night. She pushed her way into the toilets and took her place in the queue.

As Jane touched up her lipstick and did her hair in front of the mirror, two girls she recognised as friends of Angie's came in. She half-smiled and put her lipstick and comb back in her handbag.

The tallest of the pair smiled back. 'Hi, Jane. No Eddie tonight?'

'Err, no. The Raiders are playing out of the area.'

'We know,' the smaller girl smirked. 'Cathy and Angie have gone over on the train to watch them. I'm surprised at you, Jane, letting a good-looking lad like Eddie go off on his own when Angie's on the loose.'

'I can trust Eddie.' Jane made for the door. She didn't like the way the taller girl was looking at her; it was almost a look of sympathy.

The smaller girl laughed. 'Really? I wouldn't trust that one as far as I could throw him. You wanna ask him what he and Angie get up to in the back of the group's van when you're not around.'

Jane felt her stomach turn over and hurried back to her seat. She sat down and picked up her drink, but couldn't stop the tears from welling.

Sammy looked at her and frowned. 'What's wrong?'

Jane shook her head. 'Nothing. Well... yeah, there is. Come outside.' She got to her feet and made for the door.

Sammy followed her. 'Jane, what is it?'

Jane told her what the girl had said. Sammy chewed her lip and looked down at the floor.

'It's true, isn't it?' Jane sobbed. 'He's seeing her again. I knew it, I just knew it. Why didn't you tell me, Sam?'

Sammy leant back against the wall and sighed. 'Oh, believe me, I've been tempted to many times, but Roy and I think Eddie should be the one to do that.'

'He's been sort of distant for a while now,' Jane said. 'Since the summer. Like his mind's elsewhere half the time. When I ask what's wrong, he says he's thinking about the group and where things will take them. It's been going on for a while, hasn't it? Is he sleeping with her?'

Sammy shrugged, dug in her pocket for a hanky and handed it to Jane. 'I don't honestly know. I thought it was all off again, but if the girl says that, then it must be still going on and yes, I suppose he's getting up to something in the back of the van. You need to ask him point-blank.'

'I will.' Jane wiped her eyes. 'And believe me, if he's cheating, that's it, we're finished. I'm seeing him tomorrow at his mum's. I'll have it out with him. Don't tell Roy, I don't want him pre-warned.'

'I won't. Come on back inside, it's freezing with no coats on. Have a dance with Mark. He's not taken his eyes off you all night. The only reason you won't dance with him is because of Eddie. Well, stuff him, you enjoy yourself.'

And although her heart felt like it was being ripped in two, Jane accepted Mark's next invite to dance. She had to give him his due, he never gave up. His face split into a big grin when she said yes and took to the floor with him. She tried to concentrate on her steps but her mind was all over the place. How could Eddie do this to her? In spite of him seeming preoccupied, he was always telling her he loved her and buying her little gifts. He met her from school as often as he could, but the group took up a lot of time with rehearsals and gigs. And on the odd midweek night he was free, she wasn't allowed out because of her mother's stupid, rigid rules. Why she couldn't go out Tuesday or Thursday instead of Wednesday occasionally she didn't know. It was so unfair. No wonder he got fed up of waiting and chose a girl who could spend more time with him. But that still didn't excuse the cheating.

As the music ended, Mark led her over to the counter, draping his arm loosely around her shoulders as they waited to be served.

'Not with Eddie tonight then?' A female voice spoke beside her, adding, 'I don't know, Jane, you're as bad as your boyfriend is. He's probably with Angie and you're with Mark, acting like butter wouldn't melt. You're a right cheating pair.'

Jane turned around to see who was speaking and realised it was another of Angie's cronies. 'Mind your own business.' She turned back to Mark, who pulled her close. The girl turned and walked away, but not before Jane saw her grinning like a Cheshire Cat. Jane struggled not to cry again. It seemed like all of Angie's friends knew the bitch was seeing Eddie and were laughing behind Jane's back. Why was she the last to know? Her stomach churned so much, she felt she might be sick at any moment. She looked at Mark, who shrugged his shoulders.

'I'll go and find Sammy.' He walked away and returned with an anxious Sammy on his heels.

'Just keep your beak out, you stupid cow,' Sammy shouted to the girl, who was sitting with her friends, and judging by their smug faces, all obviously party to the Eddie and Angie affair. 'Thanks, Mark, I'll look after her now. You go back to Tony, I've left him sitting with Pat.' She took Jane by the arm and led her outside again.

'They all know. I can't bear it,' Jane sobbed.

Sammy put her arms around her as Pat came to find out what was going on. 'Get our coats, Pat, we're going home,' Sammy ordered.

Pat went back inside and came out a few minutes later, followed by a worried-looking Mark.

'Jane.' He put his hand on her shoulder. 'I'm so sorry. If you need me, call me. I've given Pat my phone number.'

Jane smiled through her tears as he gave her a tentative hug. 'Thank you, Mark. I'll see you soon.'

'We'll get a taxi to our place, and then we can talk properly.' Sammy linked her arm through Jane's.

'Okay,' Jane said. 'I can't go home. Mum will wonder why I'm crying and I don't want to tell her. She'll only say I told you he was no good. I need to speak to Ed first, see what he says.'

'He's a bastard!' Sammy spat. 'You're better off without him.'

'I don't understand,' Pat said. 'It wasn't that long ago he couldn't bear to be in the same room as her.'

'Well, he can just get lost,' Jane said. 'The bitch is welcome to him. Nobody's two-timing me.'

* * *

On Sunday afternoon, wearing a new red sweater dress, bought with her Saturday-job money, black stockings and long black boots, Jane hurried down the road towards Eddie's parents' house. With her glossy brown hair swinging on her shoulders and knowing that she looked her best, she rang the doorbell and stood back. She was freezing with only her little black jacket over her outfit, but didn't want to spoil her new look with her big winter coat.

Eddie's eyes opened wide when he saw her. She hoped his parents had gone out as planned. 'You look gorgeous.' He stepped back to let her in. She made straight for the front parlour and sat down on the edge of the sofa, crossed her legs and let her dress ride up her thighs. Eddie sat down next to her and pulled her into his arms. She allowed him to kiss her and slide his hand up her leg. When he reached the soft flesh above her stocking top, she smacked him away and turned her face from his. She felt angry: he was so bloody sure of himself.

He stared at her, looking puzzled. 'Why won't you let me touch you?' He tried again, laid her back against the sofa cushions and nibbled her ear.

She fought the feelings he was giving her and pushed him away. 'Leave me alone, you two-timing bastard!'

His jaw dropped. 'What you on about?'

Jane laughed and got to her feet. 'What am *I* on about?' she mimicked. 'Let me see now, where shall I begin?' She placed one finger against her chin. 'First of all, where did you go after last night's gig? Secondly, where are you on nights when I don't see you?'

He shrugged. 'Nights I don't see you I'm usually playing and last night I came straight back here.'

'And you expect me to believe that when I know Angie was at your gig last night? Do you think I'm stupid? I know you're seeing her again, and I also know you're sleeping with her.'

His blue eyes narrowed. 'Who told you that?'

'No one. I worked it out for myself. And Angie's friend at the coffee bar kindly told me I shouldn't trust you out on your own, and that I should ask you what you and Angie get up to in the back of the van after gigs.'

'The gobby cow! She had no right to say anything.'

'Well, she did, and the least you owe me is to stop lying and tell me why.' Jane threaded her fingers together and tried not to cry in front of him.

Eddie hung his head, as though realising the game was up. 'Okay,' he muttered. 'I'm seeing Angie again. This'll sound like a poor excuse, but I can't help myself. I felt so jealous when I first saw her with Richard that I came home and punched the door, which is how I hurt my hand. When you stayed behind at Mario's with Roy and Sammy, she followed me out and came back home with me. One thing led to another and we... well, you don't want to know the details.'

'That was the day you met my parents. How could you do this to me? I thought we were really special, that we meant something to each other.' Jane sat down again and burst into tears.

* * *

Eddie sat with his head in his hands; he couldn't bear to see her crying. He didn't know what to say or do. He was confused. He wanted Jane, but Angie's body was like a drug. The relationship wasn't particularly good, but he couldn't seem to finish it.

'I'm so sorry.' He knelt in front of Jane and took hold of her shaking hands. 'I don't want us to split up. I love you, I really do. I don't want to lose you. I don't love Angie.'

'Well, finish with her then. Tell her you can't see her anymore,' Jane sobbed, tears running down her cheeks.

Eddie stared at her, wondering if she could see the turmoil in his eyes.

'You can't do it, can you? Well, you can't have us both. I'll make it easy for you. It's over, I couldn't trust you again anyway.' Jane got up and made for the door but Eddie was quicker and blocked her path.

'You can't go. I won't let you.'

'You don't have a choice. Now move or I'll scream and the neighbours will wonder what's going on.'

He grabbed her arms. 'Jane, please, give me another chance.'

'No, I can't, not while she's around.' She shook him off. 'Finish with her, and prove to me that you've finished with her, and I'll see how I feel. But until then just stay out of my way. I don't want to see you at all.'

* * *

Jane ran down the street feeling sick and betrayed. She walked into town and all the way back to Primrose Avenue to cool off. Sammy would be at Roy's, but Pat would be doing her homework before going to Tim's for tea.

'How did it go?' Pat asked as tears rolled down Jane's cheeks.

'I told him he has to finish with her,' she sobbed. 'If he does, I might give him another chance.'

'I wouldn't even give him that choice, Jane. He doesn't deserve it.'

'I don't want to lose him, but I'm not sharing him.' Jane blew her nose and continued, 'I feel it's partly my fault. If I could get out more often or had let him go all the way, he wouldn't have gone off with Angie. He wouldn't have needed to.'

Pat shook her head. 'No, Jane, you're underage, it's not right. Tim and I haven't gone all the way yet. He respects the way I feel. Eddie should be the same for you. He can't have a substitute to be going on with. It's not your fault his brains are in his Levi's.'

Jane smiled through her tears. 'That sounds like something Roy would come out with, not you.'

Pat blushed. 'Actually, that was from Roy. Mark Fisher was very worried about you last night. He said you deserve better than Eddie. He's really nice, and he does fancy you, Jane.'

'I know. I like him too. He's such a gent, something Eddie could never be if he tried.' The tears welled up again as Jane mentioned his name.

'It's okay, cry if it makes you feel better,' Pat said. 'If you can't cry in front of me, who can you cry in front of? Do you want to come to Tim's with me?'

Jane shook her head. 'No, I'll go home when you go out. Will Sammy be back at teatime?'

'I think so.'

'I'll come over later. Tag along with her and Roy to Mario's. Mark might be in and it'll take my mind off Eddie for a while.'

Christmas approached and John Grey asked Jane if she'd work in the shop during the school holidays. It was very busy, giving her little time to think about Eddie. To spare her feelings, John had spoken privately to him and asked him to stay away while Jane was working, and although he desperately wanted to see her again to apologise for what he'd done, Eddie respected John's wishes and stayed away.

The weeks flew by, with Jane refusing to go to the coffee bar whenever The Raiders were playing. She still had strong feelings for Eddie and it hurt her to even think of him and how close they'd been. She threw herself into her schoolwork; something she'd neglected while dating him and determined to do well in her end-of-year exams.

* * *

Mark Fisher wasted no time in asking Jane for a date when he realised she'd finished with Eddie. They grew closer and he enjoyed buying Jane and her mother chocolates and flowers and fussing around her. She liked the attention and so did her mother, but there was something missing in the relationship and Jane held her feelings back, determined not to be hurt again.

Enid hadn't been unduly surprised when Jane told her that Eddie had two-timed her and they'd split up. In her eyes, Mark Fisher seemed a really decent boy by comparison and far more suitable for Jane. He was steady and had a good job with prospects. Even the fact that he was a part-time musician and occasionally wore a leather jacket and tight jeans didn't worry her too much. Mark, unlike Eddie, wasn't the sort of boy who would throw caution and prospects to the wind for the sake of a vague chance of fame and fortune.

Jane told her mother that Mark's friend, Tony, had met a nice girl called Sarah at Mario's and they were now dating as a regular foursome. She missed the company of Pat and Sammy. She still saw them at school, and when The Raiders were playing out of the area, but it wasn't the same.

* * *

Sammy and Pat made it quite clear to Angie that she wasn't welcome in their circle of friends, even though Angie tried to win them round, reminding them that she'd been there first, having been at school with the boys.

'Why does Eddie want to be with her?' Sammy asked Roy after a painful night out with the couple, where Angie had been draped over Eddie all night, contributing nothing to the conversation, and sulking when he'd spoken to Roy about the group and its future plans.

'He's not serious,' Roy said. 'Not like he was with Jane. But he won't back down first. He's convinced now that Jane was seeing Mark while he was playing out of the area. Angie's friend told him that Jane was holding hands with Mark and dancing with him that night she found out about him and Angie. He's now got a bee in his bonnet that Jane was two-timing him.'

Sammy told Jane what Eddie had said to Roy.

'That's ridiculous,' Jane said. 'He was already seeing the cow then and he'd been seeing her for ages before that night. How dare he blame me? I tell you, I never want to speak to the bastard again.'

\* \* \*

The untimely death of Eddie Cochran in April, however, briefly re-united the six friends. Mario held a special Rock 'n' Roll evening as a tribute to the popular young singer, whose death followed a tragic road accident in Bristol on Easter Sunday.

Vincento asked The Raiders to play Eddie Cochran songs as their part of the tribute. Mark's group had a gig in Manchester that night and Angie had gone away to the seaside with her sister and young nephews for a few days.

Jane's stomach tied itself in knots as she got ready to go to Mario's. The coffee bar had recently been the subject of a bit of an overhaul and had been extended into the back office to make a bigger stage and dance area and tonight was the first night in its new format.

An insistent Sammy and Pat had persuaded Jane to accompany them to the tribute night and grand re-opening.

'You loved Eddie Cochran, Jane,' Sammy said. 'Why should you miss out on paying your respects, so to speak?'

'I can't face seeing her with Eddie.' Jane couldn't even bear to say Angie's name.

'She's not coming, she's away. And you can just ignore him if it makes it easier for you,' Pat said.

Jane sighed, knowing that would be impossible. 'All right then. But don't leave me on my own with him, please.'

\* \* \*

As Roy parked the group's van in Mario's car park, Eddie's heart thumped so hard, he felt it might explode from his chest. Knowing Jane was a fan of Eddie Cochran, he fully expected her to be there. He hadn't seen or spoken to her since the Sunday afternoon when they'd split up and he missed her more than he would admit to anyone, except Roy and Tim. Without Jane in his life, the relationship with Angie had paled. He soon realised the only thing keeping them together was sex and the fact that Angie never said no. But it didn't carry the same attraction now it was on tap. There was also the choice of willing girls after the gigs but they were one-night stands that meant nothing. He was always glad to make his escape afterwards, feeling low, cheap and angry with himself.

Angie had stopped seeing Richard as soon as Eddie was free. She made it quite clear she wanted more from the relationship than he was willing to give. She was forever going on about friends who were getting engaged and even married. He'd told her in no uncertain terms there was no chance of it happening with them and they were too young to even think about it. She reminded him that Roy and Sammy were still secretly engaged and they should do the same. Nobody needed to know.

She was doing his head in and he knew he'd have to do something about it sooner or later. Every time he tried to finish it, she'd cry and then he'd feel bad and hug her and they'd end up shagging. Then he'd feel even worse. Thank God he'd got the group to keep him occupied. It took his mind off Jane, who he was convinced wouldn't want anything more to do with him ever again. He was so glad Angie was away this weekend, and Roy had told him that Mark Fisher was playing in Manchester, so he was hoping to get the opportunity to talk to Jane and apologise for the way he'd treated her. Given half a chance, he knew he'd go down on bended knee and give the world to win her back, but first he had to give up Angie. He knew for certain he didn't love her, so why did she continue to have such a hold over him?

* * *

As The Raiders came off stage to the usual tumultuous applause, Jane caught Eddie's eye and he walked over and asked her if she'd like to dance.

She hesitated for a second and nodded. With legs like jelly and a dry mouth, her hands shook as he reached for hers. His touch shocked her like an electric volt and she saw in his eyes that he'd felt it too.

'Jane, I'm so sorry,' he began. 'I owe you a big apology. I want to make it right between us, I really miss you.'

'Like you missed me when I was in Blackpool, enough to sleep with Angie?' she retorted.

'It was a mistake, and if I could turn back the clock, I would.'

'I bet she didn't think it was a mistake. Anyway, it can't be that bad because you've made no attempt to finish it.'

'I don't see much of her,' he said. 'I'm usually playing away somewhere. It's not that easy to find the right time.'

'Well, I found it easy enough. You say it's over and you walk away, no matter how much it hurts.'

'Would you consider going out with me again?' he asked, giving her the look that melted her bones.

'Only if I could be sure you'd changed.' She was dying to yell yes of course she would and pull him close and snog his face off there and then, but she wanted to make him pay for what he did. 'I couldn't go through all that pain again. Mark treats me with respect and at least I know where I stand with him and he wouldn't cheat on me.'

Eddie sighed and put his arms around her. 'This is so good, so right.' He pulled her close and kissed her on the lips.

She pulled away from him. 'Don't do that. Cathy just walked in with her mates. I'm not having Angie blame me for coming between you.' She walked away, trembling, and sat down with Sammy and Pat. Roy and Tim were on stage packing up and Eddie joined them, glaring at Cathy's back.

'So?' Sammy raised an enquiring eyebrow.

'So, nothing. If he wants me back, he has to get rid of her.'

'Good for you,' Sammy said. 'He thinks he can wind girls around his little finger when he blinks those big blue eyes.'

Jane sighed. 'Being in his arms again for that moment was wonderful.'

'Don't you dare weaken, Jane Wilson.' Sammy rolled her eyes.

'I won't. I hope he doesn't think he's walking me to Mersey Square when Tim and Roy walk you two.'

'I'll go and tell Roy,' Sammy said. 'He'll make sure Eddie stays here. He can keep Cathy company. He'll just love that, and serves him right!'

## 19

JUNE 1961

By June the girls had finished their O level exams and were looking forward to leaving school in July. Sammy, whose engagement to Roy was no longer a secret from her family, but frowned upon by her teachers, was desperate to leave so she could wear his ring all day. She was going on to college to study art and dress design. Pat had chosen to do a shorthand and typing course, while Jane couldn't decide. John Grey asked her if she'd consider working full-time in Flanagan and Grey's. The business was expanding and two more shops were due to open that year. His father planned to promote him to area manager and he wanted John to train Jane to take over the running of the Stockport branch in time.

Her mum wasn't keen on the idea. 'I'd rather you were going to college. What's the point in having a grammar school education if you're going to throw it away and work in a shop? You could train to be a nurse or a secretary.'

Jane pulled a face. 'I don't want to. I enjoy working in the shop. I love the music and stuff.' She looked at her dad for support.

'Give her a break, Enid. I don't see why she can't continue

at the shop for a while if it's something she enjoys,' he said, smiling at Jane. 'Not often you find a job you like at her age.'

Her mum gave in with a reluctant sigh that told Jane she wasn't happy. 'All right then. Give it a trial for a few months and you can go to college later.'

'Thanks, Mum, Dad.' Jane couldn't wait and there was no chance she was going to college later if she had her way.

\* \* \*

Jane took a magazine to the top of the hill behind Rosedean Gardens and lay down on a grassy mound. She tried to read but couldn't concentrate; it was too hot and sunny. Mark and Tony were away for the week and she was supposed to be seeing Tony's girl Sarah tonight but didn't feel like going out. They'd been invited to Mark's mother's for tea. Maude Fisher, who Jane had taken an instant dislike to, seemed quite old to have a son as young as Mark. He'd told Jane that his father had passed away when he was a small boy. He couldn't remember him and he said his mother never spoke of him. Jane didn't like the way Maude sulked whenever she went to the house. It was as though she was jealous that Mark had a girlfriend. Why the woman had invited her for tea while Mark was away, she had no idea.

Maude was a miserable so-and-so who hardly ever left the house, so she and Mark never had time alone except for once when she was out and they'd gone up to his bedroom for a cuddle. Mark had tried it on but took no for an answer right away and had since respected her wishes. She didn't expect that situation to last long. Now she'd turned sixteen, he'd no doubt try again. He didn't make her feel like Eddie used to. She never got the funny feelings low down in her tummy when he kissed her. He talked about their relationship in the long-term, holidays with Tony and Sarah, getting engaged in a year or two, buying a house and mortgages and stuff that she wasn't even remotely interested in. But her mum was. Perhaps she just wanted to get rid of her and let someone else take on the responsibility of looking after her.

Although she liked Mark, Jane found him a bit overpowering at times. It was almost as though her mind wasn't her own anymore and she didn't have a right to an opinion. But he was good to her and she supposed she was lucky to have such an attentive boyfriend who didn't expect too much and would probably never cheat on her. Maybe he'd asked his mother to keep an eye on her so that she didn't go out alone, hence the invite to tea. The more she bandied the idea around, the more she was convinced of it and the more it annoyed her. She decided to cancel tonight – she was certain Sarah wouldn't mind, she didn't like Maude either.

She wondered what Eddie was doing these days. The group was busier than ever and they worked up and down the country now, sleeping in the van or tacky B&Bs if it was too late and too far to travel home. Sammy kept her up to date with group activities but usually left Eddie's name out of the conversation. She heard someone calling her and sat up as Pat came into view.

'Your mum said I'd find you up here.' Pat flopped down on the grass, blowing her fringe off her forehead. 'Phew, it's hot! Tim's tinkering in the garage. Sammy's gone to Norman's Woods with Roy. No prizes for guessing what they'll be up to. So I thought I'd take a walk. Penny for them, you were miles away.'

'I was just thinking about Ed, funnily enough. Stupid I know, but...' she tailed off and choked back a sob. It hurt, and she still loved and hated him at the same time.

'When did you last talk to him?' Pat asked, chewing a flat blade of grass.

'At the Eddie Cochran tribute,' Jane said. 'Over a year ago.'

'Why don't you come to the coffee bar on Wednesday? The Raiders are playing. Sammy and I are helping Rosa work the counter while Vinnie's away, but you can sit on a stool close by and we get breaks, so we can have a dance with you.'

'I might just do that. Mark's away with Tony so he doesn't need to know. I'd never hear the end of it if he thought I was going out without him. The only thing that puts me off is seeing her with Eddie. Still, I don't suppose I've got much choice – I'm sick of hiding away.'

'It's up to you. John and Stu will be there, so you'll have company. Don't take this as gospel, but I'm pretty sure Ed's not seeing her anymore. He finished with her just after Christmas and then according to Tim, they had a one-night stand in March but it's over as far as I know. She's never with him at the gigs and I haven't seen her for a few weeks at Mario's either. Ed told Tim he'd give his right arm to be back with you.'

'Really?'

'Yep. I know you still love him, Jane, but, well, can you trust him again? And what about Mark? You never say much about him, but you've been seeing him a while. Are you serious?'

Jane blew out her cheeks. 'Mark is, so is my mother! But it's not what I want. I should break it off, really. I just don't want to hurt him.'

'Well, if it's not right, maybe you should finish it. Have a think about Wednesday anyway. You could get Eddie a birthday card. He's eighteen on Friday. It'd be a good icebreaker.'

Jane jumped to her feet and brushed the grass from her skirt. 'Maybe I will,' she said. 'Let's walk down to the paper shop and see if there's anything suitable. Pat, has he really packed her in?' She chewed her lip, a seed of an idea taking root in her mind.

'I think so. He asked Tim about you and Mark. Wanted to know if you're still seeing him. He's changed, Jane, grown up a bit. He's so quiet these days. I know he regrets what happened.'

Jane nodded. 'I'm sure he does.' She was quiet for a minute.

'I suppose I could play Angie at her own game,' she said, a faraway look in her eyes.

'What game?' Pat frowned.

'Get back with him and go all the way. He always wanted to and I wanted to wait. But for what? I mean, what was I saving myself for? He's the one I really want when all's said and done.'

'Jane, you don't have to sleep with him to get him back,' Pat said, looking shocked. 'He wouldn't expect it.'

'I know, but she did it and won him back. Anyway, I want to, I've made my mind up. I'll definitely be at Mario's on Wednesday.'

As Eddie took his place on stage he felt nervous. Roy had told him that Jane was coming tonight and that Mark was away. This was it, his chance to put things right, if she'd talk to him. Sammy and Pat were over at the counter working with Rosa but there was no sign of Jane. The table by the stage had some of Phil's usual harem seated around it, along with John and Stuart.

Halfway through the first set, movement by the door caught his eye, and he saw Jane walk in and glance around. She chewed her lip, avoided looking across at the stage and made her way to the counter, sitting down on a stool. She wore a white strappy summer dress and her hair swung loose and shiny on her lightly tanned, bare shoulders. In spite of the heat in the club that made sweat drip down his back, Jane looked cool, good enough to eat, and his stomach lurched. He couldn't wait to get off stage and talk to her.

Back in the stuffy dressing room, he pulled on a dry T-shirt, rubbed his damp hair with a towel and ran a comb through it. He took a swig of vodka from the bottle Phil had brought in and a long drag on the joint Roy was passing around. His palms felt sweaty and he rubbed his hands on the legs of his jeans.

'What you waiting for?' Roy said, giving him a push towards the door. 'Get out there and talk to her and don't fuck it up this time. Go and sort it because you're driving us nuts, moping about all over the place.'

'Alright, I'm going.' He took a deep breath and left the room.

* * *

Jane sipped her Coke and sat with her back to the crowd. Mario switched the jukebox back on and the Everly Brothers' 'Cathy's Clown' blasted out.

'He's coming over,' Sammy whispered. 'Are you ready?'

'Oh God, I feel sick,' Jane muttered. 'Deep breath, deep breath,' she chanted to herself, and then a hand fell on her shoulder.

'Jane.'

She spun around to face him and her heart soared as he smiled. 'Hi.'

'Hi yourself,' he said. 'How are you?'

'Okay, and you?'

'Not bad. Can I get you a drink?'

'Coke, please.'

Sammy handed two Cokes over and Eddie paid her. 'Shall we find a table?' he suggested. 'There's one by the window just come vacant.' He carried the drinks and she followed him.

They both started to speak at once and then laughed. 'I've missed you,' he said.

'I've missed you too.'

'So, Sammy said you've finished your O levels? Hope you do better than me and Roy did.'

'Well, that shouldn't be too difficult,' she said with a laugh.

'Nah, waste of blooming time. Not a one between us. Still,

Tim did us proud with his five good grades. Not that he needs them anyway.'

'Neither do I. I'm going to be working full-time in Flanagan and Grey's.'

'Oh, that's great, Jane. Well done.'

Jane smiled. He seemed genuinely pleased for her. 'Err... Pat said it's over between you and Angie.' She took a sip of Coke and looked at him over the rim of her glass. Oh God, his eyes were bluer than ever and his hair had grown. He had a bit of stubble on his chin and it looked good. She just wanted to climb on to his knee and kiss him.

He nodded. 'It is, completely over. It's a big relief. What about you and Mark?'

She shrugged. 'He's away, back on Sunday.'

'So, are the pair of you serious?'

'Mark is, I'm not. I quite like his company and he treats me okay, but I don't love him, if that's what you mean.'

He lit a cigarette and didn't take his eyes off her. The jukebox went quiet and someone got up to choose some songs. The dulcet tones of Ben E. King filled the room and Jane smiled.

'Oh, I love this one.'

'Me too. It's the B-side of "Stand by Me". The group has started to learn it and I'm singing it. Fancy a dance?' He got to his feet and held out his hand.

It was the most natural thing to move into his arms and he held her as they jived to 'First Taste of Love', swinging her around and then pulling her close and as they danced, he sang along and it made her smile. They finished the dance with a gentle kiss and he led her back to the table, keeping hold of her hand as they sat down.

'Can we try again?' he asked. 'Wipe the slate clean and start afresh.'

She swallowed hard. It was what she'd hoped he'd say, but

she was terrified of being hurt again. She looked at their entwined hands and chewed her lip for a long moment. She'd have to finish with Mark. He'd be furious. But a future with him wasn't what she wanted. Sod it, she was going to take a chance.

Eddie took her silence to mean no and shook his head. 'I'm sorry. Why would you want to date me again? How could you begin to trust me?'

'I do,' she said. 'Want to, I mean.'

His eyes lit up and he let out a huge breath. 'You do? Really? Oh, Jane, you've no idea how much I needed to hear that. I love you, I really love you. I'll never let you down again, I promise.'

'I love you too, Ed. I never stopped. Even when I hated you, I still loved you.'

He smiled. 'Can I walk you to Mersey Square later?'

'Of course.'

* * *

On Friday, Jane spent all her savings on a new outfit for Saturday night. The Raiders were playing at Mario's and Eddie had told her it was a special night because Frank James, a well-respected Manchester agent, had finally agreed to come and see them play. Eddie had taken her out last night for a meal and they'd talked about their feelings and the future. He was coming to the shop tomorrow to take her for lunch. She liked that. Lunchtime was what Mac's girl Jackie called dinnertime, and she also called tea, dinner. Bit confusing, but it sounded so much posher. And now she and Ed were back together, they may end up living in Wilmslow if this Frank James fellow liked The Raiders enough to take them on. They might get really famous and rich.

She was dreading Sunday when Mark came home and she had to tell him it was over. He'd called her at work yesterday and it had been difficult to make conversation with him. He'd asked why she'd cancelled going to his mum's with Sarah. She told him she felt a bit poorly and didn't want to pass any germs on to his mum. They'd left it at that, but for the rest of the conversation, he was a bit snappy and she'd been glad when he hung up.

* * *

'Can I go now?' Jane asked John as Eddie arrived for their lunch date.

'Of course,' John said. 'See you in a bit.'

She grabbed her handbag and followed Eddie up the stairs.

'Where would you like to eat?' he asked after a while.

They'd wandered hand in hand around the market, where she'd completed her outfit for tonight with pale-coloured silky stockings that'd look lovely with the new cream lace underwear she'd bought.

'The Black Horse does a decent pie and chips,' he continued.

'Am I allowed in pubs? Thought you had to be eighteen.'

'You do, but it'll be alright if you just have Coke.'

'Okay.'

Inside the smoky pub, Eddie led her to a small alcove and went to order. She glanced at her surroundings and hoped there was no one in here that knew her parents. She daren't even begin to tell her mother they were back together. She'd go crazy.

Eddie came back with the drinks – 'Food won't be long. Cheers.' He clinked his glass to hers and took a sip of cider.

'Ed.' She touched his hand. 'I'm staying over at Sammy's tonight. Tom and Molly are away.'

'Right. And...'

'Well, it means I don't have to rush off for the last bus or anything. I can come back to yours with you and then get a taxi back to theirs later.' She knew his mum and dad were also away until late Sunday, but she couldn't chance staying all night with him. She wasn't that brave and her mum would be sure to find out one way or another. 'What I'm saying is, we can have lots of time together before I have to go. And well, err, I'm ready now.'

'Ready?'

'Yeah, you know.'

'Jane, are you sure?'

She nodded. 'Positive. Tonight's the night. Will you get some, err...'

He took her hand across the table. 'Yes, leave that to me. But are you really sure? I'm just glad we're back together and I'm happy to wait.'

'Well, I'm not,' she said. She wasn't losing him to Angie again, she was ready to make a commitment. 'I want to.'

'If it's what you want,' he said, 'then so do I.' He leant across the table and planted a kiss on her lips.

* * *

Halfway through the first set, Jane spotted Angie, Cathy and a crowd of girls, making their way into Mario's. Pat had told her she hadn't been in for ages. Trust her to pick tonight to show up. She leant back behind John Grey and observed as Angie, wearing a loose, low-cut black dress and red stilettos, looked across and stared at Eddie with a hungry look in her eyes. Jane felt her stomach lurch.

She saw Eddie look away as Angie raised her hand in a wave and then walked over to the bar and ordered a round of drinks from a frosty-faced Rosa, who slammed the glasses down on a tray and snatched the money, before turning her back on the girl. Jane smiled. Rosa didn't like Angie either and had been happy to learn that Jane was giving Eddie another chance.

Angie's eyes narrowed and her lips formed a thin line as she spotted Jane. Jane looked away and started talking to Stuart.

\* \* \*

Angie put the tray of drinks on the table and flopped down on the chair next to Cathy.

'Why the glum face?' Cathy asked.

'Jane's here. And she looks a million dollars.'

She watched as Jane got up to dance with Stuart, noting the way Eddie's eyes followed her onto the floor.

'That dress she's wearing is gorgeous,' Cathy muttered, a hint of envy in her voice. 'Looks like real silk. Bet it cost a packet. How on earth can a kid like her afford something like that?'

'She probably saved up for it,' Angie said, staring at Jane's low-cut cream shift that emphasised her curves and showed off her shapely legs. 'She's got a Saturday job at Flanagan and Grey's. Oh God, Cathy, Eddie hasn't taken his bloody eyes off her. It's obvious he still fancies her. I bet he'll be in a stinking mood tonight when I try and talk to him.'

'You're definitely going to say something then?'

'I have to. Get it over with, then I can put my plan into action and get on with my life.'

'And what about Richard?'

'What about him?'

'Well, shouldn't you say something to him, too?'

'There's nothing to say, it's got nothing to do with him.'

'But I thought...' Cathy tailed off. 'Oh well, you know best. Good luck.' She stood up and walked over to the bar to replenish their drinks while Angie chewed her lip and tried to catch her ex-boyfriend's eye.

\* \* \*

Eddie played and sang better tonight than he'd done for a long time. He felt on top of the world and it showed. He beat the hell out of his drums in a final energetic crescendo, tossed the sticks into the air and jumped to his feet. He caught Roy's eye and grinned. Roy grinned back and swaggered to the edge of the stage. The audience went wild, screaming for more. But that was it, the final encore. They'd had four and Eddie's arms felt like they were about to drop off. He swiped his hand across his sweaty forehead and joined Roy, Tim and Phil to take a bow.

Ponytailed girls in brightly coloured, full-skirted dancing dresses were reaching out to touch them, to shake their hands, waving their pens and autograph books. Eddie grabbed the nearest book and scribbled his mark. He looked up, eyes searching the crowd for Jane. She waved and blew him a kiss. He blew one back, mouthed 'See you later', and filed off stage with the rest of the group.

\* \* \*

Jane couldn't stop smiling. She was dying to be alone with Eddie.

Sammy tapped her on the arm. 'You okay? Now you are sure about later, aren't you?'

'Yes, dead sure.' She looked across to where Angie was sitting, glaring at her as she'd done all night. 'She's not getting her claws in him again.'

'I don't think that will ever happen anyway,' Sammy said. 'But just make sure he takes care. I showed you what to do to make certain it's on right.'

'I'll be fine,' Jane said, feeling her cheeks heating. She saw Mario leading a thickset man to the dressing room. 'Is that Frank James?'

'Must be,' Sammy said. 'He's been here for the last set of

songs. I'm sure I've seen him at other clubs too. Let's hope he wants them – they deserve it.'

\* \* \*

'That was fantastic.' Eddie peeled off his black satin shirt and flung it in a heap on the dressing-room floor with Roy's. 'Best night this week.' He grabbed a towel and rubbed himself down, stripped off his leather pants, pulled on jeans and a black T-shirt and dragged a comb through his damp brown hair. 'Was Frank in tonight?' He gathered up his stage clothes and bundled them into a holdall.

'Yeah,' Roy said, standing in front of the cracked mirror. He smiled at his reflection and combed his black hair, arranging it into a neat quiff. Someone hammered on the door. 'Get that, Ed. Fingers crossed it's Frank.'

Eddie opened the door and let in Mario, and Frank James of the Frank James Organisation.

'Mr James wants a word,' Mario said and left the room with a click of his Cuban heels.

Frank James's smartly-suited presence squeezed into the small, overcrowded room, where the dingy yellow walls were plastered with black and white pin-ups of Eddie Cochran, Elvis, Little Richard, and other stars who had never been within a mile of Mario's club. The scent of woody aftershave filled Eddie's nostrils. He pushed the only chair towards Frank as though he were royalty. Frank inspected the chair, brushed crumbs off the shabby upholstery and sat down. He fished a packet of Benson & Hedges and an embossed gold lighter from his pocket and handed them round.

'Posh cigs,' Eddie whispered to Roy as Frank contentedly puffed a cloud of smoke into the air.

'Well, boys, as you know, I've been following you around for a few weeks. I'm impressed. But you need a manager and I'm looking for a new group. I think The Raiders fit the bill. Come to my office at two next Wednesday and sign a contract.' He sat back, a benevolent smile on his clean-shaven face and waited for a response.

They didn't disappoint him. Eddie flung his arms around Roy. Phil almost knocked Tim flying as he leapt around the room and they were all yelling at once as they shook Frank's hand.

'I'll take it that's a yes then?' Frank said, laughing as he stood up. 'I'll leave you to celebrate. See you Wednesday.'

Eddie saw him out and turned to the others, whose grins were splitting their faces. 'Fucking hell! I can't believe it. Best agent in town and he wants *us*.'

''Bout time though,' Roy said. 'He's kept us dangling for weeks. That's it, lads, we've made it, well… almost.'

'Let's do what Frankie Boy says and celebrate,' Phil said. 'Your folks are away, Ed, we could go back to your place. I got some sweet dope off Mac earlier, and there's a bottle of whisky in the van.'

'Not tonight, Phil.' Eddie shook his head. 'I've got a date with Jane and I want her all to myself. We'll celebrate after we've signed up.'

'You're a lucky sod, Mellor. I wouldn't mind giving Jane one myself.'

'Piss off, Phil!'

'Touchy bugger!' Phil smirked. 'Go flash your big blue eyes at her, she'll be putty in your hands. Right, let's get the gear loaded. I've had my eye on the little blonde dancing near the stage. Hope she's not cleared off.'

'Be out soon,' Eddie said as the others left the room. He needed a minute to himself. Phil's flippant comments about Jane had annoyed him.

* * *

The man reappeared, smiling after several minutes and the group came out on stage to pack away their instruments. They looked happy enough so Jane guessed all went well. Eddie hadn't come out yet. She got to her feet as Angie gave her the evil eye again. 'I'm going to find Ed,' she said to Sammy and made her way into the dressing room. She knocked on the closed door, popped her head inside to see Eddie grinding out the butt of a cigarette on the worn lino. He pulled her inside.

'What's wrong? Did Phil say something?'

'No. Why?'

'Oh, nothing.'

'Angie Turner's out there with her mates. They were all looking daggers, so I thought I'd meet you in here rather than outside.'

He nodded. 'I spotted them dancing. Ignore them. Angie's jealous 'cos we're back together.' He kissed her again. 'Can't wait for later,' he whispered into her long, dark hair. 'You still sure?'

She nodded. 'Did you remember to get some...?'

'Yeah. They're in my pocket. Let's get my stuff packed away then we can go.' He grabbed her hand and pulled her with him onto the stage, where the others were taking their gear out to the van. Dismantling his kit, he stroked the bass drum. Jane grinned at him. 'You might well laugh,' he said. 'This kit means everything to me, well... almost everything,' he added when she raised an eyebrow. 'Not only that, my old man's still paying for it. Least I can do is look after it properly. Here, you carry this.' He handed her the cymbal case and Roy came back to help him with the drums.

'I'll take everything back to my place and leave it in the van,' Roy said. 'Save us re-loading. You two get going if you want. See you tomorrow.'

'Bye,' Eddie called. He slung an arm around Jane's shoulders. 'We'll jump in a taxi, it'll only cost a couple of bob.' On the walk to the taxi rank he told her about Frank James's visit. 'It's gonna be brilliant. He's the best agent in Manchester. We might make a record soon. It's all happening at once. We're back together, new manager for the band, Mum and Dad away and the house to ourselves.'

They took their place in the queue and leant against the wall. Eddie unbuttoned her jacket, slid his hands inside and kissed her. The taxi queue grew shorter and then it was their turn and they clambered into a black cab.

* * *

Jane threw her jacket over the back of the parlour sofa as Eddie poured them a drink of his dad's whisky. Her stomach was tying itself in knots. 'Will your dad mind us drinking this?'

He was quiet, as though miles away but looking at her as though she might suddenly vanish.

'You're in a trance, Ed. You okay? I asked if your dad will mind you nicking his whisky.'

'I'm fine,' he said, handing her a glass. 'Dad won't know. I'll top the bottle up with water.'

She took a sip and grimaced. 'Ugh! It's burning the back of my throat. You have it.'

He knocked his own and hers back as well and she laughed as his eyes opened wide.

'That's hit the spot.' He put both glasses on the coffee table, pulled her into his arms and kissed her. They dropped to the floor on the rug, rolling together, their kisses becoming more demanding.

He caressed her breasts through the silkiness of her dress, undid the back zip and slid the dress over her shoulders. She reached out, pulled off his T-shirt and snuggled into his chest. 'Let's go to my room,' he said after a while and pulled her to her feet. He led her upstairs. By the time they tumbled onto his single bed they were naked and there was a trail of clothes across the landing and on the bedroom floor. Jane saw him push a box of Durex under the pillow. He leant across to switch on the Dansette, already stacked with singles. The harmonious Everly Brothers filled the room and he sang along to 'All I Have to Do Is Dream', looking deep into her eyes.

Jane felt like she was floating. She'd never felt so happy in her life. 'That's our song from now on,' she whispered and gasped as he circled her nipples with his fingertips. He kissed each breast in turn and explored her. She reached to touch and stroke him and he groaned.

'You're still sure?' He reached under the pillow.

She nodded, took the box from him, pulled out a packet and tore off the top. She heard him take a deep breath as she rolled a Durex onto his erection.

'Where did you learn to do that?'

'Sammy showed me,' she said. 'We practised on a carrot!'

He kissed her again and she groaned as he slid inside her. He looked down. 'You okay? Did I hurt you?'

'I'm fine.' She pulled him closer, moving with him as he built up a rhythm. He cried out her name and collapsed on top, burying his face in her neck. 'I love you, Jane,' he whispered. 'I'll make it better for you later, I promise.'

'Ed, it was wonderful. How on earth can it be better?'

'It can.' He stroked her cheek. 'I love you,' he repeated.

'I love you, too.'

He was quiet for a few moments, just looking at her. She wondered what he was thinking and hoped he wasn't going to say she was rubbish in bed compared to Angie.

Then he sat up and took her hand. 'Marry me!'

'Marry you?' She stared at him. It was the last thing she expected to hear. 'Don't be daft, Ed. We're far too young.'

'I don't mean right away. Maybe in a couple of years when you're eighteen. We could get engaged now.'

She looked at the ceiling for a long moment. The Dansette clicked and whirred as another record dropped onto the turntable and Buddy Holly warbled 'True Love Ways'. God, what would her mother say? She'd go crackers. But sod it, it was her life and she loved him so much.

'Jane,' he whispered.

She smiled and pulled his face to hers and kissed him. 'Okay, Ed. I'll marry you in two years.'

He crushed her in his arms and she could see tears in his eyes as her own filled. 'You won't regret it,' he said and rained kisses on her face. 'I'll make you the happiest girl in Stockport, no – make that the world. When Frank signs The Raiders, we'll be famous. I'll buy you everything. We'll have that posh house in Wilmslow. That'll show your mother there's money in rock 'n' roll and that I'm not a total waste of time.'

She laughed and rolled her eyes. 'Well, you know what Mum's like. She says drumming's not a proper job. But I'm sure you'll prove her wrong one day.'

'I will, believe me. We're gonna have the most fantastic life.'

A loud bang from downstairs made them jump.

'What if it's your mum and dad come back early?' Jane clutched the bedspread around her. 'They'll go mad if they catch us.'

'They're away all weekend. Maybe the door's blown open.'

'But there's no wind,' she began as footsteps thundered on the stairs.

A female voice called out, 'Ed, we need to talk. You in your room?'

'Fuck, it's Angie,' he said as the door flew in and hit the wall.

Jane snuggled into him and he flung his arm around her. They both stared at Angie, whose face looked pale, eyes red-rimmed from crying and her hair an untidy mass of curls.

'The door was unlocked,' she said, glaring at them. 'I thought you'd be up here.'

He pulled Jane closer. 'What the fuck do you think you're doing, barging into my room? It's over. Jane and I are back together. She's just agreed to marry me.'

'Is that a fact?' Angie moved towards the bed. 'Well, here's another one for you.' She yanked up the welt of her Sloppy Joe sweater, revealing a slightly swollen belly. 'I'm pregnant. You're the father. So what you gonna do about it?'

## 20

Jane pulled away from Eddie as the room began to spin.

'I swear, Jane, I had no idea...' he began, his voice echoing in her ears.

She pushed him away, wrapped the bedspread around her and fled to the bathroom, where she was sick in the washbasin. She sank to the floor trembling. She could hear raised voices coming from his bedroom. All she wanted to do was get out of the house as fast as she could, but she needed her clothes and her legs wouldn't work. Her whole world was tumbling down and she just wanted to curl up and die. How could he, how could he? At that moment she loved and hated him equally.

Through her noisy sobs, she heard a knock on the door.

'Jane, let me in, love, please.'

She opened the door a crack. He had her clothes in his hands, his face completely drained, and his blue eyes wide with disbelief. Upset as she was, her heart went out to him. She drew him inside as he shook his head in bewilderment. 'I'm so sorry. I can't believe this, it's a nightmare. I'm hoping I'll wake up in a minute.'

'Is she okay?' Jane stammered.

'She's very upset. I need to talk to her. It's probably a false alarm and she's panicking. Christ, I haven't even seen her since March. I'll phone for a taxi to take you to Sammy's. I'll call Sammy too and tell her to expect you, shall I?'

'Please. Why does everything go wrong? Ten minutes ago, I was so happy.' She burst into fresh sobs.

Eddie put his arms around her and hugged her. 'It'll be alright. I'll sort it, don't worry.'

'How? How can you sort it? If she's pregnant, you'll have to marry her. We can't be together, Ed. It's all just a dream.'

Her shoulders shook as she gazed into his eyes and saw the despair there. It was all just a dream, with the frightening reality sitting in the bedroom across the landing.

Eddie waved Jane off in the taxi and, without giving anything away, called Sammy to warn her that she was on her way. With leaden legs and a sinking heart, he walked slowly back upstairs. Angie was slumped on the end of his bed, twiddling her pony-tail around her fingers and sobbing. He stood in front of her, hands thrust into his jeans' pockets and stared at his bare feet, lost for words.

She looked at him, eyes spilling with tears. 'Well, aren't you going to say anything?'

He shrugged and ran his hands through his hair, where only a short time ago Jane had been running hers. 'Like what? What do you want me to say?'

'Oh, I don't know... anything.'

'How did it happen?'

She gave a hollow laugh. 'The usual way, Eddie. How the bloody hell do you think it happened? It wasn't the Immaculate Conception, and in case you hadn't noticed, my name's not Mary.'

'There's no need for sarcasm. You know full well what I mean. I haven't had sex with you for months so how the hell can you be pregnant?'

She looked at the ceiling for a long moment. 'It was that one-night stand we had in March.'

He frowned, trying to remember back. They'd shared a joint, a few glasses of her dad's rum, followed by a shag on the rug in front of the fire. It had been quick, her parents were asleep in the bedroom above and he'd made a hurried escape before they woke up. He'd not used anything but he'd been careful. It couldn't be his. And why the hell was she telling him now after months of silence? 'You sure it's mine?'

She gasped, picked up one of his boots and hurled it at his head. He ducked out of the way and it hit the dressing table mirror. 'You bastard! Of course it's yours. What do you take me for?'

He smacked his forehead with the palm of his hand. 'Why didn't you say something sooner? Shit, what the fucking hell are we going to do? Can you get rid of it?'

'How?'

He chewed his lip for a moment. 'Mac knows someone, a woman in Manchester. His girl Jackie went there.'

Angie looked horrified. 'You mean that posh blonde from Wilmslow? She nearly died. Some girls were talking about her in Mario's. Something went wrong. It sounded awful. I can't face that, I'd rather have it.'

'Adoption then. You could go away, have it secretly, and then we can sign it over.'

Angie started to cry again. 'No, we couldn't. I want to get married and keep it. I love you, you know I do, and I want our baby.'

'Angie, get real. Christ, we're both only just eighteen. I don't want to get married yet and I don't want to be lumbered with a kid either. Not now, not at this time. The band's taking off in a big way.' He lit a cigarette and offered her one, but she shook her head.

'It makes me feel sick at the moment.'

'You are sure, aren't you? Could it be a false alarm?'

'I've been praying it was for nearly four months now. I had a test done at the chemist last Wednesday. It's definite.'

'Why didn't you tell me sooner?' he repeated and paced the floor, sucking hard on his cigarette and wishing it was a joint. He needed more than nicotine to get him through this. Fuck, his folks would go nuts and he daren't even think what hers would say.

She shrugged. 'I was scared of your reaction. You know how you are with me – one minute you want me, next you don't.'

He gazed at her, sitting there twiddling her thumbs, and felt guilty for upsetting her. She didn't need it. He sat down and slipped an arm around her shoulders. 'I'm sorry. Sorry for asking if it's mine, I mean.' What he was about to say made him feel sick. He'd probably choke on his words, but felt he had no choice as his mum would make him do it anyway. He took a deep breath. 'I'll stand by you. Marry you if I have to.' He tried to keep his tone from sounding too grudging.

She smiled through her tears. 'Will you, Ed? I do love you, you know.'

'I know.' He sighed, wishing he could return the compliment, but knowing the words would stick in his throat if he said them so soon after saying them to Jane. 'God only knows what our parents are going to say.'

'I'll be glad to get it out in the open,' she said, rubbing her hand across her eyes. 'I've had morning sickness for weeks and had to turn the bathroom taps on to drown out the noise. Mum's gonna go crazy. I'm terrified of telling her. She warned me I'd end up in trouble, going out with you.'

'Did she? Well, she obviously knows me better than I know myself. She'll either go for my jugular or castrate me, or both.

It'll probably be the only kid I'll ever have.' He tried to make light of it, but didn't succeed very well.

'What about Jane?' Angie had the grace to ask.

He shook his head. 'She's devastated. What do you expect? I'll have to see her, tell her what's happening.'

'But you won't see her after that, will you?'

'I don't expect she'll want to see me again after this.' He sighed. 'I'd better get you a taxi home. My parents are away until late tomorrow. I'll tell them when they get back and then come over to you Monday night about seven thirty and we'll tell yours together. Make sure they're both in. I might stand a better chance of survival if your mother's not alone when we give her the news.'

* * *

Sammy was waiting at the door, an anxious expression on her face as the taxi carrying Jane arrived.

'Come on in. You look awful, what the hell's happened? Ed sounded like the end of the world had come, but he wouldn't say why. Have you had a row?'

As Sammy bombarded her with questions, Jane burst into fresh floods of tears. 'Sit down and tell us, for goodness' sake,' Sammy said, guiding Jane to the sofa and gently pushing her down.

Sammy and Pat stared in shocked silence as Jane poured out her tale, in between sobs.

Sammy's hand flew to her mouth. 'Oh my God! You are joking? Well, I hope he's been more careful with you than he was with her.'

Jane nodded. 'He was. Oh God, I just wanted him back. What have I done?' She put her head in her hands, tears running through her fingers.

'What's he going to do – about her, I mean?' Sammy asked.

'I don't know. I hate Angie, but I have to admit I felt sorry for her. Coming round to tell him her news and finding us in bed like that must have come as an awful shock. And Ed told her he'd asked me to marry him and I'd said yes. He wanted us to get engaged.'

'Shit, he asked you to marry him? Oh, Jane.' Sammy stroked her arm.

'I know. I was so happy, and then it all turned upside down.'

'She might miscarry,' Sammy said. 'You know, with the shock. It would be for the best,' she finished, as Pat and Jane glared at her.

'That's not very nice, Sam, it's Eddie's baby too,' Pat said.

'Well, it'll be the last thing Eddie wants right now,' Sammy said. 'I could just imagine Roy's reaction if I announced I was in the club. He'd have a coronary, and we're engaged. It would be best all round, solve the problem for them both.'

'You know something?' Pat said a thoughtful expression on her face. 'What if it's not Ed's? You know what she's like. Flirts with anything in trousers.'

'I never thought of that,' Jane said. 'But I would think it's Ed's. She was very upset and he didn't say anything to her, like, is it mine?'

'Well no, but he'll ask her in private, not in front of you,' Sammy said.

'Oh, Jane, what a disaster,' Pat said. 'It should have been such a special time for you both as well. Do you regret it, after everything that's happened?'

'No. It was special, in fact it was wonderful. I wish we'd done it sooner and then all this wouldn't have happened. I feel numb and drained. We were all snuggled up and cosy when she burst in.'

'Well, finish your tea and go straight up to bed,' Sammy said. 'Things might look brighter in the morning.'

* * *

Eddie got up from the sofa, turned off the radiogram and went to help his parents in with their suitcase. He'd been rehearsing what he'd tell them, or trying to, and had decided to just go with the flow and see what happened.

'Go and sit down, I'll make some tea,' he said.

He loaded up a tray, carried it through to the parlour and put it down on the coffee table. 'Did you enjoy yourselves?' he asked. They'd been to Southport for their wedding anniversary and had stayed in the same guest house where they'd spent their short wartime honeymoon.

'It was lovely.' His mum accepted the cup of tea he offered. 'This is very nice of you, Ed,' she said as he sat down on the rug in front of the tiled fireplace. He handed a cup to his dad, spooning in sugar.

'That's more sugar than he usually takes. But never mind, love, it's the thought that counts.'

He half-smiled, knowing he was about to tip their steady world upside down. 'Hot sweet tea,' he began. 'It's supposed to be good for shock, isn't it?'

His dad frowned. 'Aye, so they say; that, and a drop of brandy. Why, what have you been up to? What shock have you got in store for us?'

His mum smiled and reached out to ruffle Eddie's hair. 'Don't be so cynical, Fred. He hasn't got any shocks for us, have you, son? Mind you, him making tea is a shock in itself. Still, there's a first time for everything.' She looked closely at him. 'You're a bit pale, Ed. Is something wrong?'

He took a deep breath, get it over with. 'Err, I've got Angie pregnant!'

His mum continued to drink her tea, as though she'd not taken in what he'd said.

His dad's cup clattered back into the saucer, knocking the

teaspoon onto the floor. He looked at Eddie, his face an angry shade of red. 'What did you say?'

Eddie hung his head, not daring to look at either of them. 'I said, Angie's pregnant,' he repeated quietly.

His mum's left hand flew to her mouth as his dad removed the cup and saucer from her trembling right hand.

'But, Ed, she can't be,' she began.

'She is, Mum, I'm sorry.'

His dad remained silent, the angry red replaced by a furious white as he gazed at his wife's stricken expression and his young son's anxious face.

His mum spoke up. 'But how? You're only a child yourself. How could you have been so stupid and irresponsible? I hope it hasn't happened under this roof. What on earth will everyone say? The neighbours, your auntie Minnie down the road, and your aunt Celia in Brighton... she thinks the world of you. Oh, Ed, how could you do this to us? After everything we've done for you. Bought your drums, let you join the group, against our better judgement. You've had too much freedom, my lad, too much of your own way all along. Well, you'll be in for a shock now, I can tell you. There'll be no more freedom. You'll have to marry the girl and give up the group, get a respectable job. If you're grown-up enough to get her in the family way, then you're grown-up enough to accept the responsibility and take care of her. What on earth have her parents said? I'm surprised her father hasn't lynched you.'

Before Eddie had a chance to reply, his dad spoke up, pointing an accusing finger. 'You've been nothing but trouble for years. How could you let your mother and me down like this? You're no son of mine, I wash my hands of you.' He got up and left the room, slamming the door behind him.

His mum turned her tearstained face to Eddie. 'He'll come round, just give him time. He's in shock.'

Eddie nodded. 'We're telling Angie's parents tomorrow

night and then we'll decide what to do. I suppose we'll have to get married. I don't want to, but there's not much choice, is there? She's nearly four months gone already.'

'Oh, Ed, you were only seventeen, you silly lad. Well, God only knows how you'll cope. I'll help all I can, but at the end of the day, it's down to you two. You'll have to give up the group and look for a proper job to support you all. What does Roy have to say about all this? I bet he and Sammy wouldn't get themselves into a mess, they've got more sense.'

'He doesn't know yet. I only just found out myself last night. It's such a shock, I can't take it in. Roy'll go mad, the group's really taking off and we're signing with an agent this week. I don't want to leave them at this stage.'

'Well, you'll have to. You can't be cavorting around the country playing drums, leaving a young wife and baby at home.'

Eddie sighed, feeling close to tears. 'I know. Oh, how did I get into this mess?'

'By trying to be grown-up before your time. Didn't I always warn you that you'd end up in trouble? I was right, although I didn't expect this at your age.'

'Everybody does it. It's not just me, Mum,' he protested.

'I don't suppose it is. But it's you that's made the mistake. I mean, if you were going to mess about with that girl, you should have been more careful, used something.' His mum's cheeks were crimson as he looked at her, raising an eyebrow at her embarrassment.

Sex was a subject rarely discussed under their roof and certainly never with him.

She cleared her throat and continued, 'I suppose we're as much to blame. Your dad should have had a word with you about such matters. Well, it's too late to worry now, what's done is done.'

'Mum, for heaven's sake, I'm not completely stupid. I know what's what. I was careful, that's why it's such a shock.'

'Well, in that case are you sure it's yours? I mean, Angie's a right flighty piece at times.'

He nodded. 'She is, I know, but yes, she says it's mine.'

She tutted and shook her head. 'You should have stuck with that nice little Jane instead of getting mixed up with Angie again. She was such a sensible girl, quiet and well behaved. You wouldn't have had your wicked way with her. She's the sort of girl who would have made you wait until you put a ring on her finger.'

Eddie could feel his cheeks heating and hoped his mother wouldn't find out what he and Jane had been up to last night. A sudden awful thought struck him: if being careful with Angie had failed him, what if being careful with Jane hadn't worked either? But surely not, they'd used something and anyway lightning never struck twice in the same place. He pushed such horrendous thoughts away and stood up.

'I'm going to bed, Mum. I'm drained and I've got early rehearsals tomorrow.'

She nodded wearily. 'Bit of a waste of time for you, but I suppose it'll give you a chance to talk to Roy and Tim privately. Well, goodnight, love. What a way to end your birthday weekend.'

'Goodnight, Mum.'

He bent to kiss her, feeling terrible. She looked grey and old. The shock had been too much for both his parents. He wished now that he'd tried a bit harder to be the model son they'd hoped he'd be. One they could be proud of, with good exam results, and a job with future prospects. Instead of which they were ashamed of him. He vowed that from now on, he'd try and do his utmost to make his parents proud, by facing up to his responsibilities like a man and looking after Angie and the expected baby properly.

He paused by the parlour door and looked back. 'Mum, don't suppose I can still have my driving lessons, can I?' He'd

chosen lessons for his birthday present and had been looking
forward to starting them next week.

As she looked up, Eddie saw the look of disbelief in her eyes
and realised, given the circumstances, he'd pushed his luck a bit
too far. But you got nothing if you didn't ask, he reasoned.

'Eddie Mellor, get to bed before I do something I might
regret forever.'

He fled, closing the door quietly behind him.

Jane was unable to concentrate on anything at work on
Monday. Eddie hadn't been in touch yet and she just wanted to
know what was happening. Mark had called to ask her to meet
him outside the bank for lunch. She'd fibbed and told him she
was unable to get out and would call him after work. She
couldn't face him and after a week away, he'd be expecting
kisses and cuddles and she couldn't deal with that right now.
Her stomach lurched each time the phone rang and eventually
she took a call from Eddie late afternoon. He apologised for the
delay, said he'd had a lot of stuff to deal with, and asked her to
meet him on the rec at six thirty. As she put down the phone,
she just knew it was over and dreaded him telling her.

He was waiting, cigarette dangling from his lips as he came
forward to meet her. They walked hand in hand to the far end
away from the swings and the road and sat down on a bench.
Jane thought he looked pale and sad-eyed, as though he hadn't
slept a wink.

'So, what's happening?' she asked, biting her lip to stop the
threatening tears. His face told her the news was not what she
wanted to hear.

'I've got to go to Angie's when I leave you,' he began. 'That's
why I've only got half an hour or so.'

'So, it's definite, she is pregnant?'

'Nearly four months. She was too scared to tell me and hoped it was a false alarm. Huh, some false alarm,' he said, shaking his head.

'Are you going to marry her then?' Jane felt sick as she said it.

'I'll have to. We're telling her parents tonight. I told mine last night. Mum's upset, Dad's not speaking to me. Mum says I have to do right by Angie and marry her, give up the group, get a job. I don't want to give up the group. I told Roy, Tim and Phil earlier that I might have to leave. Roy's not happy. We've worked so hard and we're supposed to be signing with Frank James on Wednesday. God knows what her parents are gonna say, her dad will probably want to kill me, and if he doesn't, her bloody mother will. I don't want to get married yet, not to her anyway. I don't love her. It's you I love and want to marry.' He ran his shaking hands through his hair. 'Saturday night was wonderful, Jane. Special and absolutely perfect. I've made a right fucking mess of everything. I'm so sorry.'

She put her arms around him and held him close. He kissed her as tears splashed down her cheeks. 'Saturday was wonderful,' she sobbed, 'and this is probably the hardest thing we're ever going to have to do in our lives, but we need to be grown-up about it. I have to let you go, for the baby's sake, not hers. Does she love you, Ed, and is it definitely yours?'

He nodded, sniffing back tears. 'Yes, she says she loves me, and yes, I asked her if it's mine and she says it is.' He got to his feet. 'Well, I guess this is it, Jane. Do you have any regrets about Saturday, before Angie caught us, I mean?'

'None at all. I can't believe this is happening to us.' She put her arms around him and kissed him one last time. 'Goodbye, Ed, and good luck. I guess I'll see you around.'

She walked away, her heart breaking and feeling like her whole reason for being had ended.

* * *

Eddie stared after her; his girl, his Jane. She was the only one he'd ever really wanted and now he'd lost her forever. Tears trickled down his cheeks as he walked in the direction of Angie's parents' house and the awful ordeal that awaited him.

He crunched up the gravel drive of the smart detached house. Angie answered his knock and let him in, her face pale, eyes downcast. He gave her a quick peck on the cheek.

'Are they in?' he whispered.

She nodded, took his jacket and hung it on the hallstand. 'They're in the lounge. They've just had dinner and a couple of drinks, so might be feeling mellow with a bit of luck. Best not to go in with a leather jacket on, it'll put my mother's back up right away.'

He shrugged. At his mum's insistence he'd put on a clean white shirt and fresh jeans, drawing the line at trousers and a tie. What they see is what they get, he'd told her. If they don't like it, they can lump it. He was doing them a big favour marrying their daughter when it was the last thing in the world he wanted to do.

'I'm dreading this,' she whispered.

'That makes two of us,' he muttered and squeezed her hand. 'I've just talked with Jane.'

'Oh, is she okay? You haven't changed your mind though, about us I mean?' she said.

'Like I've got a choice,' he said, raising an eyebrow. 'And no, she's not okay.' He swallowed a sob. 'But then, what can you expect?'

'I'm sorry, Ed.'

She seemed genuinely upset, which surprised him. He thought she'd be acting all smug now she knew she'd well and truly got her claws in him.

'Yeah, me too.' He shrugged. 'Let's get it over with.'

He followed her into the plush lounge, where her mother was reclining on the red velvet sofa, reading a glossy magazine, and her father, perched in his high-back leather chair by the fireplace, still suited and booted from work, *The Times* newspaper obscuring his face. Angie grabbed his hand and pulled him to stand beside her on the rug in front of them both. Neither looked up from their reading.

'Mum, Dad,' Angie began, 'can we talk to you, please?'

Her mother looked up over her reading glasses. 'Can't it wait, Angela?' she snapped and then her eyes fell on Eddie and she put down her magazine. 'And who gave you permission to bring him into the house?'

Her father lowered his paper. 'Lydia, give the girl a chance, woman.' He glared at his wife then turned his attention to Angie: 'What is it, Angela?'

'Err, Eddie wants to ask you something,' Angie said, squeezing Eddie's hand.

Eddie took a deep breath and blurted out, 'I'd like your permission to marry Angie, please.' The silence that followed was deathly. He thought her mother's eyes were about to pop out of her head, her thin lips twisted into a sneer and she looked down her nose at him as though he was dog shit on her shoe.

'Don't be ridiculous,' she screeched. 'As if we'd give permission for our daughter to marry the likes of you.'

Angie's eyes filled. 'Mum, that's a horrible thing to say.'

'Well, for goodness' sake. You can do better than him.' She glared at Eddie, who glared back.

'Suit yourself,' he said and made for the door but Angie pulled him back.

'Tell them, Ed, please,' she begged. 'Don't leave me.'

Her mother jumped to her feet, her eyes, green like Angie's, but cold, hard and narrow. 'Tell us what? I hope this isn't what I think it is. If you've got my girl into trouble, I'll, I'll...' She sat back down again, fanning her face with her hand.

Angie's father got to his feet and stared at them. 'Angela, is this true?' He went to his wife and put his arms around her.

'Yes,' Angie said. 'We're having a baby and we want to get married as soon as possible.'

All hell broke loose then and Eddie just wanted the ground to open up and swallow him. Her mother shrieked at the top of her voice, Angie burst into tears and screamed back and her father yelled at them all. Eddie blew out his cheeks and let them get on with it. He silently looked down at the floor, realising he was standing on the rug where the quick, March, life-changing shag had taken place. God almighty, what a nightmare and what the fuck had he let himself in for?

## 21

Jane went straight to Sammy's after leaving Eddie. She couldn't face going home and have her mother asking what was wrong.

Molly answered the door and Jane burst into tears before she could stop herself.

'Jane, what's the matter?' Molly put her arm around Jane's shoulders and led her into the hallway. 'Are you in some sort of trouble, love?'

Before Jane could reply, Sammy burst out of the sitting room followed by Pat. 'We'll go upstairs, Jane. We can talk in our room.' Turning to Molly, she said, 'You wouldn't understand, Mum.'

'You've seen him then?' Sammy handed Jane a hanky as the threesome sat down on the beds.

'Yes,' she sobbed, 'and she's definitely pregnant. He's gone to tell her parents now. He's already told his and they're not happy with him.'

'No surprise there,' Sammy said. 'Roy's would be just the same.'

'What's he going to do?' Pat asked.

'Marry her. He doesn't want to, but he's not got much choice.'

'Poor Ed,' Pat sympathised.

Sammy sighed. 'Should have been more careful. Let's hope you're okay, Jane. I know you used something, but Durex isn't a hundred per cent safe.'

'Oh, don't tell me that,' Jane said. 'I daren't even think about the alternative.'

\* \* \*

A reluctant Eddie married Angie at Stockport Registry Office on a hot and sunny day at the end of July. With Roy as his best man and Cathy as Angie's bridesmaid, the marriage was celebrated with a small gathering of family and friends at Angie's parents' home.

Lydia Turner strolled around her well-tended garden like the Queen presiding over a royal garden party, greeting guests and doing her best to be cheerful under the circumstances. Her flower-bedecked hat trembled with indignation every time she looked in the direction of her wilful pregnant daughter, uncouth new son-in-law, who'd taken his tie off and stuffed it in his pocket as soon as he'd said his vows, and the scruffy members of that dreadful group he belonged to. His equally uncouth best man insisted on swigging cider from a bottle and winking brazenly every time she caught his eye. Not only that, they'd all shared the same home-made cigarettes, passing one another God knew what germs, and were now laughing drunkenly and trampling on her flower beds. The sooner they went home, the better.

\* \* \*

Within a week of his marriage, Eddie told Roy that he'd definitely be leaving The Raiders as soon as they could find a replacement drummer. The group had signed with Frank as planned and nothing had been said to him with regards to Eddie's situation. Roy just hoped he wouldn't drop the group after Eddie departed. Frank's comment about his and Ed's harmonies being the soul of the group weighed on Roy's shoulders. They'd be hard-pushed to find another drummer with a voice like Ed's. The group had been together for so long and no one could replace Eddie in their eyes, but they understood his need for a regular and consistent income. Raiders' money was great for a single bloke but not enough to keep a family on.

His dad, getting over his initial anger, had relented and offered to help the young couple financially, along with Angie's parents. But the condition was that Eddie gave up the group and found himself a proper job. Under those circumstances he felt he had no choice. The responsibility to provide for his wife and unborn baby lay heavily on his young shoulders, and any help, whatever the conditions, had to be gracefully accepted. He found a full-time labouring job in a local paint factory, and in the hopes of finding a better job in the future, enrolled on an evening book-keeping course at college.

He and Angie moved into a poky, second-floor, one-bedroomed flat close to Stockport town centre, and struggled to make ends meet. It broke his heart to sell his precious drum kit and he reluctantly handed the money to Angie to buy a pram, cot, and baby clothes.

Enforced married life was no bed of roses. He and Angie argued all the time about everything and anything, he missed the group, his social life, and his friends, but most of all, he missed Jane and thought about her constantly. He tried hard to be cheerful for Angie's sake, but deep down he knew he'd made the worst mistake of his life and he'd only himself to blame.

* * *

In August the girls received the long-awaited O level results. Much to their respective parents' delight, all three had done well, but Jane couldn't have cared less about hers.

'Don't need them anyway,' she told her mum as she stared at the slip of paper, informing her of five grade ones and a two.

'But it's nice that you've got them,' her mum said. 'You might want to go to college sometime in the future.'

Jane was adamant she wouldn't. All she wanted to do was work in Flanagan and Grey's. She'd told her mum that Eddie had married Angie, and why, but Molly had beaten her to it. Her mum's folded arms and barbed comment was only to be expected: 'I told you he was no good. And according to Molly, that girl he's married is a wild one as well. God help that baby when it arrives. You're very lucky to have Mark – he's steady and he'll look after you properly.'

*Yeah*, Jane thought, *steady, but boring.*

Although she was still dating him, she'd kept quiet about her night with Eddie. She knew she should have finished with Mark, but he'd got her through the weeks following Angie's announcement. She'd been glad to go out with him and to just have him put his arms around her and hold her. She cried herself to sleep most nights. Missing Eddie was like a physical pain that just wouldn't go away. She tried to carry on as normal, and was supported by Sammy and Pat through the longest week of her life when her period was late. After Sammy told her Durex weren't always safe, she'd worried herself into a right old state.

'We need to tell Eddie,' Sammy said.

'No, we can't,' Jane said. 'He's got enough on his plate and there's nothing to tell really. I'll do the worrying for both of us for now.'

'Well, the more you worry, the worse you're gonna make it,'

Sammy said. 'There's an old wives' tale that if you drink gin while sitting in a very hot bath it might do the trick.'

Jane agreed to try it and Sammy sent Roy out to buy a bottle of gin. She made Jane drink most of it on Sunday afternoon while sitting in a hot bath at Roy's parents' house. Far from curing the problem, Jane felt very sick.

'Any more bright ideas?' she said, emerging white-faced from the bathroom following a vomiting session.

'Well, let's hope it's only the gin making you sick,' Sammy said.

'Oh, Sam, don't.' Jane was on the verge of tears as Sammy patted her arm.

Jane made an excuse not to see Mark on the Tuesday night as planned and met up with Sammy and Pat at their place. Roy and Tim arrived with an address given to them by Mac, of the ex-nurse in Manchester who might be able to help.

'You haven't told Mac, surely?' Jane said. 'I don't want anyone to know, Roy. It might get back to Mark.'

'Mac won't blab,' Roy said. 'Anyway, I told him it was Sammy who might be up the duff.'

'Oh, great! Well, thank you, Roy,' Sammy said. 'Let's just hope that doesn't get back to my mum then, or she'll be after your blood.'

'Sorry, Sam. Didn't think you'd mind helping your mate out. Anyway, Jane, what do you think? Me and Tim will find the money. You can skip work for a day and I'll drive you into town and back.'

Jane shook her head. 'Thanks for the offer, Roy, but I'll run away from home before I'd consider it. You heard about poor Jackie, she almost died. And I'd need a lot longer than one day off work as well. I'd never get away with it. Anyway, if I'm pregnant – and it is a big if – it's Eddie's baby and I could never get rid of it.'

'Okay,' Roy said. 'It's up to you. But we're all here for you if you need us.'

* * *

When her late period turned out to be just that, Jane and her friends breathed a sigh of relief. She realised that Mark probably wondered why his girlfriend had a dramatic change of character overnight, from being a snappy, secretive cow to a carefree teenager once more. He didn't say anything, just kept giving her odd looks. Jane knew Mark couldn't fathom her out. One minute she was loving and friendly and the next he told her it was like dating the Ice Queen.

* * *

Eddie's replacement in The Raiders was a drummer called Kris. Older than the rest of them, in his early twenties, he was the best of the three they auditioned. He could sing, but not as well as Eddie could. Roy offered him the position and called Frank to explain the situation. Frank turned up at a few local gigs and within two weeks had called Roy and pulled the contract. He told Roy he'd planned to put The Raiders on a theatre tour, but their sound without Eddie wasn't quite what he wanted: 'Persuade your lad back and I'll sign you again,' he promised.

Roy was disappointed but there was little he could do at this stage to persuade Eddie to rejoin them.

* * *

In mid-December, Angie gave birth to a baby boy. Eddie told Roy that she'd had a difficult time and that both she and the baby had nearly died.

'Hmm, pity she didn't!' Sammy said.

'Sammy, you don't mean that,' Jane gasped.

'Jane, how can you be so forgiving, after what she did to you and everything you and we four went through in August?'

'I'm not forgiving, believe me. But you can't wish that on her. What have they called the baby anyway?'

'Jonathon Edward, apparently,' Sammy said.

'I like that, it's a lovely name.' Jane smiled. 'I wonder if he looks like Eddie,' she said, almost to herself.

## 22

MAY 1962

Eddie waved at Jane as she walked across the recreation ground. She had on the cream dress she'd worn the night they made love. He recognised it, because as she walked, the soft silky fabric moulded itself to her curves. She smiled and called out his name, waving back as he waited by the swings for her.

As she came closer, he tried to run towards her, but his feet felt strange, almost like lead weights. No matter how he tried, he was unable to move. He would have to wait until she reached him. A baby's cry rent the air, stopping her in her tracks, and her eyes opened wide. She shook her head and called 'No!' then turned and ran back in the opposite direction, her long glossy hair flying out behind her.

In desperation, Eddie tried calling her name, but no sound came out. He woke with a start, drenched in sweat. Damn it, he hated waking up to reality. Jane hadn't even got close to him tonight before the crying had turned her away. He rolled over with a sigh and climbed out of bed. The baby cried day and night lately. His mother said he was teething. Eddie wasn't convinced. If that was the case then he was teething all the time. Face it, what he knew about babies wouldn't fill the back of a postage stamp, and Angie was no better. He picked Jonny out of the cot and cuddled him, stroking his damp curls as the sobs subsided. Jonny was cold, his cheeks bright red and he was wet where his nappy had leaked.

Eddie carried him across to the bed and shook Angie by the shoulder.

She shrugged away. 'Leave me alone.'

He shook her again. 'Angie.'

'Don't touch me, go away,' she snarled, burying her head in the pillow.

'I'm not touching you, for God's sake. Jonny needs changing, he's wet through. How come you never hear him crying? He's in the same bloody room.' He felt tired and angry. Almost every night followed the same pattern, broken sleep for him while she slept right through regardless. He looked at the clock on the bedside table: four thirty and he had to be up in two hours to go to that godforsaken paint factory, while she slept in. Not for the first time he felt resentment and anger welling. Was it too much to ask that she got up and changed Jonny's nappy? He sighed and shook her again. 'Please, Angie, change the baby.'

'Change him yourself. He's yours as well as mine.' She turned her back and this time pulled the pillow over her head.

'I don't know how to. Come on, love, please. I've got to get up for work soon and I'm really tired. You can stay in bed and have a lie-in, it's okay for you.'

Angie rose like a phoenix from beneath the bedcovers and faced him, eyes blazing in her pale face. 'How dare you say it's okay for me! You got me pregnant; you ruined my life, and you tell me it's okay? I had a job I loved and a nice home. Now look at me, stuck in this bloody dump all day, bored stiff and no future. I hate you, Eddie Mellor, and I hate that screaming kid. I wish I'd never married you, and I wish he'd been aborted.' She burst into angry tears.

Eddie shook his head wearily and carried Jonny through into the living room. He'd no idea where the clean nappies were stored and even less idea how to put one on, but at least he could try. He pushed a pile of magazines and newspapers to one side and lay Jonny on the old red and black sofa. The sideboard cupboard was the only storage space in the cluttered room. The flat was tiny, cold and damp, with peeling wallpaper and dingy flaking paintwork and he hated living here.

The last few months had been an absolute nightmare and at that moment he felt like running away with Jonny and going back to live with his mum, if she'd have them. Tears of frustration pricked the backs of his eyelids as he rooted in the cupboard for nappies and pyjamas, but his search proved fruitless. He didn't relish the thought of going back into the bedroom to ask Angie where she kept them, she'd be sure to bite his head off again. A quick glance around the small room for inspiration and he spotted a clothes maiden standing in the corner by the window. He sighed with relief at the sight of clean nappies and baby clothes hanging on it. At least she did the washing occasionally. His only problem now, how did he go about putting a nappy on? Jonny smiled through his tears as Eddie laid him on the threadbare carpet and peeled off his damp pyjamas, leaky plastic pants and soaking-wet nappy.

His heart filled with love for the little boy he'd created. Jonny was the only reason he stayed with Angie, the marriage was shit and she was never satisfied. He worked long hours at the factory for a pittance and knew he'd have been better off financially by staying with the group. He felt increasingly bitter about leaving them. No matter how much overtime he did, they never had any spare money. Both sets of parents paid the rent between them, but it was still an uphill struggle to pay the bills, put food on the table and clothes on their backs.

They hardly ever went out together as a couple. Angie went for a drink midweek with Cathy and the girls from the salon.

On those welcome occasions Eddie asked Roy over for a chat and a drink. Roy always obliged if he wasn't playing and tried to keep Eddie's spirits up by bringing him gifts of cigarettes, cider, and the odd ready-rolled joint. For a short time, Eddie felt relaxed and almost happy again, chatting with Roy about the group and Jane and blotting out the nightmare of reality.

Roy also encouraged him to try and write songs and lent him an old acoustic guitar. The two of them played and sang duets together, making Eddie wish more than ever that he was back with the group. Once Roy had gone home, and Angie and Cathy returned, shooting him baleful glances, as though begrudging him the right to any pleasures, life returned to normal again, until the next time.

Eddie sighed and picked up Jonny, complete with clean nappy and dry pyjamas. Jonny flashed him a gummy smile. 'Back to bed with you, young fella, while Daddy has another hour's kip.' He kissed Jonny and lay him in the cot in the corner of the bedroom, tucking the blankets around him.

Eddie climbed back into bed and moved closer to Angie. He put an arm around her waist. She sighed and turned towards him.

'Sorry, Ed. I don't know what's wrong with me. I'm so tired all the time. I didn't mean what I said, I don't hate you or Jonny. I love you both. It all gets on top of me at times.'

'It's okay, it's the same for me.' He kissed her forehead. 'I didn't want a baby either, but we've got him now. It's too late to be blaming one another. We're too young for all this responsibility, but we can't let Jonny down; we owe it to him to do the best we can.'

'You're right, we do, and we will. Thanks for changing him.' She kissed him lightly on the lips. He put both his arms around her and pulled her close.

'I've not done a very good job but at least he's quiet again.' He nuzzled her neck, nibbling her ears, something she used to love him doing. 'Fancy a quickie?' He unbuttoned the front of her baby-doll nightdress. 'It's been ages and I'm feeling very unloved.' He kissed her breasts, tracing her nipples with his tongue, hoping for a response. She stiffened as he slipped his hand between her thighs.

She pushed him away and turned her back to him. 'I don't want to.'

'You never bloody well do,' he snapped. 'What's the point in being married? You say you love me, so why can't you show it?' He pulled her back into his arms and tried to kiss her, but she wriggled free.

'I do love you, I just don't want sex. I can't help it, Ed. I'm sorry, and stop shouting at me, you'll disturb Jonny.'

'Why don't you want sex? You couldn't get enough of it. What's changed?'

She didn't answer and Eddie turned his back on her, punching his pillow in frustration. He couldn't stand much more of this, he felt as though he could strangle her. He'd come so close to slapping her at times and the feeling frightened him. He wasn't violent but Angie brought out his demons. She provoked him over the least little thing, like she was trying to punish him solely for their predicament. He closed his eyes and tried to sleep. Jane's smiling face came into his mind again; it was never far from his thoughts.

In his dreams her big brown eyes always had the look of love in them and he could almost conjure up the smell of her fresh clean hair and the scent of her lovely body. She was usually wearing the cream dress, and she always wanted to make love with him, except when Jonny cried and she ran away. Roy had told him that she was still going steady with Mark Fisher and seemed happy enough. Eddie's stomach had plummeted and after Roy had gone home, he'd been physically sick. The thought of Jane having sex with Mark tore him in two. The feeling was a hundred times worse than imagining Angie with

Richard. Eddie wished he could turn the clock back twelve months. He knew Jane wasn't completely over him. She'd told Sammy, and Sammy had told Roy, who, in turn, had told him. Eddie clung to that one shred of hope, that one day, somehow, he and Jane could be together again, and meantime he had his memories and dreams.

\* \* \*

Angie lay stiffly by Eddie's side, her eyes burning with unshed tears. She just couldn't go on like this; she was hurting Eddie and herself more and more as the weeks rolled by. They should never have married, but at the time it seemed the only thing to do.

She thought back to the Saturday night when she'd told him she was pregnant. The last thing on her mind that night had been marriage. She'd already made a decision to hide the pregnancy for as long as she could, and then to go away, stay with a friend in Leeds, have the baby and give it away for adoption. No one at home would ever know except herself, Eddie, and Cathy. But finding Eddie in bed with Jane had angered her so much that before she could stop herself, she'd blurted out the news to the pair and it was too late then to take it all back. She'd gone along with the charade of wanting the baby and marriage to Eddie, realising it was her best chance of hanging on to him and not losing him to Jane, as would surely happen if she went away.

Both families had insisted they do the right thing, of course, and marry for the baby's sake, each offering their financial support. Angie felt that everything had been taken out of her own and Eddie's control from that moment on and since the wedding, things had gone from bad to worse. Eddie had to give up the group and his dreams of becoming famous someday, and she knew it had broken his heart when he'd sold his drum kit.

She was under no illusion that he'd ever forgive her. Jonny's birth had been long and painful and she didn't relish the thought of going through that again for anything. She'd haemorrhaged badly and had so many stitches that she couldn't bear Eddie to touch her intimately at all. She was so terrified of becoming pregnant again, that on the rare occasions he'd tried to make love to her it had been a disaster. She felt he made little effort to understand her feelings and he was becoming increasingly angry and impatient as the months rolled by.

She hoped to go back to work at the salon soon and resume her apprenticeship, it would help them financially as well as give her back her self-esteem, but at the moment there was no one to look after Jonny. Her mother refused to mind him, saying that she'd made her bed and Jonny was her and Eddie's responsibility.

Although the relationship with her mother-in-law was not an easy one, Lillian had tried her best to help. Angie was sure Lillian thought she'd deliberately got herself pregnant to trap Eddie. Nevertheless, she offered to look after Jonny on Saturdays if Angie wanted to find herself a little job to get her out of the flat for a while.

A couple of months after his birth, she'd taken Jonny into the salon to show him off to her colleagues and was shocked to learn that Richard Price had left shortly after she had. He'd married his fiancée and they'd moved to North Wales to set up a hairdressing and beauty salon. The news devastated Angie and it slowly dawned on her why: she was in love with Richard, missed him like crazy and now it was all too late. If only she'd been more forthcoming the last time he'd taken her out. She should have told him that she wanted to give their relationship a go. He'd given her the chance to say something after making love to her and telling her that he was falling for her. Why, oh why, hadn't she said something back instead of convincing herself it was Eddie that she loved? And she did love Eddie in her own way, she always had done. There'd been a spark between them from the word go. But with hindsight, Angie realised that Cathy had been right all along, and it had just been infatuation and puppy love. She'd wanted him and he'd been determined to have her, but neither had truly loved or respected the other.

Not once in all the time they'd been together had Eddie told her he loved her. When she asked him, he'd replied of course he did, but he never said the words. Angie knew deep down that he was still in love with Jane, but she was too frightened to let him go. What would become of her and Jonny on their own? There was no choice but to try and make an effort – for Jonny's sake if nothing else.

With Eddie's encouragement and his mother's assistance in looking after Jonny, Angie began working back at the salon on Saturdays, manning reception and making coffee for clients. When Jonny was a bit older and she could find a suitable nursery place for him, she planned on going back full-time and was hoping to finish her apprenticeship. Maybe when she was a qualified hairdresser, she could face the future alone with Jonny. She'd convinced herself that Eddie wouldn't stay with her forever. He was always threatening to walk out when they argued, which was most of the time. She retaliated by saying that if he did, she wouldn't allow him to see Jonny. She knew the threat was unfair, but she also knew that Eddie, whatever else he had to put up with, would think twice before abandoning the little boy he adored.

## 23

Following the aftermath of all that had happened, Jane threw herself into learning everything John Grey could teach her about the record trade and a year later was in sole charge of the Stockport branch of Flanagan and Grey's, ably assisted by Carl Harrison, her junior assistant. A gangly teen with a mop of unruly red curls and a face full of freckles, Carl was a much-cherished only child. He blushed furiously whenever anyone spoke to him and came to work wearing Fair Isle jumpers, hand-knitted by his doting mum. He was willing to learn though and looked up to Jane with puppy-dog devotion. At her request, he'd run errands; sweep the stairs and the shop floor without complaint. But the most important qualification for a Flanagan and Grey's employee, he made the best coffee Jane had ever drunk.

Christmas loomed closer, bringing the busy and exciting time Jane loved. She and Carl made the shop a festive haven for music lovers, with colourful montages of album sleeves and a decorated tree with twinkling lights.

'Return to Sender' by Elvis Presley was the Christmas number one, and that's what Jane knew she should have done with the card she received from Eddie. It was pushed through the letterbox one morning when she opened up the shop.

Jane picked up the envelope with the rest of the post and put it on the counter, unaware that one was for her eyes only. Carl arrived and made them the first coffee of the day.

'Shall I put the invoices on the clipboard for John?' he asked, picking up the post and sifting through it.

'Please, and put any Christmas cards on the pinboard with the rest.'

The ringing phone distracted her. The caller was John Grey, announcing he'd be over in Stockport around lunchtime and could Carl get him a sandwich.

Jane hung up, glancing at Carl, who was standing by the counter, red-faced, holding a card. 'What's wrong? Is it from your secret lover?' she teased, looking at the satin-covered card, fronted by a red-breasted robin and the words TO SOMEONE SPECIAL emblazoned across the top in gold lettering.

'Err no, not mine. Might be from yours though. Sorry, Jane, didn't realise it was for you only.'

'What are you on about?' Jane grabbed the card and recognised Eddie's neat hand. 'Oh no! Why has he sent me this?'

The message inside read – To My Darling Jane, I Still Love You. I'll Never Forget The Night We Made Love. I Think About You All The Time. All My Love, Eddie, followed by a row of kisses.

'Is it from someone you know?' Carl asked as Jane felt her legs turning to jelly. 'You've gone very pale.'

She sat down heavily on the stool behind the counter. 'Carl, you don't want to know. It's complicated,' Jane said, above the sound of her heart thudding in her ears. He still loved her. She still loved him. She hadn't seen either Eddie or Angie for ages and presumed they'd settled down and were okay. She occasionally asked Roy and Sammy how they were, but the pair was fairly non-committal on the subject. Probably trying to protect her feelings. Roy had told her Eddie was doing his best to make things work, but it was an uphill struggle.

She showed the card to Sammy and Pat when they called into the shop during their Christmas shopping expedition.

'Well, he isn't happy, so I'm not really surprised,' Sammy said. 'He does try, but it's hard for him.'

'She'd go mad if she knew you had that,' Pat said. 'What you going to do with it?'

Jane sighed and shook her head. 'Well, I can't take it home. Mum would also go mad if she clapped eyes on it. Carl, will you go and get John's sandwich? He'll be here any minute. Grab some for us, too.' She turned back to Sammy and Pat. 'I can't think straight. I know I should tear it up and chuck it in the bin, but I don't suppose I will. I still love him as well, but it's too late. He's got to get on with his life like I'm trying to get on with mine. Anyway, it's like a morgue in here,' she said, changing the subject. 'Any requests? Bit of Phil Spector, perhaps?'

'Yeah, "He's A Rebel" by The Crystals,' Sammy said, winking at Pat.

'Coming right up.' Jane placed the record on the turntable. The Crystals sang their hearts out and the girls sang along with them.

'Sounds very jolly in here,' John said as he ran down the stairs, closely followed by Carl with the sandwiches. 'But don't give up your day jobs, girls.'

'Hardly,' Sammy said with a grin. 'We're playing Eddie's song.'

'Oh, that's not fair,' Pat said. 'Just 'cos he's made one mistake, bless him.'

'At least one,' Sammy said, looking pointedly at Jane, who could feel her face heating.

'Am I missing something?' John picked up Eddie's card from the counter and read the message. He raised an eyebrow in

Jane's direction. 'Better put it somewhere safe. If Angie hears about it, she'll be after your blood.'

'Angie knows, she was there.' Sammy's tongue had been loosened by a couple of lunchtime apricot brandies in nearby Turner's Wine Vaults.

'What, you mean a threesome?' John said, an incredulous expression on his face.

'Of course not,' Jane gasped. She looked daggers at Sammy and told John a little of what had happened that night. 'Don't you dare tell anyone,' she pleaded.

John sympathised, while Carl blushed and turned away.

'What's up, Carl?' John frowned.

'I thought you had to be married before you, err, well, you know...' he trailed off.

'It was a mistake, Carl,' Jane said.

'We all make mistakes,' John said.

'Yeah,' she agreed. 'It's just that between us, Eddie and I seem to make more than most.'

* * *

Christmas Eve had Jane, Stuart, John and Carl rushed off their feet with customer after customer and barely enough time for the all-important coffee breaks. At five, John cashed up the bulk of the takings and pushed the pile of bank notes into a leather money pouch. He turned to Jane: 'Would you and Carl take this to the bank's night safe, please?'

'It's okay, John, it's still busy in here and you need Carl. I'll go up to the bank on my own. I'll put the pouch in my shoulder bag, it'll be okay in there.'

'Be careful, Jane,' John called after her as she grabbed her coat and scarf and ran up the stairs and out of the shop.

The main street was still heaving with throngs of people doing their last-minute shopping before everywhere closed for the holidays. As Jane turned off to climb the steps to the High Street, a hand fell onto her shoulder, making her jump. She whipped round, holding her breath, convinced she was about to be robbed of the takings, and instead found herself looking into Eddie's big blue eyes.

'Oh, Ed, you made me jump!' she exclaimed, her stomach lurching in an all-too familiar fashion.

'Sorry. I followed you from outside the shop. I often do, but today I just had to speak to you. Can I walk with you, please?'

'Of course. I'm going up to the bank with the takings. It's so good to see you again. How are you, how's your little boy, and, err, Angie?' Jane nearly choked on her name.

'Jonny's fine, a bit of a handful, he's just turned one now. Angie's a bit down, we haven't any money to spare to go out over Christmas and she's depressed about that, but otherwise we're okay, I suppose. Did you get my card? I meant the words I wrote. I'm trying to make things work but my heart isn't in it, it's with you.'

Jane could see the longing in his eyes. She shivered, knowing she would have to be the strong one, even though it would tear her in two all over again. The rush of love she felt for him was overwhelming. He looked so good, had filled out slightly in the last year and his hair had grown much longer. He still had the floppy fringe, which he flicked back from his eyes as they walked along. He was wearing his black leather biking jacket, shabby now from years of wear, with the fur-lined collar turned up against the cold wind, faded blue jeans and a black polo-neck sweater. She just wanted to jump on him and hold him and tell him that she loved him.

Instead she laid her hand on his arm and took a deep breath: 'Ed, please don't say that. It's over between us, it has to be. You have a wife and baby and they need you. You owe it to them to try and make it work. I don't like it any more than you do, but you can't do this to me. It broke my heart that we couldn't be together. I've tried so hard to rebuild my life twice now without you. I want to be free of these feelings I have for you. Free to love Mark one day maybe, when I feel ready. He's very patient with me and I'm really horrible to him at times because he's not you, and that's not fair to him.' Looking into his eyes was too much for her and she burst into tears.

People hurrying by stopped to stare at them as Eddie put his arms around her and buried his face in her hair while she sobbed against his chest. He kissed her and his tears mingled with hers. She could see in his eyes that she'd dashed his dreams, but what could they do?

He sighed. 'Sorry, Jane. I don't know what I expected you to say. I suppose I hoped for a genie to pop up and grant me three wishes. Come on, I'll walk you to the bank and then back to the shop. It's dark and it bothers me that you're out on your own, carrying all that money.'

He took her hand and held it tight as they walked in silence up the High Street. Jane pushed the pouch into the night safe, breathing a sigh of relief as she heard it fall inside. Eddie walked her back to the shop, his arm around her shoulders. Jane sensed he needed to feel close to her; his body probably ached with longing like hers did for him.

'Are you going to Mario's tonight?' he said.

'Yes, are you?' She hoped he wasn't – she couldn't face seeing Angie again, ever.

'No, we can't afford it. We're staying with Angie's parents over Christmas. Mine have gone to Brighton to Aunt Celia's. They won't be back until New Year. Angie's family still hasn't forgiven me for getting her pregnant. Her mother really hates me and the feeling's mutual. The atmosphere's awful. I'll give you two guesses who she'd rather be stuffing instead of the turkey.' Jane smiled as he continued, 'They all love Jonny, it's just me they don't like. Are The Raiders playing tonight? I haven't seen Roy for a couple of weeks so I can't remember where he said they were on Christmas Eve.'

'They are, and I'm really looking forward to it.'

'What do you think of their new drummer? Well, he's hardly new, but you know what I mean.'

Jane shrugged. 'Kris? He's okay, I suppose. He's a bit moody and has his own set of friends. He doesn't sing as well as you did. He seems to find the harmonies a struggle. Do you know him?'

He shook his head. 'I've never met him. Roy reckons he's a bit secretive, says you can't really have a laugh with him. I hardly see any of my old friends now, except for Roy and Tim. I know the group's busy. I wish I hadn't left them. I should have stuck to my guns, shouldn't I? The parents had the final say in what happened, not me and Angie. I should have bargained with them, told them I'd only marry her if I could stay in the group. Ah well, that's hindsight for you. I think we were both so scared that we agreed to anything and now we regret it. I hate my job, that book-keeping course is worse than school ever was, and you know how much I loved school.' He threw back his head and gave a hollow laugh. 'God, listen to me, I've done nothing but moan. I'm full of self-pity. I had the world in the palm of my hand and I threw it away. I've no one to blame but myself.'

Jane sighed. 'I need to get back to work or they'll think something's happened to me. I'll see you again sometime. Keep in touch. But promise me you'll try and get to grips with yourself and work at your marriage, for everyone's sake, especially the baby's. He didn't ask to be born.'

'I wish you'd been pregnant and not her,' he said, winding a lock of her hair around his fingers and pulling her towards him.

Jane smiled and shook her head. She thought back to the nerve-racking weeks following That Night. 'You should just think yourself lucky you haven't got two kids.'

'I'm sorry, I had no idea.' He pulled her close, looking shocked. 'Why didn't you tell me?'

'You had enough on your plate, there was no point in worrying you.'

'Even so, you could have let me know through Roy. Did Sammy and Pat help you?'

'Yeah, and Roy and Tim. Got me very drunk and sick on gin, but it was a false alarm anyway.'

'Bloody hell, Roy never said a word. What must he think of me?' He shook his head. 'I really do love you, you know. Do you still love me?'

'You know I do. Go home now, Ed, please.' She didn't think she could bear the pain any longer.

He grabbed hold of her, kissed her like he'd never let her go and walked off up the street, his shoulders bowed, head down.

Jane, on legs of jelly, walked down the stairs into the shop.

'Where've you been?' John said. 'We've been worried to death. Stuart was just coming to look for you.'

Jane glanced at her watch. The trip should have taken her five minutes. She'd been thirty at least. No wonder they were panicking.

Stuart noticed her tear-stained face. 'What's happened?' he asked, putting an arm around her shoulders.

'I saw Eddie,' she said, tears streaming down her cheeks.

Carl looked puzzled. 'Who is this Eddie?'

'Tell you when you're older,' John said.

'Well, I'm only a bit younger than Jane is.'

'Ah, but Jane's got an old head on her shoulders,' John said, giving Jane a hug.

'It'll get easier,' Stuart said, rubbing her arm.

* * *

Mario's was packed with revellers that night and as Jane danced with Mark, while The Raiders played, her heart felt heavy. Nothing seemed the same anymore, even the group was apathetic lately, and lacking the raw enthusiasm and sparkle they'd had in the early years. Sammy had told her that Roy seemed to be losing interest and was desperate to persuade Eddie to come back. But Eddie said he couldn't afford to buy a new drum kit, and Angie didn't want him to work as a musician again. Jane didn't tell Mark about the Christmas card or her meeting with Eddie. He'd go nuts. He was getting more possessive with her and she found it stifling at times. Angie's friend Cathy, sitting in a corner with her mates, smiled and waved, which Jane found a bit disconcerting, but she smiled back and turned quickly away, frowning.

'Why the frown?' Mark asked.

'No reason,' she said, more sharply than she'd intended. A look of hurt flickered in his eyes and she immediately felt guilty. 'Sorry, Mark, I'm tired that's all. Been a long and very busy day.'

'Tony will give us a lift home soon. He has to get Sarah back before midnight.'

Jane nodded and looked across to where Sammy and Pat were sitting. They waved and beckoned her over.

'Listen, Mark, I'll get a lift home in the group's van. There's no point in Tony going out of his way when Pat and Sammy live around the corner from me.' She just wanted to be with her old mates tonight, but didn't want to hurt his feelings.

'Well, if you're sure. As long as Roy doesn't mind of course.'

'He won't mind at all,' Jane assured him. She kissed him goodbye and breathed a sigh of relief as she watched him walk out of the club with Tony and Sarah.

She hurried across the dance floor to join her friends. Sammy handed her a glass of Coke that was sitting spare on the table. 'There's a drop of voddy in that and you look like you need it. What's up with you? You've had a face like a wet weekend in Morecambe all night.'

Jane told them what had happened with Eddie earlier, and everything they'd talked about.

'Oh dear, Roy said last time he went to see him he was very down.'

'I didn't encourage him or anything, didn't need to, but he has to give it a bit longer before he throws in the towel completely with Angie.'

'Well, maybe now you've told him you want to be free of the feelings you have for him and that you want to make it work with Mark, he'll settle down better,' Pat said.

'Hopefully,' Jane agreed. She took a sip of her drink, knowing deep down that wasn't what she wanted at all.

## 24

---

## MARCH 1963

As 1963 got underway a group from Liverpool shot to number two in the British record charts with a self-penned song called 'Please, Please Me'. Roy had raved about The Beatles for a long time and he, Tim and Phil visited The Cavern Club in Liverpool to see them play. They'd come away impressed and determined to try penning songs of their own. Roy already had a few lyrics that he and Eddie had written so it was a start.

Tim parted company with his double bass and bought a Fender Precision. Along with the purchase of powerful new amplifiers, the changes injected a fresh lease of life into The Raiders. They began to play with renewed enthusiasm and acquired an even bigger following of fans. Roy still badgered Eddie to rejoin them, just occasionally as a guest singer if nothing else, but Eddie was adamant that it wasn't possible. He told Roy he couldn't handle any more arguments at home. Singing with the group would make life more unbearable than it already was. Instead, and to maintain some contact with them, he wrote the lyrics to a song which Roy put the melody to, and the group sang at their gigs.

The song was a melancholy ballad about lost love, which brought a lump to Jane's throat. She realised the words were written with her in mind. She knew that Eddie would know she'd hear them, and the message that she was still in his thoughts gave her some comfort.

Phil Jackson sought Roy's opinion about asking Jane for a date.

'Up to you, mate,' Roy said. 'But she's going pretty steady with Mark, although I'm not sure how serious they are, and she still holds a torch for Ed, same as he still holds one for her.'

'But that's madness!' he exclaimed. 'If Ed's still in love with her, and that song he wrote tells me he's got it bad, why does he stay in a marriage that's not working? Love 'em and leave 'em, that's my motto, baby or no baby.'

Roy grinned. 'So, can we look forward to a trail of broken hearts up and down the country, and angry fathers with shotguns?'

Phil shrugged. 'No one's caught up with me yet, but they've tried.' He produced a letter from his inside jacket pocket and waved it at Roy. 'See this? Insurance. Gets me off the hook.'

Roy took the official-looking letter, written on hospital headed paper, and read it. He burst out laughing. 'I assume it's a fake?' The letter stated that due to a severe dose of mumps, Phil was now sterile and unable to father children.

'Signed by my friend who's a doctor,' Phil said. 'I, err, got cornered by a couple of birds who claimed I'd fathered their kids. I might have done, but they're the kind who drops 'em for anybody and I wasn't getting lumbered. My mate sorted the letter to help me out. Pity Ed didn't do something like that.' It was beyond his comprehension how a talented musician like Eddie allowed himself to be saddled with an unwanted wife and kid when there was fame just around the corner, and a beautiful brown-eyed girl to share it with.

* * *

Thanks to the hard work and enthusiasm of Jane and Carl, Flanagan and Grey's Stockport store was doing excellent business, and towards the end of the year, they were each rewarded with a pay rise. Jane had plans to restock her wardrobe and even thought about taking driving lessons.

When she told Mark, he had other ideas for her money. It was one of Maude's rare nights out. They were upstairs in his bedroom and although Jane wouldn't allow him to go all the way, they'd had a petting session and were lying relaxed in one another's arms. 'Why don't we get engaged?' he said. 'We can save up to get married now we're both earning decent money.' He leapt up, knelt by the bed and took her hand. 'Will you marry me, Jane?'

She caught her breath and looked at him. She wasn't expecting that. Was he serious? A quick study of his face told her he was. She supposed she could do worse. He was a good-looking lad who told her he loved her very much and she cared for him and would probably grow to love him in time. Her mum would be thrilled to bits if she married him, but she didn't think his would be best pleased, miserable bugger that she was. Still, it wasn't up to Maude. She nodded. 'Okay, yes, I'll marry you.'

He jumped up, swept her into his arms and kissed her. For a fleeting moment she thought about the night Eddie had asked her to marry him and the feelings of love and elation that were absent now, but pushed it to the back of her mind where it would have to stay.

* * *

Mark hardly gave Jane time to draw breath before he bombarded her with plans for their future. 'We can buy a nice little semi in a good area with a subsidised mortgage from the bank,' he said. 'I'd like two children, no need to wait; we can start our family as soon as we're married.' He'd make sure she gave up work, or at least changed her job. Get her away from that record shop and all its temptations, and the lads who ogled her.

Mark swore to himself that he would look after her like Eddie never could have done, but he was also aware that the neat, organised life he planned for them both might not be quite what she wanted so he tried not to put too much pressure on her to set a date for their engagement, hoping that eventually, she'd suggest one herself. She did, and chose the twenty-third of November. He had to be content with that, for in spite of his protestations that they should do it now, she dug in her heels and wouldn't settle for anything earlier.

\* \* \*

Sammy told Jane that she and Roy had recently bumped into Eddie, Angie and young Jonny at the summer fair, and that Eddie had looked very unhappy.

'He's desperate to get back into music again. Roy's asked him to come along to the next rehearsal if he can. She just stood there with a right pained expression, looked like she was sucking a bloody lemon. Hardly said two words to me all the time Roy was talking to Ed. She obviously doesn't want him going anywhere near the group again, but Roy and I got the impression he's past caring.'

Jane felt unsettled for a few days after, but she'd taught herself not to dwell on things and to keep looking forward. Her future lay with Mark; Eddie was in the past.

\* \* \*

The month of November and Jane and Mark's planned engagement brought the shocking news of the assassination of the American president, John F. Kennedy. Jane cancelled the party she and Mark had arranged at Mario's. She also cancelled the notification in the local paper. She'd not been keen on that idea anyway, but her mum had insisted. She felt it wasn't right to be celebrating when the world was in mourning.

'Let's wait until after Christmas to make it official,' she said to Mark. 'There's no rush, is there?'

But Mark wasn't pleased. 'I don't want to wait any longer, Jane. I've waited long enough. I don't mind hanging on for the party, but I want that ring on your finger now.'

'I can't see the difference a few weeks will make,' Jane said to Sammy and Pat. 'But he insists I wear the ring.'

Sammy and Pat exchanged looks and raised eyebrows as they stared at the ruby and diamond cluster on Jane's finger.

'What?' Jane said. 'Why are you looking at one another like that?'

Sammy shrugged. 'It's a lovely ring, but are you sure this engagement is what you want, Christmas or any time come to that?'

'Yes, of course I am,' Jane said. 'The sooner Mark and I are married, the better.'

\* \* \*

December brought many new record releases including Phil Spector's Christmas Album. A firm favourite, the shop demo copy was played over and over again. Carl walked around singing 'Frosty the Snowman', Ronettes style, until Jane threatened to put a paper bag over his head if he didn't shut up.

The Beatles' 'I Want to Hold Your Hand' was the Christmas number one and made Roy more determined than ever to persuade Eddie to rejoin The Raiders. He was convinced they could be as big as The Beatles and had visions of record labels with Mellor and Cantello below the song title, as opposed to Lennon and McCartney.

\* \* \*

A close friendship had developed between Jane and Carl, who wished he were a few years older. He'd love to ask Jane out, but was shy and had never had a girlfriend. Anyway, it was no use because now she'd gone and got herself engaged to that Mark fellow; odd though that she didn't always seem particularly happy about it. There was also the mysterious Eddie who she used to go out with. She talked to Sammy about him all the time, and sometimes with tears in her eyes. Carl reckoned she must still fancy him, but didn't like to ask.

\* \* \*

Once more, as last year, a card was pushed through the door from Eddie. Not quite as intimate this time, more apologetic really. Still Missing You, Jane. Please Don't Forget Me. All My Love, Eddie, followed by a row of kisses. As if she ever could.

Sammy shook her head when Jane showed her. 'How do you feel now? Do you still love him?'

Jane nodded. 'Yep, but I'm marrying Mark next year, remember?'

'You don't have to. There are plenty of other lads out there. You still haven't had the engagement party yet. You've no enthusiasm as far as I can see, so why bother? Why tie yourself down when it's not really what you want? You've seen what it's done to Ed; two wrongs don't make a right. It's almost like you want to make yourself suffer because he is. Phil Jackson told Roy he fancies you like crazy. You should go out with him, have a bit of fun. He's such a sexy man and I bet he's a wow between the sheets.'

Jane felt her cheeks heating. She'd had a similar thought herself. 'I do like Phil, but he's only after one thing. Once he's got it, he doesn't want to know. Mark's not like that, he rarely tries it on, and when he does, he will take no for an answer.' She twisted a lock of hair around her fingers and tried to think of something complimentary to say about Mark, but was hard-pushed: 'He says he likes to look after me.' That sounded lame. He was a bit too overprotective and it made her sound like an invalid. She tried again: 'I know being around him is a bit like watching paint dry at times, but he's okay and at least I know he really loves me.'

Sammy snorted with exasperation. 'For God's sake, Jane, you don't love him though. And watching paint dry? What sort of a relationship is that? You should be having fun at your age. If you ask me, it'll all end in tears and I mean all. Somebody's going to get hurt.'

Over the next few days, Jane thought frequently of her conversation with Sammy. Perhaps she was right, maybe she should finish with Mark and have some fun with Phil. He certainly paid her a lot of attention when she was at Mario's and Mark wasn't around. Always putting his arms around her, giving her a cuddle and even stealing the odd kiss. She enjoyed flirting with him and it took her mind off Eddie for a while. But she couldn't accept a date with Phil for worrying about what would be sure to happen if they were alone.

'I went to Mario's at lunchtime and rearranged our engagement party,' Mark said to Jane, the week after Christmas. 'He can do us a buffet on Wednesday night. The Raiders are playing so all your friends will be there anyway and I'll ask a few of mine from work.' He stopped as she frowned. 'Why are you looking at me like that?'

'You might have checked with me first.'

'What's the point? Every time I bring up the subject, you make excuses. Anyway, it's sorted now. All you have to do is make an effort to be there.'

'Okay.' Jane shrugged and then she smiled. 'Looks like I haven't got much choice.'

* * *

Jane leant against Mark as Tony took a photograph of them. She laughed as the flashbulb failed and Tony cursed and fiddled with it. He tried again and this time it worked.

'That's the first one for our new family album,' Mark said, dropping a kiss on her lips.

Jane nodded. She was trying her best to look happy. She glanced across to the stage where The Raiders were coming back on for their second set. She caught Sammy's eye and waved. Sammy beckoned her over.

'Just popping across to have a chat with Sammy,' Jane said, extricating herself from Mark's arms. 'I'll take them some food over.' She picked up a plate of sausage rolls and sandwiches and walked away before he could protest. He hadn't let her out of his grasp all night and she was desperate for a few minutes away from him.

Sammy gave her a hug. 'You okay?'

Jane nodded and looked back at Mark, who was staring at them, a half-smile on his face. 'Yeah. It's done now, I can't let him down. We'll be fine. I'll make it work.'

'Oh, Jane,' Sammy said, patting her arm. 'Well, good luck. I do mean that, you know, even though I still think you've made the biggest mistake of your life.'

Jane smiled as Roy played the opening chords to 'That'll Be the Day'. She thought back to the first night she'd heard the group play the song and Eddie, with his floppy fringe, keeping time to the rhythm. She blinked away threatening tears and smiled. 'Well, that's only something time will tell. I'm sure we'll be fine.'

# A LETTER FROM PAM

Dear reader,

I want to say a huge thank you for choosing to read *The Girls of Mersey Square*. If you did enjoy it, and want to keep up to date with all my latest releases, just sign up at the following link. Your email address will never be shared and you can unsubscribe at any time.

*www.bookouture.com/pam-howes*

To my loyal band of regular readers who bought and reviewed all my previous stories, thank you for waiting patiently for another book. Your support is most welcome and very much appreciated.

As always, a big thank you to Beverley Ann Hopper and Sandra Blower and the members of their Facebook group, Book Lovers. Thanks for all the support you show me. Also, thank you to Deryl Easton and the supportive members of her Facebook group, Gangland Governors/NotRights.

A huge thank you to team Bookouture, especially my lovely editor, Maisie Lawrence. As always it's been such a pleasure to work with you again, and thanks also to copyeditor/line editor Jane Eastgate and proofreader Jane Donovan for the copyedits and proofreading side of life.

And last, but definitely not least, thank you to our amazing media team, Kim Nash, Sarah Hardy Jess Readett and Noelle

Holton, for everything you do for us. You're 'Simply the Best' as Tina would say! And thanks also to the gang in the Bookouture Authors' Lounge for always being there. As always, I'm so proud to be one of you.

I hope you loved *The Girls of Mersey Square* and if you did, I would be very grateful if you could write a review. I'd love to hear what you think and it makes such a difference helping new readers to discover one of my books for the first time.

I love hearing from my readers – you can get in touch on my Facebook page or through Twitter.

Thanks,

Pam Howes

facebook.com/Pam-Howes-Books-260328010709267
twitter.com/PamHowes1

# ACKNOWLEDGEMENTS

As always, for my partner, my daughters, grandchildren, great granddaughters and all their partners/spouses. Thanks for being a supportive and lovely family.

Printed in Great Britain
by Amazon